The Times Are
Never So Bad

The Times Are Never So Bad

A NOVELLA AND EIGHT SHORT STORIES

ANDRE DUBUS

David R. Godine, Publisher
BOSTON

First edition published in 1983 by
David R. Godine, Publisher, Inc.
Box 450
Jaffrey, New Hampshire 03452
website: www.godine.com

Copyright © 1983 by Andre Dubus

Library of Congress Cataloging-in-Publication Data
Dubus, Andre, 1936–1999.
The times are never so bad.
Contents: The pretty girl – Bless Me, Father – Goodbye – [etc.]
1. Title.
PS3554.U265T55   813'.54   82-48703

ISBN 0-87923-641-8

ACKNOWLEDGMENTS

"Bless Me, Father" first appeared in *Carleton Miscellany;* "Good-bye" and "The Captain" in *Ploughshares;* "Leslie in California" in *Redbook;* "The New Boy" in *Harper's;* "Anna" in *Playboy;* and "A Father's Story" in *The Black Warrior Review.*

Third printing, 1999
PRINTED IN CANADA

To Philip and Michel Spitzer

Contents

*. . . the man in the violent situation reveals
those qualities least dispensable in his personality,
those qualities which are all he will have to take into
eternity with him. . . .*

Flannery O'Connor, 'On Her Own Work'

*The times are never so bad but that a good man
can live in them.*

Saint Thomas More

The Pretty Girl

But because thou art lukewarm, and neither cold nor
hot, I am about to vomit thee out of my mouth. . . .
                              Saint John, *The Apocalypse*

For Roger Rath
out among the stars

I DON'T KNOW HOW I feel till I hold that steel. That was always true: I might have a cold, or one of those days when everything is hard to do because you're tired for no reason at all except that you're alive, and I'd work out, and by the time I got in the shower I couldn't remember how I felt before I lifted; it was like that part of the day was yesterday, and now I was starting a new one. Or a hangover: some of my friends and my brother too are hair-of-the-dog people, but I've never done that and I never will, because a drink in the morning shuts down the whole day, and anyway I can't stand the smell· of it in the morning and my stomach tells me it would like a Coke or a milkshake, but it is not about to stand for a prank like a shot of vodka or even a beer.

It was drunk out last night, Alex says. And I always say: *A severe drunk front moved in around midnight.* We've been saying that since I was seventeen and he was twenty-one. On a morning after one of those, when I can read the words in the *Boston Globe* but I can't remember them long enough to understand the story, I work out. If it's my off day from weights, I run or go to the Y and swim. Then the hangover is gone. Even the sick ones: some days I've thought I'd either blow my lunch on the bench or get myself squared away and, for the first few sets, as I pushed the bar up from my chest, the booze tried to come up too, with whatever I'd eaten during the night, and I'd swallow and push the iron all the way up and bring it down again, and some of my sweat was cool. Then I'd

3

do it again and again, and add some weights, and do it again till I got a pump, and the blood rushed through my muscles and flushed out the lactic acid, and sweat soaked my shorts and tank shirt, the bench under my back was slick, and all the poison was gone from my body. From my head too, and for the rest of the day, unless something really bothered me, like having to file my tax return, or car trouble, I was as peaceful as I can ever be. Because I get along with people, and they don't treat me the way they treat some; in this world it helps to be big. That's not why I work out, but it's not a bad reason, and one that little guys should think about. The weather doesn't harass me either. New Englanders are always bitching about one thing or another. Once Alex said: *I think they just like to bitch, because when you get down to it, the truth is the Celtics and Patriots and Red Sox and Bruins are all good to watch, and we're lucky they're here, and we've got the ocean and pretty country to hunt and fish and ski in, and you don't have to be rich to get there.* He's right. But I don't bitch about the weather: I like rain and snow and heat and cold, and the only effect they have on me is what I wear to go out in them. The weather up here is female, and goes from one mood to another, and I love her for that.

So as long as I'm working out, I have good days, except for those things that happen to you like dead batteries and forms to fill out. If I skip my workouts I start feeling confused and distracted, then I get tense, and drinking and talking aren't good, they just make it worse, then I don't want to get out of bed in the morning. I've had days like that, when I might not have got up at all if finally I didn't have to piss. An hour with the iron and everything is back in place again, and I don't know what was troubling me or why in the first place I went those eight or twelve or however many days without lifting. But it doesn't matter. Because it's over, and I can write my name on a check or say it out loud again without feeling like a liar. This is Raymond Yarborough, I say into the phone, and I feel my words, my name, go out over the wire, and he says the car is ready and it'll be seventy-eight dollars and sixty-five cents. I tell him I'll come get it now, and I walk out into the world I'd left for a while and it feels like mine again. I like stepping on it and breathing it. I walk to the bank first and cash a check because the garage won't take one unless you have a major credit card, which I don't because I don't believe in buying something, even gas, that I don't have the money for. I always have enough money because I don't buy anything I can't eat or drink. Or almost anything. At the bank window I write a check to Cash and sign both sides and talk to the girl. I tell her she's looking good and I like her sweater and the new way she's got her hair done. I'm not making a move; I feel good and I want to see her smiling.

But for a week or two now, up here at Alex's place in New Hampshire, the iron hasn't worked for me. While I'm pumping I forget Polly, or at least I feel like I have, but in the shower she's back again. I got to her once, back in June: she was scared like a wild animal, a small one without any natural weapons, like a wounded rabbit, the way they quiver in your hand and look at you when you pick them up to knock their heads against trees or rocks. But I think she started to like it anyways, and if I had wanted to, I could have made her come. But that's Polly. I've known her about twelve years, since I was fourteen, and I think I knew her better when we were kids than I ever did after high school when we started going together and then got married. In school I knew she was smart and pretty and tried to look sexy before she was. I still don't know much more. That's not true: I can write down a lot that I know about her, and I did that one cold night early last spring, about fifty pages on a legal pad, but all of it was what she said to me and what she thought I said to her and what she did. I still didn't understand why she was that way, why we couldn't just be at peace with one another, in the evenings drink some beer or booze, talking about this and that, then eat some dinner, and be easy about things, which is what I thought we got married for.

We were camping at a lake and not catching any trout when we decided to get married. We talked about it on the second night, lying in our sleeping bags in the tent. In the morning I woke up feeling like the ground was blessed, a sacred place of Indians. I was twenty-two years old, and I thought about dying; it still seemed many years away, but I felt closer to it, like I could see the rest of my life in that tent while Polly slept, and it didn't matter that at the end of it I'd die. I was very happy, and I thought of my oldest brother, Kingsley, dead in the war we lost, and I talked to him for a while, told him I wished he was here so he could see how good I felt, and could be the best man. Then I talked to Alex and told him he'd be the best man. Then I was asleep again, and when I woke up Polly was handing me a cup of coffee and I could hear the campfire crackling. Late that afternoon we left the ground but I kept the tent; I didn't bring it back to the rental place. I had a tent of my own, a two-man, but I rented a big one so Polly could walk around in it, and arrange the food and cooler and gear, the way women turn places into houses, even motel rooms. There are some that don't, but they're not the kind you want to be with for the whole nine yards; when a woman is a slob, she's even worse than a man. They had my deposit, but they phoned me. I told them we had an accident and the tent was at the bottom of Lake Willoughby up in Vermont, up in what they call the Northern Kingdom. He asked me what it was doing in the lake. I said I had no way of knowing because that lake was formed by a glacier and is so deep in places that nobody could know even how far down it was, much less what it was doing. He said *on* the lake, what was it doing *on* the lake? Did my boat capsize? I said, What boat? He had been growling, but this time he barked: then how did the tent get in the fucking lake? I pitched it there, I said. That's the accident I'm talking about. Then he howled: the deposit didn't cover the cost of the boat. I told him to start getting more deposit, and hung up. That tent is out here at Alex's, folded up and resting on the rafters in the garage. This place was Kingsley's, and when his wife married again she wanted to give it to me and Alex, but Alex said that wasn't right, he knew Kingsley would want her to do that, and at the same time he knew Kingsley would expect us to turn it down and give her some money; their marriage was good, and she has his kid, my niece Olivia who's nearly ten now. I was still in school, so Alex bought it.

What I thought we had—I know we had it—in the tent that morning didn't last, and even though I don't understand why everything changed as fast as our weather does, I blame her because I tried so hard and was the way I always was before, when she loved me; I changed toward her and cursed her and slapped her around when every day was bad and the nights worse. There are things you can do in the daytime that make you feel like your marriage isn't a cage with rattlesnakes on the floor, that you can handle it: not just working out, but driving around for a whole afternoon just getting eggs and light bulbs and dry cleaning and a watchband and some socks. You listen to music in the car and look at people in their cars (I've noticed often you'll see a young girl driving alone, smiling to herself; maybe it's the disc jockey, maybe it's what she's thinking), and you talk to people in their stores (I always try to go to small stores, even for food), and your life seems better than it was when you walked out of the house with the car key. But at night there's nothing to distract you; and besides at night is when you really feel married, and need to; and there you are in the living room with all those snakes on the floor. I was tending bar five nights a week then, so two nights were terrible and sad, and on the others I came home tired and crept into the house and bed, feeling like I was doing something wrong, something I didn't want her to wake up and see. Then near the end Vinnie DeLuca was in that bed on the nights I worked, and I found out and that was the end.

I treated her well. I shared the housework, like my brothers and I did growing up. I've never known a woman who couldn't cook better than I do, but still I can put a meal on the table, and I did that, either fried or barbecued; I cooked on the grill outside all year round; I like cooking out while snow is falling. I washed the dishes when she cooked, and sometimes remembered to vacuum, and I did a lot of the errands, because she hated that, probably because she went to supermarkets and never talked to anybody, while I just didn't quite enjoy it.

Never marry a woman who doesn't know what she wants, and knows she doesn't. Mom never knew what she wanted either, but I don't think she knew she didn't, and that's why she's stayed steady through the years. She still brings her Luckies to the table. When I was little I believed Mom was what a wife should look like. I never thought much about what a wife should be like. She was very pretty then and she still is, though you have to look at her for a while to see it. Or I guess other people do, who are looking for pretty women to be young, or the other way around, and when they see a woman in her fifties they don't really look at her until they have to, until they're sitting down talking to her, and seeing her eyes and the way she smiles. But I don't need that closer look. She's outdoors a lot and has good lines in her face, the kind of lines that make me trust someone.

Mom wants Lucky Strikes and coffee, iced in summer after the hot cups in the morning, and bourbon when the sun is low. When she has those she's all right, let it rain where we're camping or the black flies find us fishing. During the blizzard of 1978 Mom ran out of Luckies and Jim Beam, and the coffee beans were low; the old man laughs about it, he says she was showing a lot of courage, but he thought he better do something fast or be snowed in with a crazy woman, so he went on cross-country skis into town and came back with a carton and a bottle and a can of coffee in his parka pockets. I tried to stop you, she says when they joke about it. Not as hard as you've tried to stop me going other places, the old man says. The truth is, it was not dangerous, only three miles into town from their house, and I know the old man was happy for an excuse to get out into the storm and work up a sweat. Younger, he wouldn't have needed an excuse, but I think his age makes him believe when there's a blizzard he should stay indoors. He's buried a few friends. At the store he got to in the snow they only had regular coffee, not the beans that Mom buys at two or three stores you have to drive to. He says when he came home she grabbed the carton first and had one lit before he was out of his ski mask, and she had two drinks poured while he was taking off his boots; then she held up the can of coffee and said: Who drinks this? You have a girl friend you were thinking about? He took the drink from her and said I don't have time for a girl friend. And she said I know you don't. They didn't tell us any more of that story; I know there'd be a fire going, and I like to think he was down to his long underwear by then, and he took that off and they lay in front of the fireplace. But probably they just had bourbon and teased one another and the old man took a shower and they went upstairs to sleep.

I hope the doctors never tell Mom she has to give up her Luckies and coffee and bourbon. You may call that an addiction. So what is my pumping iron? What is Polly?

She would say I raped her in June and so would her cop father and the rest of her family, if she told them, which she probably did because she moved back in with them. But maybe she didn't tell them. She didn't press charges; Alex keeps in touch with what's going on down there, and he lets me know. But I've stayed up here anyway. It's hard to explain: the night I did it I naturally crossed the state line and came up here to the boondocks; I knew when they didn't find me at home or at work, Polly would tell them to try here, but it was a good place to wait for a night and a day, a good place to make plans. In the morning I called Alex and he spoke to a friend on the force and called me back and said, Nothing yet. Late that afternoon he called again, said, Nothing yet. So I stayed here the second night, and next morning and afternoon he called me again, so I stayed a third night and a fourth and fifth, because every day he called and said there was nothing yet. By then I had missed two nights of a job I liked, tending bar at Newburyport, where I got good tips and could have girls if I wanted them. I knew that a girl would help, maybe do more than that, maybe fix everything for me. But having a girl was just an idea, like thinking about a part of the country where you might want to live if you ever stopped loving the place where you were.

So I wanted to want a girl, but I didn't, not even when these two pretty ones came in almost every night I worked and sat at the bar and talked to me when I had the time, and gave me signs with their eyes and the way they joked with me and laughed at each other. I could have had either one, and I don't know how the other one would have taken it. Sometimes I thought about taking both of them back to my place, which is maybe what they had in mind anyway, but that wouldn't be the same as having a girl I wanted to want, and I couldn't get interested enough to go through the trouble. Once, before Polly, I went to a wedding where everyone got drunk on champagne. I noticed then something I hadn't noticed before: girls get horny at weddings. I ended up with two friends of the bride; I had known them before, but not much. They were dressed up and looking very good, and when the party broke up we went to a bar, a crowded bar with a lot of light, one of those places where the management figures it draws a crowd with all kinds in it, so one way to keep down fights and especially guys pulling knives is have the place lit up like a library. I sat between them at the bar and rubbed their thighs, and after we drank some more I had a hand up each of them; it was late spring and their legs were moist, squeezing my hands; then they opened a little, enough; I don't remember if they did this at the same time or one was first. Then I got my hands in their pants. The bar was crowded and people were standing behind us, drinking in groups and pairs, buying drinks over the girls' shoulders, and I was stroking clitoris. When I told Alex this he said, How did you drink and smoke? I said I don't know. But I do know that I kept talking and pretending to each girl that I was only touching her. I got the drinking done too. Maybe they came at the bar, but pretty soon I couldn't take it anymore, and I got them out of there. But in the car I suddenly knew how drunk and tired I was; I was afraid I couldn't make it with both of them, so I took the plump one to her apartment and we told her good night like a couple of innocent people going home drunk from a wedding. Then I brought the other one to my place, and we had a good night, but every time I thought of the bar I was sorry I took the plump one home. Probably the girl with me was sorry too, because in the morning I took a shower and when I got out, the bed was made and she was gone. She left a nice note, but it was strange anyway, and made the whole night feel like a bad mistake, and I thought since it didn't really matter who I got in bed with, it should have been the one that was plump. She was good-looking and I'm sure was not lonesome or hard up for a man, but still for the rest of the day and that night I felt sorry when I remembered her leaving the car and walking up the walk to her apartment building, because you know how women are, and she was bound to feel then that her friend was slender and she wasn't and that was the only reason she was going home alone drunk, with juicy underpants. She was right, and that's why I felt so bad. Next day I decided to stop thinking about her. I do that a lot: you do some things you wish you hadn't, and thinking about them afterward doesn't do any good for anybody, and finally you just feel like your heart has the flu. None of this is why I didn't take the two girls this summer back to my place.

What is hard to explain is why, when I knew Polly wasn't going to press charges, I stayed here instead of giving my boss some almost true story. I thought of some he would believe, or at least accept because he likes me and I do good work, something just a few feet short of saying Hey, lookit, I was running from a rape charge. But I didn't go back, except one night to my apartment for my fishing gear and guns and clothes and groceries. Nothing else in there belonged to me.

When I came up here that night I did it, I went to my place first and loaded the jeep with my weights and bench and power stands. So when I knew nobody was after me, all I did was work out, lifting on three days and running and swimming in the lake on the others. That was first thing in the morning, which was noon for everybody else. Every day was sunny, and in the afternoons I sat on a deck chair on the wharf, with a cooler of beer. Near sundown I rowed out in the boat and fished for bass and pickerel. If I caught one big enough for dinner, I stopped fishing and let the boat drift till dark, then rowed back and ate my fish. So all day and most of the night I was thinking, and most of that was about why I wasn't going back. All I finally knew was something had changed. I had liked my life till that night in June, except for what Polly was doing to it, but you've got to be able to separate those things, and I still believe I did, or at least tried to hard enough so that sometimes I did, often enough to know my life wasn't a bad one and I was luckier than most. Then I went to her house that night and I felt her throat under the Kabar, then her belly under it. I don't just mean I could feel the blade touching her, the way you can cut cheese with your eyes closed; it wasn't like that, the blade moving through air, then stopping because something—her throat, her belly—was in the way. No: I felt her skin touching the steel, like the blade was a finger of mine.

They would call it rape and assault with a deadly weapon, but those words don't apply to me and Polly. I was taking back my wife for a while; and taking back, for a while anyway, some of what she took from me. That is what it felt like: I went to her place torn and came out mended. Then she was torn, so I was back in her life for a while. All night I was happy and I kept getting hard, driving north and up here at Alex's, just remembering. All I could come up with in the days and nights after that, thinking about why I didn't go back to my apartment and working the bar, was that time in my life seemed flat and stale now, like an old glass of beer.

But I have to leave again, go back there for a while. Everything this summer is breaking down to for a while, which it seems is as long as I can keep peaceful. Now after my workout I get in the hot shower feeling strong and fresh, and rub the bar of soap over my biceps and pecs, they're hard and still pumped up; then I start to lose what the workout was really for, because nobody works out for just the body, I don't care what they may say, and it could be that those who don't lift or run or swim or something don't need to because they've got most of the time what the rest of us go for on the bench or road or in the pool, though I'm not talking about the ones who just drink and do drugs. Then again, I've known a lot of women who didn't need booze or drugs or a workout, while I've never known a man who didn't need one or the other, if not both. It would be interesting to meet one someday. So I flex into the spray, make the muscles feel closer to the hot water, but I've lost it: that feeling you get after a workout, that yesterday is gone and last night too, that today is right here in the shower, inside your body; there is nothing out there past the curtain that can bring you down, and you can take all the time you want to turn the water hotter and circle and flex and stretch under it, because the time is yours like the water is; when you're pumped like that you can't even think about death, at least not your own; or about any of the other petty crap you have to deal with just to have a good day; you end up with two or three minutes of cold water, and by the time you're drying off, the pump is easing down into a relaxed state that almost feels like muscle fatigue but it isn't: it's what you lifted all that iron for, and it'll take you like a stream does a trout, cool and easy the rest of the day.

I've lost that now: in the shower I see Polly walking around town smiling at people, talking to them on this warm dry August day. I don't let myself think anymore about her under or on top of or whatever and however with Vinnie DeLuca. I went through that place already, and I'm not going back there again. I can forget the past. Mom still grieves for Kingsley, but I don't. Instead of remembering him the way he was all those years, I think of him now, like he's forever twenty years old out there in the pines around the lake, out there on the water, and in it; Alex and I took all his stuff out of here and gave it to his wife and Mom. What I can't forget is right now. I can't forget that Polly's walking around happy, breathing today into her body. And not thinking about me. Or, if she does, she's still happy, she's still got her day, and she's draining mine like the water running out of the tub. So lately after my workout I stand in the shower and change the pictures; then I take a sandwich and the beer cooler out to the wharf and look at the pictures some more; I do this into the night, and I've stopped fishing or whatever I was doing in the boat. Instead of looking at pictures of Polly happy, I've been looking at Polly scared shitless,

Polly fucked up, Polly paying. It's time to do some more terroriz-
ing.

So today when the sun is going down I phone Alex. The lake is in
a good-sized woods, and the trees are old and tall; the sun is behind
them long before the sky loses its light and color, and turns the lake
black. The house faces west and, from that shore, shadows are
coming out onto the water. But the rest of it is blue, and so is the
sky above the trees. I drink a beer at the phone and look out the
screen window at the lake.

'Is she still living with Steve?' I say to Alex. A month ago he
came out here for a few beers and told me he heard she'd moved
out of her folks' house, into Steve Buckland's place.

'Far as I know,' Alex says.

'So when's he heading north?'

Steve is the biggest man I know, and he has never worked out;
he's also the strongest man I know, and it's lucky for a lot of people
he is also the most laid back and cheerful man I know, even when
he's managed to put away enough booze to get drunk, which is a
lot for a man his size. I've never seen him in a fight, and if he ever
was in one, I know I would've heard about it, because guys would
talk about that for a long time; but I've seen him break up a few
when he's tending bar down to Timmy's, and I've seen him come
out from the bar at closing time when a lot of the guys are cocked
and don't want to leave, and he herds them right out the door like
sheep. He has a huge belly that doesn't fool anybody into throwing a punch at him, and he moves fast. Also, we're not good friends,
I only know him from the bar, but I like him, he's a good man,
and I do not want to fuck over his life with my problem; besides,
the word is that Polly is just staying with him till he goes north,
but they're not fucking, then she'll sublet his place (he lives on a
lake too; Alex is right about New England) while he stays in a
cabin he and some guys have in New Hampshire, and after hunting
season he'll ski, and he won't come back till late spring. Alex says
he's leaving after Labor Day weekend. I have nothing against
Steve, but Vinnie DeLuca is another matter. So I ask Alex about
that gentleman's schedule.

'He's a bouncer at Old Colony. I think they call him a doorman.'

'I'll bounce his ass.'

'He might be carrying something, you know. With that job.'

'Shit. You think anybody'd let that asshole carry a gun?'

'Sure they would, but I was thinking blackjack. Want me to come along?'

'No, I'm all set.'

'If you change your mind, I'll be here.'

I know he will. He always has been, and I'm lucky to have a brother who's a friend too; I'm so lucky, I even had two of them; or unlucky because now I only have the one, depending on how I feel about things at the time I'm thinking of my brothers. I bring a beer out and sit on the wharf and watch the trees on the east side of the lake go from green to black as the sun sets beyond the tall woods. Then the sky is dark and I get another beer and listen to the lake sloshing against the bank, like someone is walking on it out there in the middle, his steps pushing the water around, and I think about Kingsley in the war. At first I don't want to, then I give in to it, and I picture him crawling in the jungle. He bought it from a mine; they didn't tell us if he was in a rice paddy or open field or jungle, but I always think of him in jungle because he loved to hunt in the woods and was so quiet in there. After a while I swallow and tighten my chest and let out some air. Polly said I was afraid to cry because it wasn't macho. That's not true. I sure the fuck cried when Mom and the old man told me and Alex about Kingsley, there in the kitchen, and I would've cried no matter who was there to watch. I fight crying because it empties you so you can't do anything about what's making you cry. So I stop thinking about Kingsley, that big good-looking wonderful son of a bitch with that look he had on his face when he was hunting, like he could see through the trees, as he stepped on a mine or tripped a wire. By the time I stop thinking about him, I know what else I'll do tonight, after I deal with Mr. DeLuca a.k.a. the doorman of Old Colony.

It is a rowdy bar at the north end of town, with a band and a lot of girls, and it draws people from out of town instead of just regulars, so it gets rough in there. I sit in my jeep in the parking lot fifteen minutes before closing. The band is gone, but the parking lot is still full. At one o'clock they start coming out, loud in bunches and couples. Some leave right away, but a lot of them stand around, some drinking what they sneaked out of the bar. The place takes about twenty minutes to empty; I know that's done when I see Vinnie come into the doorway, following the last people to leave. He stands there smoking a cigarette. He's short and wide like I am, and he is wearing a leisure suit with his shirt collar out over the lapels. He's got a chain around his neck. The cruiser turns into the parking lot, as I figured it would; the cops drive very slowly through the crowd, stopping here and there for a word; they pass in front of me and go to the end of the lot and hang a slow U and come back; people are in their cars now and driving off. I feel like slouching down but will not do this for a cop, even to get DeLuca. The truth is I'm probably the only one in the parking lot planning a felony. They pass me, looking at the cars leaving and the people still getting into cars, then they follow everybody out of the lot and up the road. Vinnie will either come right out or stay inside and drink while the waitresses and one bartender clean the place and the other bartender counts the money and puts it in the safe. It's amazing how many places there are to rob at night, when you think about it; if that's what you like. I hate a fucking thief. Polly used to shoplift in high school, and when she told me about it, years later, telling it like it was something cute she and her pals did, I didn't think it was funny, though I was supposed to. There are five cars spread around the lot. I don't know what he's driving, so I just sit watching the door, but he stays inside, the fucker getting his free drinks and sitting on a barstool watching the sweeping and table-wiping and the dirty ashtrays stacking up on the bar and the bartender washing them. Maybe he's making it with one of the waitresses, which I hope he isn't. I do not want to kick his ass with a woman there. If he comes out with a bartender or even both of them, it's a problem I can handle: either they'll jump me or try to get between us, or run for the phone; but I'll get him. With a woman, you never know. Some of them like to watch. But she might start screaming or crying or get a tire iron and knock the back of my head out my nose.

He comes out with three women. The women are smoking, so I figure they just finished their work and haven't been sitting around with a drink, they're tired and want to go home. A lot of people don't know what a long, hard job that is. I'm right: they all stand on the little porch, but he's not touching any of them, or even standing close; then they come down the steps and one woman heads for a car down on the left near the road, and the other two go to my right, toward the car at the high end of the lot, and he comes for the one straight ahead of him, off to my left maybe a couple of hundred feet. The TransAm: I should have known. I'm out the door and we're both walking at right angles to his car. He looks at me once, then looks straight ahead. Headlights are on his blue suit, and the two women drive down and pass behind him; the other one is just getting to her car, and she waves and they toot the horn, and turn onto the road. I get to the car first and plant myself in front of it and watch his chain. It's gold and something hangs from it, a disc of some kind.

'Ray,' he says, and stops. 'How's it going, Ray?' His voice is smooth and deep in his throat, but I can see his eyes now. They look sad, the way scared eyes do. His skin is dark and he is hairy and his shirt is unbuttoned enough to show this, and the swell of his pecs. I think of Alex, and look at Vinnie's hands down by his jacket pockets; I'm looking at his face too, and I keep seeing the gold chain, a short one around his neck so the disc shows high on his chest. My legs are shaky and cool and I need a deep breath, but I don't take it; I swing a left above the chain, see it hit his jaw, then my right is there in his face, and I'm in the eye of the storm, I don't hear us, I don't feel my fists hitting him, but I see them; when my head rocks he's hit me; I hit him fast and his face has a trapped look, then he's inside my arms, grabbing them, his head down, and I turn with him and push him onto the car, his back on the hood. There is a light on his face, and blood; I hold him down with my left hand on his throat and pound him with the right. There is a lot of blood on his mouth and nose and some on his forehead and under an eye. He is limp under my hand, and when I let him go he slides down the hood and his back swings forward like he's sitting up, and he drops between me and the grill. He lies on his side. My foot cocks to kick him but I stop it, looking at his face. The face is enough. The sky feels small, like I could breathe it all in. Then I look into the light. It's the headlights of the waitress's car, the one alone; it's stopped about twenty feet away with the engine running and the lights aimed at me. She's standing beside the car, yelling. I look around. Nobody else is in the lot; it feels small too. I look down at DeLuca, then at her. She's cursing me. I wave at her and walk to my jeep. She is calling me a motherfucking, cocksucking string of other things. I like this girl. With the lights off, I back the jeep up away from the club and make a wide half-circle around her to the road, so she can't read my plates. I pull out and turn on the lights.

I take a beer from the cooler on the floor and light a cigarette. My hands are shaky, but it's the good kind. Kingsley taught me about adrenaline, long before he used it over there, when I started first grade, which for boys means start learning to fight too. He said when you start to tremble, that's not fear, it just feels like it; it's to help you, so put it to use. That is why I didn't say to DeLuca the things I thought of saying. When I know I have to fight I never talk. Adrenaline makes guys start talking at each other, and you can use it up; I hold it in till I've got to either yell or have action.

The street is wide and quiet, most of the houses dark. I pass a cemetery and a school. I don't know why it is, but I know of four schools in this town either next to or across the street from a cemetery. I'm talking elementary schools too. Maybe it's an old custom, but it's weird looking at little girls and boys on a playground, and next door or across the street are all those tombstones over the dead. King is buried in one with trees and no school or anything else around but woods and the Merrimack River. The sky is lit up with stars and moon, the kind of night you could drive in with your lights off if you were the only one on the road, just follow the grey pavement and look at the dark trees and the sky and listen to the air rushing at the window. I turn on the radio and get onto 495 north. My knuckles are sore but the fingers work fine. I suck down the beer and get another from under the ice, and it feels good on my hand. I'm getting WOKQ from Dover, New Hampshire. Every redneck from southern Maine to Boston listens to that station. New Hampshire is also a redneck state, though the natives don't know it because they get snow every winter. When King was at Camp LeJeune he wrote to the family and said they could move New Hampshire down there and everybody would be happy except for the heat, which he wasn't happy with either. The heat got to him in Nam too; he wrote and said the insects and heat and being wet so much of the time were the worst part. I think about that a lot; was he just saying that so we wouldn't worry, or did he mean it? Most of the time I think he meant it, which taught me something I already knew but didn't always know that I knew: it gets down to what's happening to you right now, and if you're hot and wet and itching, that's what you deal with. You'll end up tripping a mine anyways, so you might as well fight the bugs and stay cool and dry till then.

Mostly there's woods on the sides of the highway. People are driving it fast tonight. I pull into the right lane, Crystal Gayle is singing sad, and take the exit. I hope Waylon comes on; I'm in a Waylon mood. I cross the highway on the overpass, cars going under me without a sound I can hear over Crystal, and go on a two-lane into the town square of Merrimac, where they leave off the *k*. I don't know why. The square has a rotary and some lights and is empty. I turn right onto 110, two-lane and hilly with curves, and I have to piss. It's not just beer, it's nerve-piss, and I shiver holding it in. Nobody's on the road, and when I turn left toward the lake I cut the lights and can see clearly: the road is narrow with trees on its sides, and up ahead where the road turns left, there are trees too, a thin line of them at the side of the lake. I shift down and turn and back up and turn, and park it facing 110. I take the gasoline can from behind my seat, then piss on the grass, looking up at the stars and smelling the pines among the trees. I carry the gasoline can in my left hand, the side away from the road, and walk on grass, close to the trees. I have on my newest jeans, the darkest I've got, and a dark blue shirt with long sleeves. My fingers try to stiffen, holding the can. That's from DeLuca, maybe the first one, that came up from behind my ass and got his jaw; he saw it but only in time to turn his face from it a little, so all he did was stretch his jaw out for me to hit. He should have dropped his chin, caught it on the head. I hear the lake, then see it through the trees. It's bigger than ours but there are more houses too, all around it, and in summer they're filled. We only have a few houses, on the east and north sides, because it's way out in the boondocks and the west and south sides belong to some nature outfit that a rich guy gave his land to, and all you can do there is hike and look at trees and birds. The road turns left, between the woods and the backs of houses, and I follow it near the trees. A dog barks and some others pick it up. But it's just the bitchy barking of pets, there's not a serious one in there, and I keep walking, and nobody talks to the dogs or comes out for a look, and they stop.

All the houses are so close together I won't see Steve's until I'm at it. I know it's on this road and it's brown. King wrote to me and

Alex once from there; he didn't want the folks to read it; he wrote about patrols and ambushes. He said *Don't get me wrong, I wish right now I was back there with you guys and a case of Bud in the cooler out on a boat pulling in mackerel. They must be in, about now. But I'll say this: I'll never feel the adrenaline like this again, not even with bluefish or deer or kicking ass. I understand now what makes bankers and such go skydiving on Saturdays.* Then I see Polly's red Subaru and Steve's van, and I freeze, then lower the can to the ground and kneel beside it. I wonder if this is close to what King felt. When I think of the arsenal Steve's got inside, I believe maybe it is. I kneel listening. There's a breeze and the water lapping in front of the house. I listen some more, then unscrew the cap and get up to a crouch and cross the road. I stand behind his van and look up and down the road and in the yards next door. Every yard is small, every house is small, no rich man's lake here, but people that work. Her car and the van are side by side in a short dirt driveway; on the right, by the corner of the house, there's a woodpile. I look at the dark windows, then go for the wood. I'm right under a window, and all I can hear is the breeze and the water. I move up the side of the house, under windows, toward the lake. At the front yard I stop, breathing through my mouth but slow and quiet as I can. There's a tree that looks like an oak in the yard, then the wharf. He's got a cement patio with some chairs and a hammock and a barbecue grill and table with empty beer bottles on it. I run to the lake side of the tree and press my back against it; he has a short wharf with an outboard and a canoe. I look around the tree at the front of the house. Then I step toward the lake, move out far enough so I'm past the branches—it's an oak— and I start pouring: walking backward parallel to the house that I'm watching all the time, and when I clear it, I turn and back toward the road, watching Steve's and the house on my left too. The gasoline is loud, back and forth in the can, and pouring onto the grass.

I back up past their cars and my back is stiff, I'm breathing short and quiet and need more of it but won't; I make a wide circle around their cars, and take the can cap from my pocket and drop it there, and go around the house again, the corner with the woodpile, and I back toward the lake, checking the other house on my left now, my head going back and forth but mostly forth, waiting for

Steve to stick a Goddamn .30-06 or 12-gauge out one of the windows, then I'm past the house and feeling the lake behind me and I keep going to the tree and around it, and all I can smell is gasoline. I empty the can near where I started so the lines will meet. Then I straighten up and step down off a low concrete wall to the beach. I go up the beach past three houses, then out between them to the road, and I cross it and lay the can in the woods. Then I cross again and stand at the road with her car and his van between me and the house. I look down till I see the gas cap. Then I take one match from a book and strike it and hold it to the others; they catch with a hiss, and I toss them at the cap: the gasoline flares with a whoosh and runs left and right and dances around the corners into the breeze, curving every which way, and I run back into the road where I can look past the house in time to see the flames coming at each other around the house, doing some front-yard patterns like ice skaters where I emptied the can. Then they meet and I am running on the grass beside the road, down the road and around the corner, on the grass in the dark by the woods, to my jeep up there. The key is in my hand.

In the upstairs bedroom she wakes to firelight and flickering shadows on the walls that do not yet feel like her own, and she is so startled out of sleep that she is for a moment displaced, long enough for this summer's fear—that no walls and roof will ever feel like her own—to rise in her heart before it is dissipated by this new fear she has waked to; then she is throwing back the sheet and crossing the floor. Out the front window she looks at sinuous flames surrounding the yard between her and the lake; calling Steve, she goes to the side window and looks down at fire, then into the back room where Steve's mattress on the floor is empty, still made since morning. She steps on and over it, to the rear window overlooking the yard and car and van and the ring of fire. She switches on the stair light and descends, calling; by the bottom step she knows she is not trapped and her voice softens, becomes quizzical. Downstairs is a kitchen, darkened save for the wavering light on the walls, and a living room where he sleeps sitting on the couch, his feet on the coffee table, the room smelling of beer and cigarette smoke.

'Steve?' He stirs, shakes his head, drops his feet to the floor. She points out the wide front window. 'Look.'

He is up, out the front door, turning on the faucet and pulling the coiled hose across the patio. In places the fire has spread toward the house, but it is waning and burns close to the ground.

'It's all around,' she says, as, facing the lake, he moves the hose in an arc; neighbor men shout and she trots to either side of the house and sees them: the men next door with their hoses and wives and children. Steve belches loudly; she turns and sees him pissing on the fire, using his left hand, while his right moves the hose. He yells thanks over each shoulder; the men call back. The fire is out, and Steve soaks the front lawn, then both sides, joining his stream with the others. He asks her to turn it off, and he coils the hose and she follows him to the backyard. The two men come, and their wives take the children inside.

'Jeesum Crow,' one says. 'What do you figure that was about?'

'Tooth fairy,' Steve says, and offers them a beer. They accept, their voices mischievous as they excuse themselves for drinking at this hour after being wakened. They blame the fire. Polly has come to understand this about men: they need mischief and will even pretend a twelve-ounce can of beer is wicked if that will make them feel collusive while drinking it. Steve brings out four bottles, surprises her by handing her one he had not offered; she is pleased and touches his hand and thanks him as she takes it. She sits on the back stoop and watches the men standing, listens to their strange talk: about who would want to do such a thing, and what did a guy want to get out of doing it, and if they could figure out what he was trying to get done, then maybe they could get an idea of who it might be. But their tone will not stay serious, moves from inquisitive to jestful, without pattern or even harmony: while one supposes aloud that teenaged vandals chose the house at random and another agrees and says it's time for the selectmen to talk strict curfew and for the Goddamn cops to do some enforcing, the first one cackles and wheezes about a teenaged girl he watched water skiing this afternoon, how she could come to his house any night and light some fire. They clap hands on shoulders, grab an arm and pull and push. Steve takes in the empties and brings out four more.

Polly goes upstairs for cigarettes and stands at the back window, looking down at them. Steve has slept in here since she moved in; some nights, some days, one of them has stood in the short hall between their rooms and tapped on the door, with a frequency and need like that of a couple who have lived long together: not often, and not from passion, but often enough for release from carnal solitude. She does not want to join the men in the yard and does not want to be alone in the house; she goes downstairs and sits on the stoop, smoking, and staring at the woods beyond them. She imagines Ray lying under the trees, watching, his knife in his hand. One of the men stoops and rises with something he shows the others. A cap from a gasoline can, they say. Sitting between the house and the men, she still feels exposed, has the urge to look behind her, and she smokes deeply and presses her fingers against her temples, rubs her eyes to push away her images of him softly paddling a canoe on the lake, standing on the front lawn, creeping into hiding in the living room, up the stairs to her bedroom; in the closet there. The men are leaving. They tell her good night, and she stands and thanks them. Steve comes to her, three bottles in his large hand. He places the other on her shoulder.

'Looks like your ex is back,' he says.

'Yes.'

'Dumb asshole.'

'Yes.'

Vinnie is a bruise on the pillow, and from a suspended bottle of something clear, a tube goes to his left arm and ends under tape. He is asleep. She stands in the doorway, wanting to leave; then quietly she goes in, to the right side of the bed. His flesh is black and purple under both eyes, on the bridge of his nose, and his right jaw; cotton is stuffed in his nostrils; his breath hisses between swollen lips, the upper one stitched. Polly has not written a card for the zinnias she cut from her mother's garden but, even so, she can let him wake to them and phone later, come back later, do whatever later. When she puts them on the bedside table, his eyes open.

'I brought you some flowers,' she says. She looks over her shoulder at the door, then takes from her purse a brown-bagged pint of vodka. Smiling, she pulls out the bottle so he can see the label, then drops it into the bag. He only watches her. She cannot tell whether his eyes show more than pain. She pushes the vodka under his pillows.

'Do you hurt?'

'Drugs,' he says, through his teeth, only his lips moving, spreading in a grimace.

'Oh Jesus. Your jaw's broken?'

He nods.

'Will you hurt if I sit here?'

'No.'

She sits on the side of the bed and takes his right hand lying on the sheet, softly rubs his bare forearm, watching the rise and fall of his dark hair, its ends sun-bleached gold. His arm is wide and hard with muscle, her own looks delicate, and as she imagines Ray's chest and neck swelling with rage, a cool shiver rises from her legs to her chest. She reaches for her purse on the bedside table.

'Can I smoke in here?'

'I guess.'

He sounds angry; she knows it is because his jaw is wired, but still she feels he is angry at her and ought to be. She finds an ashtray in the drawer of the bedside table, cocks her head at the hanging bottle of fluid, and says: 'Is that your food?'

'Saline. Eat with a straw.'

'Can you smoke?'

'Don't know.'

She holds her cigarette between his lips, on the right side, away from the stitches. She cannot feel him drawing on it; he nods, she removes it, and he exhales a thin stream.

'Are you hurt anywhere else? Your body?'

'No. How did you know?'

'My father called me.' She offers the cigarette, he nods, and as he draws on it, she says: 'He said you're not pressing charges.'

His face rolls away from the cigarette, he blows smoke toward the tube rising from his arm, then looks at her, and she knows what she first saw in his eyes and mistook for pain.

'I don't blame you,' she says. 'I wouldn't either. In June he came into my apartment with a fucking knife and raped me. I was afraid to do anything, and I kept thinking he was gone. *Really* gone, like California or someplace. Because Dad checked at where he worked and his apartment, and he never went back after that night. Even if I knew he hadn't gone, I wouldn't have. Because he's fucking *crazy*.'

She stands and takes her cigarettes and disposable lighter from her purse and puts them on the table.

'I'll leave you these. I have to go. I'll be back.'

Her eyes are filling. Besides Steve, Vinnie is the only person outside her family she has told about the rape, but his eyes did not change when she said it; could not change, she knows, for the sorrow in them is so deep. She has known him in passion and mirth, and kissing his forehead, his unbruised left cheek, his chin, she feels as dangerous as Ray, more dangerous with her slender body and pretty face.

'I guess it wasn't worth it,' she says.

'Nothing is. I'm all broken.'

Sometimes, on her days off that summer, she put on a dress and went to Timmy's in early afternoon to drink. It was never crowded then, and always the table by the window was empty, and she sat there and watched the Main Street traffic and the people walking outside in the heat; or, in the rain, cars with lights and windshield wipers on, the faces of drivers and passengers blurred by rain and dripping windows.

She slept late. She was twenty-six and, for as long as she could remember, she had hated waking early; now that she worked at night, she not only was able to sleep late, but had to; she lived at home and no longer felt, as she had when she was younger and woke to the family voices, that she had wasted daylight sleeping while everyone else had lived half a day. There had been many voices then, but now two brothers and a sister had grown and moved away, and only Margaret was at home. She was seventeen and drank a glass of wine at some family dinners, had never, she said, had a cigarette in her mouth, had not said but was certainly a virgin, and early in the morning jogged for miles on the country roads near their home; during blizzards, hard rain, and days when ice on the roads slowed her pace, she ran around the indoor basketball court at the YMCA. She received Communion every Sunday and, in the Lenten season, every day. She was dark and pretty, but Polly thought all that virtue had left its mark on her face, and it would never be the sort that makes men change their lives.

Polly liked her sister, and was more amused than annoyed by the way she lived. She could not understand what pleasures Margaret drew from running and not drinking or smoking dope or even cigarettes, and from virginity. She did understand Margaret's religion, and sometimes she wished that being a Catholic were as easy for her as it was for Margaret. Then she envied Margaret, but when envy became scorn she fought it by imagining Margaret on a date; certainly she felt passion, so maybe her sacramental life was not at all easy. Maybe waking up and jogging weren't either; and she would remember her own high school years when, if you wanted friends and did not want to do what the friends did, you had to be very strong. So those times when she envied, then scorned Margaret ended with her wondering if perhaps all of Margaret's life was good because she willed it.

Polly went to Mass every Sunday, but did not receive communion because she had not been in the state of grace for a long time, and she did not confess because she knew that she could not be absolved of fornication and adultery while wearing an intrauterine device whose presence belied her firm intention of not sinning again. She was not certain that her lovemaking since the end of her marriage was a sin, or one serious enough to forbid her receiving, for she did not feel bad about it, except when she wished during and afterward that she had not gone to bed with someone, and that had to do with making a bad choice. She had never confessed her adultery while she was married to Raymond Yarborough, though she knew she had been wrong, had felt wicked as well as frightened; but, remembering now (she had filed for divorce and changed her name back to Comeau), her short affair with Vinnie when the marriage was in its final months was diminished by her sharper memory of Raymond yelling at her that she was a spoiled, fucked-up cunt not worth a shit to anybody, Raymond slapping her, and, on the last night, hitting her with his fist and leaving her unconscious on the bedroom floor, where she woke hearing Jerry Jeff Walker on the record player in the living room and a beer bottle landing on others in the wastebasket. Her car key was in there with him, so she climbed out the window and ran until she was nauseated and her legs were weak and trembling; then she walked, and in two hours she was home. She had to wake them to get in, and her mother put ice on her jaw, Margaret held her hand and stroked her hair, and her father took his gun and nightstick and drove to the apartment, but Raymond was gone in his jeep, taking with him his weights and bench and power stands, fishing rods and tackle box, two shotguns and a .22 rifle, the hunting knife he bought in memory of his brother, his knapsack and toilet articles and some clothes. When she moved from that apartment two weeks later, she filled a garbage bag with his clothes and Vietnam books, most of them hardcover, and left it on the curb; as she drove away, she looked in the rear view mirror at the green bulk and said aloud: 'Adiós, motherfucker.'

She also did not go to confession because, as well as not feeling bad about her sexual adventures, and knowing that she would not give them up anyway, she did believe that in some way her life was not a good one, but in a way the Church had not defined. Neither could she: even on those rare and mysterious nights when drinking saddened her and she went to bed drunk and disliking herself and woke hung over and regretful, she did not and could not know what about herself she disliked and regretted. So she could not confess, but she went to Mass with her family every Sunday and had gone when she lived alone, because it was one religious act she could perform, and she was afraid that neglecting it would finally lead her to a fearful loneliness she could not bear.

Dressing for Mass was different from dressing for any other place, and she liked having her morning coffee and cigarette while, without anticipating drinks or dinner or a man or work or anything at all, she put on makeup and a dress and heels; and she liked entering the church where the large doors closed behind her and she walked down the aisle under the high, curved white ceiling, and between stained-glass windows in the white walls whose lower halves were dark brown wood, as the altar was and the large cross with a bronze Christ hanging from the wall behind it. When she was with her family, her father chose a pew and stood at it while Margaret went in, then Polly, then her parents; alone, she looked for a pew near the middle with an aisle seat. She kneeled on the padded kneeler, her arms on the smooth old wood of the pew in front of her, and looked at the altar and crucifix and the stained-glass window behind them; then sat and looked at people sitting in front of her on both sides of the aisle. There was a scent of perfume and sometimes leather from purses and coats, tingeing that smell she only breathed here: a blending of cool, dry basement air with sunlight and melting candle wax. As the priest entered wearing green vestments, she rose and sang with the others, listened to her voice among theirs, read the Confiteor aloud with them, felt forgiven as she read *in what I have done and in what I have failed to do*, those simple and general words as precise as she could be about the life, a week older each Sunday, that followed her like a bridal train into church where, for forty minutes or so, her mind was suspended, much as it was when she lay near sleep at the beach. She did not pray with concentration, but she did not think either, and her mind wandered from the Mass to the faces of people around her. At the offertory she sang with them and, later, stood and read the Lord's Prayer aloud; then the priest said *Let us now offer each other a sign of peace* and, smiling, she shook the hands of people in front of her and behind her, saying *Peace be with you.*

She liked to watch them receive communion: children and teen-agers and women and men going slowly in two lines up the center aisle and in single lines up both side aisles, to the four waiting priests. Coming back, they chewed or dissolved the host in their mouths. Sometimes a small boy looked about and smiled. But she only saw children when they crossed her vision; she watched the others: the old, whose faces had lost any sign of beauty or even pleasure, and were gentle now, peacefully dazed, with God on their tongues; the pretty and handsome young, and the young who were plain or homely; and, in their thirties and forties and fifties, women and men who had lost the singularity of youth, their bodies unat-tractive, most of them too heavy, and no face was pretty or plain, handsome or homely, and all of these returned to their pews with clasped hands and bowed heads, their faces both serious and calm. She tenderly watched them. Now that she was going to Mass with her family, she watched them too, the three dark faces with down-cast eyes: slender Margaret with her finely concave cheeks, and no makeup, her lips and brow bearing no trace of the sullen prudery she sometimes turned on Polly, sometimes on everyone; her plump mother, the shortest in the family now, grey lacing her black hair, and her frownlike face one of weariness in repose, looking as it would later in the day when, reading the paper, she would fall asleep on the couch; her father, tall and broad, his shirt and coat tight across his chest, his hair thick and black, and on his face the look of peaceful concentration she saw when he was fishing; and she felt merciful toward them, and toward herself, not only for her guilt or shame because she could not receive (they did not speak to her about it, or about anything else she did, not even—except Margaret—with their eyes), but for her sense and, often at Mass, her conviction that she was a bad woman. She rose and sang as the priest and altar boys walked up the aisle and out the front of the church; then people filled the aisle and she moved with them into the day.

She had always liked boys and was very pretty, so she had never had a close girl friend. In high school she had the friends you need, to keep from being alone, and to go with to places where boys were. Those friendships felt deep because at their heart were shared guilt and the fond trust that comes from it. They existed in, and because of, those years of sexual abeyance when boys shunned their company and went together to playing fields and woods and lakes and the sea. The girls went to houses. Waiting to be old enough to drive, waiting for those two or three years in their lives when a car's function would not be conveyance but privacy, they gathered at the homes of girls whose mothers had jobs. They sat on the bed and floor and smoked cigarettes.

Sometimes they smoked marijuana too, and at slumber parties, when the parents had gone to bed, they drank beer or wine bought for them by an older friend or brother or sister. But cigarettes were their first and favorite wickedness, and they delightfully entered their addiction, not because they wanted to draw tobacco smoke into their lungs, but because they wanted to be girls who smoked. Within two or three years, cigarette packs in their purses would be as ordinary as wallets and combs; but at fourteen and fifteen, simply looking at the alluring colored pack among their cosmetics excited them with the knowledge that a time of their lives had ended, and a new and promising time was coming. The smooth cellophane covering the pack, the cigarette between their fingers and lips, the taste and feel of smoke, and blowing it into the air, struck in them a sensual chord they had not known they had. They watched one another. They always did that: looked at breasts, knew who had gained or lost weight, had a pimple, had washed her hair or had it done in a beauty parlor, and, if shown the contents of a friend's closet, would know her name. They watched as a girl nodded toward a colored disposable lighter, smiled if smoke watered her eyes, watched the fingers holding the cigarette, the shape of her lips around the tip, the angle of her wrist.

So they were friends in that secret life they had to have; then they were older and in cars, and what they had been waiting for happened. They shared that too, and knew who was late, who was taking the pill, who was trusting luck. Their language was normally profane, but when talking about what they did with boys, they said *had sex, slept with, oral sex, penis*. Then they graduated and spread outward from the high school and the houses where they had gathered, to nearby colleges and jobs within the county. Only one, who married a soldier, moved out of the state. The others lived close enough to keep seeing each other, and in the first year out of high school some of them did; but they all had different lives, and loved men who did not know each other, and soon they only met by chance, and talked on sidewalks or at coffee counters.

Since then Polly had met women she liked, but she felt they did not like her. When she thought about them, she knew she could be wrong, could be feeling only her own discomfort. With her girlhood friends she had developed a style that pleased men. But talking with a woman was scrutiny, and always she was conscious of her makeup, her pretty face, her long black hair, and the way her hands moved with a cigarette, a glass, patting her hair in place at the brow, pushing it back from a cheek. She studied the other woman too, seeing her as a man would; comparing her, as a man would, with herself; and this mutual disassembly made them wary and finally mistrustful. At times Polly envied the friendships of men, who seemed to compete with each other in everything from wit to strength, but never in attractiveness or over women; or girls like Margaret, who did nothing at all with her beauty, so that, seeing her in a group of girls, you would have to look closely to know she was the prettiest. But she knew there was more, knew that when she was in love she did not have the energy and time to become a woman's friend, to go beyond the critical eye, the cautious heart. Even men she did not love, but liked and wanted, distracted her too much for that. She went to Timmy's alone.

But not lonely: she went on days when, waking late, and eating a sandwich or eggs alone in the kitchen, she waited, her mind like a blank movie screen, to know what she wanted to do with her day.

She saw herself lying on a towel at the beach; shopping at the mall or in Boston; going to Steve's house to swim in the lake or, if he wanted to run the boat, water-ski; wearing one of her new dresses and drinking at Timmy's. That was it, on this hot day in July: she wanted to be the woman in a summer dress, sitting at the table by the window. She chose the salmon one with shoulder straps, cut to the top of her breasts and nearly to the small of her back. Then she took the pistol from the drawer of her bedside table and put it in her purse. By one o'clock she was at the table, sipping her first vodka and tonic, opening a pack of cigarettes, amused at herself as she tasted lime and smelled tobacco, because she still loved smoking and drinking as she had ten years ago when they were secret pleasures, still at times (and today was one) felt in the lifted glass and fondled pack a glimmer of promise from out there beyond the window and the town, as if the pack and glass were conduits between the mysterious sensuous rhythms of the world and her own.

She looked out the window at people in cars and walking in the hot sunlight. Al was the afternoon bartender, a man in his fifties, who let her sit quietly, only talking to her when she went to the bar for another drink. Men came in out of the heat, alone or in pairs, and drank a beer and left. She drank slowly, glanced at the men as they came and went, kept her back to the bar, listened to them talking with Al. For the first two hours, while she had three drinks, her mood was the one that had come to her at the kitchen table. Had someone approached and spoken, she would have blinked at the face while she waited for the person's name to emerge from wherever her mind had been. She sat peacefully looking out the window, and at times, when she realized that she was having precisely the afternoon she had wanted, and how rare it was now and had been for years to have the feeling you had wanted and planned for, her heart beat faster with a sense of freedom, of generosity; and in those moments she nearly bought the bar a round, but did not, knowing then someone would talk to her, and what she had now would be lost, dissipated into an afternoon of babble and laughter. But the fourth drink shifted something under her mood, as though it rested on a foundation that vodka had begun to dissolve.

Now when she noticed her purse beside her hand, she did not think of money but of the pistol. Looking out at people passing on foot or in cars, she no longer saw each of them as someone who loved and hoped under that brilliant, hot sky; they became parts again, as the cars did, and the Chevrolet building across the street where behind the glass front girls spoke into telephones and salesmen talked to couples, and as the sky itself did: parts of this town, the boundaries of her life.

She saw her life as, at best, a small circle: one year as a commuting student, driving her mother's car twenty minutes to Merrimack College, a Catholic school with secular faculty, leaving home in the morning and returning after classes as she had since kindergarten, discovering in that year—or forcing her parents to discover what she had known since ninth grade—that she was not a student, simply because she was not interested. She could learn anything they taught, and do the work, and get the grades, but in college she was free to do none of this, and she chose to do only enough to accumulate eight Cs and convince her parents that she was, not unlike themselves, a person whose strengths were not meant to be educated in schools.

She did not know why she was not interested. In June, when her first and last year of college was a month behind her, she remembered it with neither fondness nor regret, as she might have recalled movies she had seen with boys she did not love. She had written grammatical compositions she did not feel or believe, choosing topics that seemed both approachable and pleasing to the teacher. She discovered a pattern: all topics were approachable if she simply rendered them, with an opening statement, proper paragraphs, and a conclusion; and every topic was difficult if she began to immerse in it; but always she withdrew. In one course she saw herself: in sociology, with amusement, anger, resignation, and a suspended curiosity that lasted for weeks, she learned of the hunters, the gatherers, the farmers, saw herself and her parents defined by survival; and industrialization bringing about the clock that, on her bedside table, she regarded as a thing which was not inanimate but a conscience run on electricity, and she was delighted, knowing that people had once lived in accord with the sun and weather, and that punctuality and times for work and food and not-work and sleep were later imposed upon them, as she felt now they were imposed upon her.

In her other classes she listened, often with excitement, to a million dead at Borodino, Bismarck's uniting Germany, Chamberlain at Munich, Hitler invading Russia on the twenty-second of June because Napoleon did, all of these people and their actions equally in her past, kaleidoscopic, having no causal sequence whose end was her own birth and first eighteen years. She could say 'On honeydew he hath fed / And drunk the milk of paradise' and '. . . the women come and go / Talking of Michelangelo,' but they, and Captain Vere hanging Billy Budd, and Huck choosing Nigger Jim and hell, joined Socrates and his hemlock and Bonhoeffer's making an evil act good by performing it for a friend, and conifers and deciduous trees, pistils and stamens, and the generals and presidents and emperors and kings, all like dust motes in the sunlight of that early summer, when she went to work so she could move to an apartment an hour's walk from the house she had lived in for nineteen years, and which she forced herself to call *my parents' house* instead of home until that became habitual.

She was a clerk in a department store in town. The store was old and had not changed its customs: it had no cash registers. She worked in the linen department, and placed bills and coins into a cylinder and put that in a tube which, by vacuum, took the money to a small room upstairs where women she never met sent change down. She worked six days a week and spent the money on rent and heat and a used Ford she bought for nine hundred and eighty-five dollars; she kept food for breakfasts and lunches in her refrigerator, and ate dinners with her parents or dates or bought pieces of fish, chicken, or meat on the way home from work. On Sundays she went to the beach.

A maternal uncle was a jeweler and owned a store, and in fall she went to work for him, learned enough about cameras and watches to help customers narrow their choices to two or three; then her uncle came from his desk, and compared watches or cameras with a fervor that made their purchase seem as fraught with possibilities of happiness and sorrow as choosing a lover. She liked the absolute cleanliness of the store, with its vacuumed carpets and polished glass, its lack of any distinctive odors, and liked to believe what she did smell was sparkle from the showcases. Her grey-haired uncle always wore a white shirt and bow tie; he told her neckties got in the way of his work, the parts of watches he bent over with loupe and tweezers and screwdriver and hand remover.

She said nothing about a tie clasp, but thought of them, even glanced at their shelf. She liked them, and all the other small things in their boxes on the shelves: cuff links and rings and pins and earrings. She liked touching them with customers.

She worked on Saturdays, but on Wednesday afternoons her uncle closed the store. It was an old custom in the town, and most doctors and lawyers and dentists and many owners of small stores kept it still. She had grown up with those Wednesday afternoons when she could not get money at the bank or see a doctor or buy a blouse, but now they were holidays for her. She had been in school so much of her life that she did not think of a year as January to January, but September to June and, outside of measured time, the respite of summer. Now her roads to and from work wound between trees that were orange and scarlet and yellow, then standing naked among pines whose branches a month later held snow, and for the first time in her memory autumn's colors did not mean a school desk and homework, and snow the beginning of the end of half a year and Christmas holidays. One evening in December, as she crossed her lawn, she stopped and looked down at the snow nearly as high as her boots; in one arm she cradled a bag of groceries; and looking at the snow, she knew, as if for the first time, though she had believed she had known and wanted it for years, that spring's trickle of this very snow would not mean now or ever again the beginning of the end of the final half-year, the harbinger of those three months when she lived the way they did before factory whistles and clocks.

The bag seemed heavier, and she shifted its weight and held it more tightly. Then she went inside and up two flights of stairs and into her apartment. She put the groceries on the kitchen table and sat looking from the bag to her wet boots with snow rimming the soles and melting on the instep. She took off her gloves and unbuttoned her coat and put her damp beret on the table. For a long time she had not been afraid of people or the chances of a day, for she believed she could bear the normal pain of being alive: her heart had been broken by girls and boys, and she had borne that, and she had broken hearts and borne that too, and embarrassment and shame and humiliation and failure, and she was not one of those who, once or more wounded, waited fearfully for the next mistake or cruelty or portion of bad luck. But she was afraid of what she was going through now: having more than one feeling at once, so that feeling proud and strong and despairing and resigned, she sat suspended in fear: *So this is the real world they always talked about.* She said it aloud: 'the real world,' testing its sound in the silence; for always, when they said it, their tone was one of warning, and worse, something not only bitter and defeated but vindictive as well, the same tone they had when they said *I told you so.* She groped into the bag, slowly tore open a beer carton as she looked at the kitchen walls and potted plants in the window, drew out a bottle, twisted off the cap, but did not drink. Her hand went into her purse, came out with cigarettes and lighter, placed them beside the beer. She hooked a toe under the other chair, pulled it closer, and rested both feet on it. *I don't believe it. And if you don't believe it, it's not true, except dying.*

What she did believe through that winter and spring was that she had entered the real world of her town, its time and work and leisure, and she looked back on her years of growing up as something that had happened to her outside of the life she now lived, as though childhood and her teens (she would soon be twenty) were, like those thirteen summers from kindergarten until the year of college, a time so free of what time meant to her now that it was not time but a sanctuary from it. Now, having had those years to become herself so she could enter the very heart of the town, the business street built along the Merrimack, where she joined the rhythmic exchange of things and energy and time for money, she knew she had to move through the town, and out of it. But, wanting that motion, she could not define it, for it had nothing to do with place or even people, but something within herself: a catapult, waiting for both release and direction, that would send her away from these old streets, some still of brick, and old brick leather factories, most of them closed but all of them so bleak, so dimly lit beyond their dirty windows that, driving or even walking past one, you could not tell whether anyone worked inside.

On a Wednesday afternoon in May, at a bar in Newburyport, where the Merrimack flowed through marshes to the sea, she sat alone on the second-floor sun deck, among couples in their twenties drinking at picnic tables. She sat on a bench along the railing, her back to the late-afternoon sun, and watched the drinkers, and anchored sailboats and fishing boats, and boats coming in. A small fishing boat followed by screaming gulls tied up at the wharf beside the bar, and she stood so she could look down at it. She had not fished with her father since she started working; she would call him tonight—no, she would finish this drink and go there for dinner and ask him if he'd like to go Sunday after Mass. Then Raymond Yarborough came around the cabin, at the bow, swinging a plastic bag of fish over his left shoulder. One of the men—there were six— gave him a beer. Her hand was up in a wave, her mouth open to call, but she stopped and watched. He had a beard now, brown and thick; he was shirtless and sunburned. She wore a white Mexican dress and knew how pretty she looked standing up there with the sun on her face and the sky behind her, and she waited. He lifted the bag of fish to the wharf and joined the others scrubbing the cleaning boards and deck. Then he went into the cabin and came out wearing a denim work shirt and looked up and laughed.

'Polly Comeau, what are you doing up there?'

She wondered about that, six years later, on the July afternoon at Timmy's; and wondered why, from that evening on, she not only believed her life had changed but knew that indeed it had (though she was never comfortable with, never sure of, the distinction between believing something about your life and that something also being true). But something did happen: when Ray became not the boy she had known in high school but her lover, then husband, she felt both released and received, no longer in the town, a piece of its streets and time, but of the town, having broken free of its gravity, so that standing behind the jewelry counter she did not feel rooted or even stationary; and driving to and from work, or pushing a cart between grocery shelves, were a new sort of motion whose end was not the jewelry store, the apartment, the supermarket cash register, but herself, the woman she saw in Raymond's face.

In her sleep she knew she was dreaming: she was waitressing at the Harbor Schooner, but inside it looked like the gymnasium in high school with tables for prom night, and the party of four she was serving changed to a crowd, some were familiar, and she strained to know them; then her father was frying squid in the kitchen and she was there with a tray, and he said *Give them all the squid they want*; then a hand was on her mouth and she woke with her right hand pushing his wrist and her left prying his fingers, and in that instant before opening her eyes, when her dream dissolved into darkness, she knew it was Ray. She was on her back and he was straddling her legs. She kneed him but he moved forward and she struck bone. He sat on her thighs and his right hand went to his back and she heard the snap, and the blade leaving its sheath; then he was holding it close to her face, his dark-bladed knife; in the moonlight she saw the silver line of its edge. Then its point touched her throat, and his hand left her mouth.

'Turn over,' he said.

He rose to his knees, and she turned on her stomach, her back and throat waiting for the knife, but then his knees were between her legs, his hand under her stomach, lifting: she kneeled with her face in the pillow, heard his buckle and snap and zipper and pants slipping down his legs; he pushed her nightgown up her back, the knife's edge touched her stomach, and he was in, rocking her back and forth. She gripped the pillow and tensed her legs, trying to remain motionless, but his thrusts drove her forward, and her legs like springs forced her to recoil, so she was moving with him, and always on her tightened stomach the knife flickered, his breathing faster and louder then Ah Ah Ah, a tremor of his flesh against hers, the knife scraping toward her ribs and breasts, then gone, and he was too; above his breathing and her own she heard the ascent of pants, the zipper and snap and buckle, but no sheathing of the blade, so the knife itself had, in the air above her as she collapsed forward, its own sound of blood and night: but please God oh Jesus please not her gripping the pillow, her chin pressed down covering her throat, not her in the white Mexican dress with her new sunburn standing at the rail, seeing now Christ looking down through her on the sun deck that May afternoon to her crouched beneath the knife—

'Good, Polly. You got a little juiced after a while. Good.'

His weight shifted, then he was on the floor. She heard him cut the telephone cord.

'See you later, Polly.'

His steps on the floor were soft: he shut the door and in the corridor he was quiet as night. Her grip on the pillow loosened; her hands opened; still she waited. Then slowly and quietly she rolled over and got out of bed and tiptoed to the door and locked it again. She lit a cigarette, sat on the toilet in the dark, wiped and flushed and went to the window beside the bed, where she stood behind the open curtain and looked down at the empty street. She listened for his jeep starting, heard only slow and occasional cars moving blocks away, in town, and the distant voices and laughter of an outdoor party, and country music from a nearby window. She dressed and went down the hall and three flights of stairs and outside, pausing on the front steps to look at the street and parked cars and, on the apartment's lawn and lawns on both sides of it and across the street, the shadowed trunks of trees. She could not hear the sounds of the party or the music from the record player. Then he was dripping out of her and she went up the stairs and sat on the toilet while he pattered into the water, then scrubbed her hands, went out again, down the walk, and turned left, walking quickly in the middle of the sidewalk between tree trunks and parked cars, and looked at each of them and over her shoulders and between the cars for two and a half blocks to the closed drugstore, lighted in the rear where the counter was. In the phone booth she stood facing the street; the light came on when she closed the door, so she opened it and called her father.

She knew his steps in the hall and opened the door before he knocked. He was not in uniform, but he wore his cartridge belt and holstered .38. She hugged his deep, hard chest, and his arms were around her, one hand patting her back, and when he asked what Ray had done to her, she looked up at his wide sunburned face, his black hair and green eyes like her own, then rested her face on his chest and soft old chamois shirt, and said: 'He had his knife. He touched me with it. My throat. My stomach. He cut the phone wire—' His patting hand stopped. 'The door was locked and I was asleep, he doesn't even *have* a credit card, I don't know what he used, I woke up with his hand on my mouth then he had that big knife, that *Marine* knife.'

His mouth touched her hair, her scalp, and he said: 'He raped you?'

She nodded against his chest; he squeezed her, then his hands vere holding her waist and he lifted her and his shoulders swung ⟩ the left and he put her down, as though moving her out of his path so he could walk to the bed, the wall, through it into the third-story night. But he did not move. He inhaled with a hiss and held it, then blew it out and did it again, and struck his left palm with his right fist, the open hand gripping the fist, and he stood breathing fast, the hand and fist pushing against each other. He was looking at the bed, and she wished she had made it.

'You better come home.'

'I want to.'

'Then I'm going look for him.'

'Yes.'

'You have anything to drink?'

'Wine and beer.'

When he turned the corner into the kitchen, she straightened the sheets; he came back while she was pulling the spread over the pillows.

'I'll call Mom,' he said. He stood by the bed, his hands on the phone. 'Then we'll go to the hospital.'

'I'm all right.'

He held the cord, looking at its severed end.

'They take care of you, in case you're pregnant.'

'I'm all right.'

He swallowed from the bottle, his eyes still on the cord. Then he looked at her.

'Just take something for tonight. We can come back tomorrow.'

She packed an overnight bag and he took it from her; in the corridor he put his arm around her shoulders, held her going slowly down the stairs and outside to his pickup; with a hand on her elbow he helped her up to the seat. While he drove he opened a beer she had not seen him take from the apartment. She smoked and watched the town through the windshield and open window: Main Street descending past the city hall and courthouse, between the library and a park, to the river; she looked across the river at the street climbing again and, above the streetlights, trees and two church steeples. On the bridge she saw herself on her knees, her face on the pillow, Ray plunging, Ray lying naked and dead on her apartment floor, her father standing above him. She looked at the broad river, then they were off the bridge and climbing again, past Wendy's and McDonald's and Timmy's, all closed. She wanted to speak, or be able to; she wanted to turn and look at her father, but she had to be cleansed first, a shower, six showers, twelve; and time; but it was not only that.

It was her life itself; that was the sin she wanted hidden from her father and the houses and sleeping people they passed; and she wanted to forgive herself but could not because there was no single act or even pattern she could isolate and redeem. There was something about her heart, so that now glimpsing herself waiting on tables, sleeping, eating, walking in town on a spring afternoon, buying a summer blouse, she felt that her every action and simplest moments were soiled by an evil she could not name.

Next day after lunch he brought her to a small studio; displayed behind its front window and on its walls were photographs, most in color, of families, brides and grooms, and what she assumed were pictures to commemorate graduation from high school: girls in dresses, boys in jackets and ties. The studio smelled of accumulated cigarette smoke and filled ashtrays, and the woman coughed while she seated Polly on a stool in the dim room at the rear. The woman seemed to be in her fifties; her skin had a yellow hue, and Polly did not want to touch anything, as if the walls and stool, like the handkerchief of a person with a cold, bore traces of the woman's tenuous mortality. She looked at the camera and prepared her face by thinking about its beauty until she felt it. They were Polaroid pictures; as she stood beside her father at the front desk, glancing at portraits to find someone she knew, so she could defy with knowledge what she defied now with instinct, could say to herself: *I know him, her, them; they're not like that at all; are fucked up too*, and, her breath recoiling from the odor of the woman's lungs that permeated the walls and pictures, she looked down at the desk, at her face as it had been only minutes ago in the back room. With scissors, the woman trimmed it. She watched the blade cutting through her breasts. The black-and-white face was not angry or hating or fearful or guilty; she did not know what it was but very serious and not pretty.

At City Hall they went to the detectives' office at the rear of the police station. Two detectives sat at desks, one writing, one drinking coffee. They greeted her father, and she stood in the doorway while he went to the desk of the coffee-drinker, a short man wearing a silver revolver behind his hip. Then her father leaned over him, hiding all but his hand on the coffee cup, and she watched her father's uniformed back, listened to his low voice without words. The other detective frowned as he wrote. Her father turned and beckoned: 'Okay, Polly.'

The detective rose to meet her, and she shook his hand and did not hear his name. His voice was gentle, as if soothing her while dressing a wound; he led her across the room and explained what he was doing as he rolled her right forefinger on ink, then on the license. There was a sink and he told her to use the soap and water, the paper towels, then brought her to his desk where her father waited, and held a chair for her. It had a cushioned seat, but a straight wooden back and no arms, so she sat erect, feeling like a supplicant, as she checked answers on a form he gave her (she was not a convicted felon, a drunk, an addict) and answered questions he asked her as he typed on her license: *one twenty-six, black* (he looked at her eyes and said: 'Pretty eyes, Polly'), *green.* He gave her the card and signed the front and looked at the back where he had typed *Dark* under Complexion, *Waitress* under Occupation, and, under Reason for Issuing License: *Protection.* He said the chief would sign the license, then it would go to Boston and return laminated in two weeks; he offered them coffee, they said no, and he walked them to the office door, his hand reaching up to rest on her father's shoulder. The other detective was still writing. In the truck, she said: 'He was nice.'

The gun, her father said, looked like a scaled-down Colt .45: a .380 automatic which they bought because it was used and cost a hundred and fifteen dollars (though he would have paid three hundred, in cash and gladly, for the .38 snubnose she looked at and held first; they were in the store within twenty hours of his bringing her home, then driving to Newburyport, to Ray's empty apartment, where he had kicked open the locked door and looked around enough to see in the floor dust the two bars of clean wood where the weight-lifting bench had been, and the clean circles of varying sizes left by the steel plates and power stands); and because of the way it felt in her hand, light enough so it seemed an extension of her wrist, a part of her palm, its steel and its wooden grips like her skinned bone, and heavy enough so she felt both safe and powerful, and the power seemed not the gun's but her own; and because of its size, which she measured as one and a half Marlboro boxes long, and its shape, flat, so she could carry it concealed in the front pocket of her jeans, when she left home without a purse.

They bought it in Kittery, Maine, less than an hour's drive up New Hampshire's short coast, at the Kittery Trading Post, where as a virgin, then not one but still young enough to keep that as secret as the cigarettes in her purse, she had gone with her father to buy surf rods and spinning rods, parkas, chamois and flannel shirts. It was also the store where Ray, while shopping for a pocketknife, had seen and bought (*I had to*, he told her) a replica of the World War II Marine knife, with the globe and anchor emblem on its sheath. It came in a box, on whose top was a reproduction of the knife's original blueprint from 1942. When he came home, he held the box toward her, said *Look what I found*, his voice alerting her; in his face she saw the same nuance of shy tenderness, so until she looked down at the box she believed he had brought her a gift. *I don't need it*, he said, as she drew it from the sheath, felt its edge, stroked its blood gutter. *But, see, we gave all his stuff away*. That was when she understood he had been talking about Kingsley, and she had again that experience peculiar to marriage, of entering a conversation that had been active for hours in her husband's mind. Now she brought her father to the showcase of knives and showed him, and he said: 'Unless he's good with it at thirty feet, he might as well not have it at all. Not now, anyways.'

Next day, in the sunlit evening of daylight savings time, at an old gravel pit grown with weeds and enclosed by woods on three sides, with a dirt road at one end and a bluff at the other, her father propped a silhouette of a man's torso and head against the bluff, walked twenty paces from it, and gave her the pistol. He had bought it in his name, because she was waiting for the license, and he could not receive the gun in Maine, so a clerk from the Trading Post, who lived in Massachusetts where he was also a gun dealer, brought it home to Amesbury, and her father got it during his lunch hour.

'It loads just like the .22,' he said.

A squirrel chattered in the trees on the bluff. She pushed seven bullets into the magazine, slid it into the handle, and, pointing the gun at the bluff, pulled the slide to the rear and let it snap forward;

the hammer was cocked, and she pushed up the safety. Then he told her to take out the magazine and eject the chambered shell: it flipped to the ground, and he wiped it on his pants and gave it to her and told her to load it again; he kept her loading and unloading for ten minutes or so, saying he was damned if he'd get her shot making a mistake with a gun that was supposed to protect her.

'Shoot it like you did the .22 and aim for his middle.'

He had taught her to shoot his Colt .22, and she had shot with him on weekends in spring and summer and fall until her midteens, when her pleasures changed and she went with him just often enough to keep him from being hurt because she had outgrown shooting cans and being with him for two hours of a good afternoon; or often enough to keep her from believing he was hurt. She stood profiled to the target, aimed with one extended hand, thumbed the safety off, and, looking over the cocked hammer and barrel at the shape of a man, could not fire.

'The Miller can,' she said, and, shifting her feet, aimed at the can at the base of the bluff, held her breath, and squeezed to an explosion that shocked her ears and pushed her arm up and back as dust flew a yard short of the can.

'Jesus *Christ*.'

'Reminds me of what I forgot,' he said and, standing behind her, he pulled back her hair and gently pushed cotton into her ears. 'Better go for the target. They didn't make that gun to hit something little.'

'It's the head. If we could fold it back.'

He patted her shoulder.

'Just aim for the middle, and shoot that piece of cardboard.'

Cardboard, she told herself as she lined up the sights on the torso's black middle and fired six times, but *shoulder* she thought when she saw the first hole, *missed, stomach, chest, shoulder, stomach*, and she felt clandestine and solemn, as though performing a strange ritual that would forever change her. She was suddenly tired. As she loaded the magazine, images of the past two nights and two days assaulted her, filled her memory so she could not recall doing anything during that time except kneeling between a knife and Ray's cock, riding in her father's truck—home, to the studio, to City Hall, to Kittery, home, to this woods—and being photographed and fingerprinted and questioned and pointing guns at the walls and ceiling of the store, and tomorrow night she had to wait tables, always wiping them, emptying ashtrays, bantering, smiling, soberly watching them get drunk, their voices louder than the jukebox playing music she would like in any other place. She fired, not trying to think *cardboard*, yielding to the target's shape and going further, seeing it not as any man but Ray, so that now as holes appeared and her arm recoiled from the shots muted by cotton and she breathed the smell of gunpowder, and reloaded and fired seven more times and seven more, she saw him attacking her and falling, attacking her and falling, and she faced the target and aimed with both hands at head and throat and chest, and once heard herself exhale: '*Yes.*'

Two weeks later her father brought her license home, but he had told her not to wait for it, no judge would send her to jail, knowing she had applied, and knowing why. So from that afternoon's shooting on, she carried it everywhere: in her purse, jeans, shorts, beach bag, in her skirt pocket at work and on the car seat beside her as, at two in the morning, she drove home, where she put it in the drawer of her bedside table and left her windows open to the summer air. At Timmy's on that sunlit afternoon in July she rested her hand on it, rubbed its handle under the soft leather of her purse. She knew she was probably drunk by police or medical standards, but not by her own. Her skin seemed thickened, so she could feel more sharply the leather and the pistol handle beneath it than her fingers themselves when she rubbed them together. For a good while she had been unaware of having legs and feet; her cheeks and lips were numb; sometimes she felt an elbow on the table, or the base of her spine, or her thighs when they pressed on the chair's edge, then she shifted her weight. But she was not drunk because she knew she was: she knew her reflexes were too slow for driving, and she would have to concentrate to walk without weaving to the ladies' room. She also knew that the monologue coming to her was true; they always were. She listened to what her mind told her when it was free of the flesh: sometimes after making love, or waking in the morning, or lying on the beach for those minutes before the sun warmed her to sleep, or when she had drunk enough, either alone or with someone who would listen with her; but for a long time there had been no one like that.

Only three men were at the bar now. She brought her glass and ashtray to it, told Al to fill one and empty the other, and took two cocktail napkins. She paid and tipped, then sat at the table and wiped it dry with the napkins, and waited for Steve. At ten to five he came in, wearing a short-sleeved plaid shirt, his stomach not hanging but protruding over his jeans. Halfway to the bar he saw her watching him and smiled, his hand lifting. She waved him to her and looked at his narrow hips as he came.

'Steve? Can I talk to you a minute?'

He glanced over her at the bar, said he was early, and sat. Even now in July, his arms and face looked newly sunburned, his hair and beard, which grew below his open collar, more golden.

'You're one of those guys who look good everywhere,' she said. 'Doing sports outside, drinking in a bar—you know what I mean? Like some guys look right for a bar, but you see them on a boat or something, and they look like somebody on vacation.'

'Some girls too.'

She focused on his lips and teeth.

'You're always smiling, Steve. Don't you ever get down? I've never seen you down.'

'No time for it.'

'No time for it. What did you do today, with all your time?'

'Went out for cod this morning—'

'Did you catch any?'

'Six. Came back to the lake, charcoaled a couple of fillets, and crapped out in the hammock. What's wrong—you down?'

'Me? No, I'm buzzed. But let me tell you: I've been thinking. I'm going to ask you a favor, and if it's *any* kind of *hass*le, you say no, all right? But I think it might be good for both of us. Okay? But if it's not—'

'What is it?'

'No, but wait. I'm sitting here, right? and looking out the window and thinking, and I've got to leave home. See'—she leaned forward, placed her hands on his wrists, and lowered her voice—'I'm living with my folks because I had a nice apartment and I liked being there, but last month, last month Ray broke in one night while I was sleeping and he held a knife on me and raped me.' She did not know what she had expected from his face, but it surprised her: he looked hurt and sad, and he nodded, then slowly shook his head. 'So I moved in with my folks. I was scared. I mean, it's not as bad as some girls get it, from some stranger, like that poor fifteen-year-old last year hitchhiking and he had a knife and made her *blow* him; it was just Ray, you know, but still—I've got a gun too, a permit, the whole thing.' He nodded. 'It's right here, in my purse.'

'That's the way it is now.'

'What is?'

'Whatever. Women need things; you're built too small to be safe anymore.'

'Steve, I got to move. But I'm still scared of having my own place. I was thinking, see, if I could move in with you, then I could do it gradually, you know? And when you leave in the fall I could sublet, I'd pay the whole rent for you till you get back, and by then—when do you come back?'

'Around April.'

'I'd be ready. Maybe I'd move to Amesbury or Newburyport. Maybe even Boston. I don't know why I said Boston. Isn't it funny it's right there and nobody ever goes to live there?'

'Not me. Spend your life walking on concrete? Sure: move in whenever you want.'

'Really? I won't be a problem. I can cook too—'

'So can I. Here.' He reached into his pocket, brought out a key ring and gave her a key. 'Anytime. Call me before, and I'll help you move.'

'No. No, I won't bring much: just, you know, clothes and cassette player and stuff. My folks won't like this.'

'Why not?'

'They'll think we're shacking up.'

'What are you, twenty-five?'

'Six.'

'So?'

'I know. It'll be all right. It's just I keep giving them such a bad time.'

'Hey: *you*'re the one having the bad time.'

'Okay. Can I move in tonight? No, I'm too buzzed. Tomorrow?'

'Tonight, tomorrow. Better bring sheets and a pillow.'

'I can't believe it.' He looked at the bar, then smiled at her and stood. 'All worked out, just like that. Jesus, you're saving my life, Steve. I'll start paying half the rent right away, and look: I'll stay out of the way, right? If you bring a girl home, I won't *be* there. I'll be shut up in my room, quiet as a mouse. I'll go to my folks' for the night, if you want.'

'No problem. Don't you even want to know how much the rent is?'

'I don't even *care*,' and she stood and put her arm around his back, her fingers just reaching his other side, and walked with him to the bar.

Polly's father comes down the slope of the lawn toward the wharf and I'm scared even while I look past him at the pickup I heard on the road, then down the driveway, and I look at his jeans and shirt; then I'm not scared anymore. For a second there, I thought Polly or maybe Vinnie had pressed some charges, but it all comes together at once: he's not in a cruiser and he's got no New Hampshire cops with him and he's wearing civvies, if you can call it that when he's wearing his gun and his nightstick too. I decide to stay in the deck chair. He steps onto the wharf and keeps coming and I decide to take a swallow of beer too. The can's almost empty and I tilt my head back; the sun is behind me, getting near the treetops across the lake. I'm wearing gym shorts and nothing else. I open the cooler and drop in the empty and take another; I know what my body looks like, with a sweat glisten and muscles moving while I shift in the chair to pull a beer out of the ice, while I open it, while I hold it up to him as he stops spread-legged in front of me.

'Want a beer, John?'

I don't know what pisses him off most, the beer or *John*; his chest starts working with his breath, then he slaps the can and it rolls foaming on the wharf, stops at the space between two boards.

'You don't like Miller,' I say. 'I think I got a Bud in there.'

He unsnaps his nightstick, moves it from his left hand to his right, then lowers it, holding it down at arm's length, gripping it hard and resting its end in his left hand. This time I don't shift: I watch his eyes and pull the cooler to me and reach down through the ice and water. I open the beer and take a long swallow.

'*Ass*hole,' he says. 'You want to *rape* somebody, *ass*hole? You want to set fucking *fires*?'

I watch his eyes. At the bottom of my vision I see the stick moving up and down, tapping his left hand. I lower the beer to the wharf and his eyes go with it, just a glance, his head twitching left and down; I grab the stick with my left hand and let the beer drop and get my right on it too. He holds on and I pull myself out of the chair, looking up at his eyes and pushing the stick down. My chest is close to his; we stand there holding the stick.

'What's the gun for, John?' I've got an overhand grip; I work my wrists up and down, turning the stick, and his face gets red as he holds on. I don't stop. 'You want to waste me, John? Huh? Go for it.'

I'm pumping: I can raise and lower the stick and his arms and shoulders till the sun goes down, and now he knows it and he knows I know it; he is sweating and his teeth are clenched and his face is very red with the sun on it. All at once I know I will not hurt him; this comes as fast as laughing, is like laughing.

'Go for the gun, John. And they'll cut it out of your ass.' I walk him backward a few steps, just to watch him keep his balance. 'They can take Polly's nose out too.'

'Fucker,' he says through his teeth.

'Yes I did, John. Lots of times. On the first date too. Did she tell you that?' He tries to shove me back and lift the stick; all he does is strain. 'It wasn't a date, even. I came in from fishing, and there she was, drinking at Michael's. We went to her place and fucked, and know what she said? After? She said, Once you get the clothes off, the rest is easy. Now what the fuck does *that* mean, John? What does that *mean?*'

I'm ahead of him again. Before he gets to the gun my left hand is on it; I swing the stick up above my head, his left hand still on it; I unsnap the holster and start lifting the gun up against his hand pressing down; it comes slowly but it never stops, and his elbow bends as his hand goes up his ribs. When the gun clears the holster he shifts his grip, grabs it at the cylinder, but his fingers slip off and claw air as I throw it backward over my shoulder and grab his wrist before the gun splashes. I lift the stick as high as I can. He still has some reach, so I jerk it down and free, and throw it with a backhand sidearm into the lake. He is panting. I am too, but I shut my mouth on it.

'Go home, John.'

'You leave her alone.'

He is breathing so hard and is so red that I get a picture of him on his back on the wharf and I'm breathing into his mouth.

'Go get some dinner, John.'

'You—' Then he has to cough; it nearly doubles him over, and he turns to the railing and holds it, leans over it, and hacks up a lunger. I turn away and pick up the beer I dropped. There's still some in it; I drink that and take one from the ice, then look at him again. He's standing straight, away from the rail.

'You leave her alone,' he says. 'Fire last night. What are you, crazy? DeLuca.'

'DeLuca who?'

He lifts a hand, waves it from side to side, shakes his head.

'I don't care shit about DeLuca,' he says. 'Let it go, Ray. You do anything to her, I'll bring help.'

'Good. Bring your buddies. What are friends for, that's what I say.'

'I mean it.'

'I know you do. Now go on home before that club floats in and we have to start all over.'

He looks at me. That's all he does for a while, then he turns and goes up the wharf, wiping his face on his bare arm. He walks like he's limping, but he's not. I get another beer and follow him up the lawn to his pickup. By the time he climbs in and starts it, I'm at his window. I toss the beer past him, onto the seat. He doesn't look at me. He backs and turns and I wait for gravel to fly, but he goes slowly up the driveway like the truck is tired too. At the road he stops and looks both ways. Then the beer comes out the window onto the lawn, and he's out on the blacktop, turning right, then he's gone beyond a corner of woods.

Last night waiting tables she was tired, and the muscles in her back and legs hurt. She blamed that afternoon's water skiing, and worked the dining room until the kitchen closed, then went upstairs to the bar and worked there, watching the clock, wiping her brow, sometimes shuddering as a chill spread up her back. She took orders at tables, repeated them to the bartender, garnished the drinks, subtracted in her mind, made change, and thanked for tips, but all that was ever in her mind was the bed at Steve's and herself in it. At

one o'clock the Harbor Schooner closed, and when the last drinkers had gone down the stairs, the bartender said: 'What'll it be
tonight?' and she went to the bar with the other two waitresses,
scanned the bottles, shaking her head, wanting to want a drink
because always she had one after work, but the bottles, even vodka,
even tequila, could have been cruets of vinegar. She lit a cigarette
and asked for a Coke.

'You feeling all right?' he said.

'I think I'm sick,' and she left the cigarette and carried the Coke,
finishing it with long swallows and getting another, as she helped
clean the tables, empty the ashtrays, and stack them on the bar.

She wakes at two o'clock in the heat of Labor Day weekend's
Sunday afternoon, remembers waking several times, once or more
when the room was not so brightly lit, so hot; and remembers she
could not keep her eyes open long enough to escape the depth of
her sleep. Her eyes close and she drifts downward again, beneath
her pain, into darkness; then she opens her eyes, the lids seeming
to snap upward against pressing weight. She grasps the edge of the
mattress and pulls while she sits and swings her legs off the bed,
and a chill grips her body and shakes it. Her teeth chatter as she
walks with hunched shoulders to the bathroom; the toilet seat is
cold, her skin is alive, crawling away from its touch, crawling up
her back and down her arms, and she lowers her head and mutters:
'Oh Jesus.'

She does not brush her teeth or hair, or look in the mirror. She
goes downstairs. There are no railings, and she slides a palm down
the wall. She drinks a glass of orange juice, finds a tin with three
aspirins behind the rice in the cupboard, swallows them with juice,
and phones the Harbor Schooner. Sarah the head waitress answers.

'Is Charlie there?'

'No.'

'Who's tending bar?'

'Sonny.'

'Let me talk to him.'

She ought to tell Sarah, but she does not like to call in sick to
women; they always sound like they don't believe her.

'I'm sick,' she says to Sonny. 'I think the flu.'

He tells her to go to bed and take care of herself, and asks if she
needs anything.

'No. Maybe I'll come in tomorrow.'

'Get well first.'

'I'll call.'

She takes the glass and pitcher upstairs, breathing quickly as she climbs. The sun angles through her bedroom windows, onto the lower half of the bed. There are shades, but she does not want to darken the room. She puts the pitcher and glass on the bedside table, lies on the damp sheet, pulls up the top sheet and cotton spread, and curls, shivering, on her side. Her two front windows face the lake; she hears voices from there, and motors, and remembers that she has been hearing them since she woke, and before that too, from the sleep she cannot fight. It is taking her now; she wants juice, but every move chills her and she will not reach for it. She stares at the empty glass and wonders why she did not fill it again, drinking would be so much easier, so wonderfully better, if she did not have to sit up and lift the pitcher and pour, so next time she drinks she will refill the glass because then it won't be so hard next time, and if she had a hospital straw, one of bent glass. Vinnie was last week with the tube in his arm and the bandages, but in memory he is farther away than a week, a summer; last night is a week away, going from table to table to table to bar to table to table and driving home, hours of tables and driving. Her memory of making love with Vinnie is clear but her body's aching lethargy rejects it, denies ever making love with anyone, ever wanting to, so that Vinnie last spring, early when the rivers began to swell with melting snow, is in focus as he should be: not loving him then she made love because, it seems to her now, he was something to do, one of a small assortment of choices for a week night; and she remembers him now without tenderness or recalled passion.

When she wakes again she is on her left side, facing the front windows, and the room's light has faded. The chills are gone, and she is hungry. There is ham downstairs, and eggs and cheese and bread, and leftover spaghetti, but her stomach refuses them all. She imagines soup, and wants that. But it is down the stairs and she would have to stand as she opened and heated it, then poured it into a cup so she could climb again and drink it here; she turns onto her right side and waits, braced against chills, but they don't come. Evening sunlight beams through the side window, opposite the foot of her bed, which is now in the dark spreading across the floor and dimming the blue walls. As though she can hear it, she senses the darkness in all the downstairs rooms, and more of it flowing in from the woods and lake. There are no motors on the water. Voices rise and waft from lawns touching the beach. She switches on the bedside lamp, pushes herself back and up till she sits against the pillows, and pours a glass of orange juice. She drinks it in three swallows, refills the glass, then lies on her back, closes her hot eyes, thinks of Ray, of danger she cannot feel, and lets the lamp burn so she will not wake in the dark.

For a while she sleeps, but she is aware that she must not, there is something she must do, and finally she wakes, her head tossing on the pillow, legs and arms tense. She reaches for the drawer beside her, takes the gun, holds it above her with both hands; she pulls the slide to the rear and eases it forward, watching the bullet enter the chamber. She lowers the hammer to half-cock and pushes up the safety. She turns on her side, slips the gun under the pillow, and goes to sleep holding the checkered wood of its handle.

She wakes from a dream that is lost when she opens her eyes to light, though she knows it was pleasant and she was not in it, but watched it. The three windows are black. Steve is looking down at her, his smell of beer and cigarettes, his red face and arms making her feel that health, that life even, are chance gifts to the lucky, kept by the strong, and she was not to have them again.

'Sorry,' he says. 'You want to go back to sleep?'

'No.' Her throat is dry, and she hears a plea in her voice. 'I'm sick.'

'I figured that. Can I do anything?'

'I think I want to smoke.'

He takes cigarette papers from his shirt pocket, a cellophane pouch from his jeans.

'No, a cigarette. In my purse.'

He lights it and hands it to her.

'Could I have some soup?'

'Anything else?'

'Toast?'

'Coming up.'

He goes downstairs, and she smokes, looking at the windows; she cannot see beyond the screens. Neither can her mind: her life is this room, where her body's heat and pain have released her from everyone but Steve, who brings her a bowl of soup on a plate with two pieces of toast. He pushes up the pillows behind her, then pulls a chair near the bed.

'I'm leaving in the morning.'

'What time is it?'

'Almost one.'

She shakes her head.

'That way I beat the traffic.'

'Good idea.'

'I can leave Tuesday, though. Or Wednesday.'

'You're meeting your friends there.'

'They'll keep.'

'No. Go tomorrow, like you planned.'

'You sure?'

'It's just the flu.'

'No fun having it alone.'

'All I do is sleep.'

'Still. You know.'

'I'll be all right.'

'What'll you do about the ex?'

'Maybe he won't come back.'

'Don't bet on it.'

'My father went to see him.'

'Yeah? What did he say?'

'Who, Ray? I don't know.'

'No, your dad.'

'He told him if he harassed me again, he'd take some people out there and break bones.'

'Thing about Ray is he doesn't give a shit.'

'He doesn't?'

'Think about it.'

'He gives a shit about a lot of things.'

'Not broken bones. That little gun you got: if he comes, fire a couple over his head.'

'Why?'

'Because I don't think you could use it on him, and you might just leave it in the drawer. Then there's nothing you can do. So think about scaring him off.'

'I'd use it. You don't know what it's like, a man—what's the *mat*ter with him?'

He shrugs and takes the bowl and plate.

'Think two shots across the bow,' he says and stands; then, leaning over her, he is huge, blocking the ceiling and walls, his chest and beard lowering, his face and breath close to hers; he kisses her forehead and right cheek and smooths the hair at her brow. She watches him cross the room; at the door he turns and says: 'I'll leave this open; mine too. If you need something, give a shout.'

'You've got a nice ass,' she says, and smiles as his eyes brighten and his beard and cheeks move with his grin. She listens to his steps going down, and the running water as he washes her dishes. When he starts upstairs she turns out the lamp. In his room his boots drop to the floor, there is a rustle of clothes, and he is in bed. He shifts twice, then is quiet. She sits against the pillows in the dark; and wakes there, Steve standing beside her, the room sunlit and cool. The lake is quiet.

'You're going?'

'It's time.'

'Have fun.'

'Sure. You want breakfast?'

'No.'

She takes his hand, and says: 'I'll see you in April, I guess. Good hunting and all. Skiing.'

'If you don't find a place, or you want to stay on in spring, that's fine.'

'I know.'

'Well—' His thumb rubs the back of her hand.

'Thanks for everything,' she says.

'You too.'

'The room. Good talks. Whatever.'

'Whatever,' he says, smiling. Then he kisses her lips and is gone.

In early afternoon she phones the Harbor Schooner and tells Charlie, the manager, that she is still sick and can't make it that night but will try tomorrow. She eats a sandwich of ham and cheese, makes a pitcher of orange juice, and brings it upstairs. She reaches the bed weak and short of breath. Through the long hot afternoon she lies uncovered on the bed, asleep, awake, asleep, waking always to the sound of motorboats, the voices of many children, and talk and shouts and laughter of men and women. When the sun has moved to the foot of the bed and the room is darkening, she smells charcoal smoke. She turns on the lamp and lies awake listening to the beginning of silence: the boats are out of the water, most of them on trailers by now; she hears cars leaving, and on the stretch of beach below her windows, families gather, their voices rising with the smells of burning charcoal and cooking meat. Tomorrow she will wake to quiet that will last until May.

She closes her eyes and imagines the frozen lake, evergreens, the silent snow. After school and on weekends boys will clean the ice with snow shovels and play hockey; she will hear only burning logs in the fireplace, will watch them from the living room, darting without sound into and around one another. She will have a Christmas tree, will eat dinner at her parents', but on Christmas Eve she could have them and Margaret here for dinner before midnight Mass. She will live here—she counts by raising thumb and fingers from a closed fist—eight months. Or seven, so she can be out before Steve comes back. Out where? She shuts her eyes tighter, frowning, but no street, no town appears. In the Merrimack Valley she likes Newburyport but not as much since she started working there, and less since Ray moved there. Amesbury and Merrimac are too small, Lawrence is mills and factories, and too many grocery stores and restaurants with Spanish names, and Haverhill: Jesus, Haverhill: some people knew how to live there, her parents did, Haverhill for her father was the police department and their house in the city limits but in the country as well, with the garden her mother and father planted each spring: tomatoes, beans, squash, radishes, beets; and woods beyond the garden, not forest or anything, but enough to walk in for a while before you came to farmland; and her father ice-fished, and fished streams and lakes in spring, the ocean in summer. Everyone joked about living in Haverhill, or almost everyone: the skyline of McDonald's arch and old factories and the one new building on the corner of Main Street and the river, an old folks' home and office building that looked like a gigantic cinder block. But it wasn't that. The Back Bay of Boston was pretty, and the North End was interesting with all those narrow streets and cluttered apartments of Italians, but Jesus, Boston was dirtier than Haverhill and on a grey winter day no city looked good. It was that nothing happened in Haverhill, and she had never lived outside its limits till now, and to go back in spring was going downhill backward. A place would come. She would spend the fall and winter here, and by then she would know where to go.

She looks at the walls, the chest with her purse and cassette player on its top, the closed door of the closet; she will keep this room so she'll have the lake (and it occurs to her that this must have been Steve's, and he gave it up), and she'll hang curtains. She will leave his room, or the back room, alone; will store in it whatever she doesn't want downstairs, that chair with the flowered cover he always sat in, and its hassock, the coffee table with cigarette burns like Timmy's bar; she will paint the peeling cream walls in the kitchen. For the first time since moving in, she begins to feel that more than this one room is hers; not only hers but her: her sense of this seems to spread downward, like sentient love leaving her body to move about the three rooms downstairs, touching, looking, making plans. Her body is of no use to her but to move weakly to the bathroom, to sleep and drink and, when it will, to eat. Lying here, though, is good; it is like the beach or sleeping late, better than those because she will not do anything else, cannot do anything else, and so is free. Even at the beach you have to—what? Go into the water. Collect your things and drive home. Wash salt from suit, shower, wash hair, dry hair. Cook. Eat. But this, with no chills now, no pain unless she moves, which she won't, this doesn't have to end until it ends on its own, and she can lie here and decorate the house, move furniture from one room to another, one floor to another, bring all her clothes from her parents' house, her dresser and mirror, while outside voices lower as the smell of meat fades until all she smells is smoke. Tomorrow she will smell trees and the lake.

She hears a car going away, and would like to stand at the window and look at the darkened houses, but imagines them instead, one by one the lights going out behind windows until the house becomes the shape of one, locked for the winter. She is standing at the chest, getting her cigarettes, when she hears the people next door leaving. *Do it*, she tells herself. She turns out the bedside lamp, crouches at a front window, her arms crossed on its sill, and looks past trees in the front lawn at the dark lake. She looks up at stars. To her right, trees enclose the lake; she cannot see the houses among them. Water laps at the beach and wharf pilings. She can see most of the wharf before it is shielded by the oak; below her, Steve's boat, covered with tarpaulin, rests on sawhorses. Her legs tire, and she weakens and gets into bed, covers with the sheet and spread, and lights a cigarette, the flame bright and large in the dark. She reaches for the lamp switch, touches it, but withdraws her hand. She smokes and sees the bathroom painted mauve.

For a long while she lies awake, filling the ashtray, living the lovely fall and winter: in a sweater she will walk in the woods on brown leaves, under yellow and red, and pines and the blue sky of Indian summer. She will find her ice skates in her parents' basement; she remembers the ponds when she was a child, and wonders how or why she outgrew skating, and blames her fever for making her think this way, but is uncertain whether the fever has made her lucid or foolish. She is considering a snow blower for the driveway, has decided to buy one and learn to use it, when he comes in the crash of breaking glass and a loud voice: he has said something to the door, and now he calls her name. She moves the ashtray from her stomach to the floor, turns on her side to get the gun from under the pillow, then lies on her back.

'Polly?' He is at the foot of the stairs. 'It's me. I'm coming up.'

He has the voice of a returning drunk, boldly apologetic, and she cocks the hammer and points the gun at the door as he climbs, his boots loud, without rhythm, pausing for balance, then quick steps, a pause, a slow step, evenly down the few strides of hall, and his width above his hips fills the door; he is dark against the grey light above him.

'You in here?'

'I've got a gun.'

'No shit? Let me see it.'

She moves her finger from the trigger, and pushes the safety down with her thumb.

'It's pointed at you.'

'Yeah? Where's the light in here?'

'You liked the dark before.'

'I did? That's true. That little apartment we had?'

'I mean June, with that fucking knife.'

'Oh. No knife tonight. I went to the Harbor Schooner—'

'Shit: what *for*.'

'—So I goes Hey: where's Polly? Don't she work here? Sick, they said. To see you, that's all. So I did some shots of tequila and I'm driving up to New Hampshire, and I say what the fuck? So here I am. You going to tell me where the light is?'

His shoulders lurch as he steps forward; she fires at the ceiling above him, and he ducks, his hands covering his head.

'Pol*ly*.' He lowers his hands, raises his head. 'Hey, Polly. Hey: put that away. I just want to talk. That's all. That was an asshole thing I did, that other time. See—'

'Go away.'

Her hand trembles, her ears ring, and she sits up in the gunpowder smell, swings her feet to the floor, and places her left hand under her right, holding the gun with both.

'I just want to ask you what's the difference, that's all. I mean, how was it out here with Steve? You happy, and everything?'

'It was *great*. And it's going to be better.'

'Better. Better without Steve?'

'Yes.'

'Why's that? You got somebody moving in?'

'No.'

'But it was good with Steve here. Great with Steve. So what's the difference, that's what I think about. Maybe the lake. The house? I mean, what if it was with me? Same thing, right? Sleep up here over the lake. Do some fucking. Wake up. Eat. Swim. Work. How come it was so good with Steve?'

'We weren't *mar*ried.'

'Oh. Okay. That's cool. Why couldn't it be us then, out here? What did I ever do anyways?'

'Jesus, what is this?'

'No, come on: what did I do?'

'Nothing.'

'Nothing? I must've done something.'

'You didn't do anything.'

'Then why weren't you happy, like with Steve? I mean, I thought about it a lot. It wasn't that asshole DeLuca.'

'You almost killed him.'

'Bullshit.'

'You could have.'

'You see him?'

'I brought him flowers, is all.'

'See: it wasn't him. And I don't think it was me either. If it was him, you'd be with him, and if it was me, well, you got rid of me, so then you'd be happy.'

'I *am* happy.'

'I don't know, Polly.'

She can see the shape and muted color of his face, but his eyes are shadows, his beard and hair darker; his shoulders and arms move, his hands are at his chest, going down, then he opens his shirt, twists from one side to the other pulling off the sleeves.

'Don't, Ray.'

Flesh glimmers above his dark pants, and she pushes the gun toward it.

'Let's just try it, Polly. Turn on the light, you'll see.' He unbuckles his belt, then stops, raises a foot, holds it with both hands, hops backward and hits the doorjamb, pulls off the boot, and drops it. Leaning there, he takes off the other one, unzips his pants, and they fall to his ankles. He steps out of them, stoops, pushing his shorts down. 'See. No knife. No clothes.' He looks down. 'No hard-on. If you'd turn on a light and put away that hogleg—'

He moves into the light of the door, into the room, and she shakes her head, says No, but it only shapes her lips, does not leave her throat. She closes her eyes and becomes the shots jolting her hands as she pulls and pulls, hears him fall, and still pulls and explodes until the trigger is quiet and she opens her eyes and moves, leaping over him, to the hall and stairs.

In the middle of the night I sit out here in the skiff and I try to think of something else but I can't, because over and over I keep hearing him tell me that time: *Alex, she's the best fuck I've ever had in my life.* I don't want to think about that. But I look back at the house that was Kingsley's and I wish I had put on the lights before I got in the boat, but it wasn't dark yet and I didn't think I'd drift around half the night and have to look back at it with no lights on so it looks like a tomb, with his weights and fishing gear in there. I'll have to get them out. It looks like we're always taking somebody's things out of that house, and maybe it's time to sell it to somebody who's not so unlucky.

He bled to death, so even then she could have done something. I want to hate her for that. I will, too. After he knew he loved her, he didn't talk about her like that anymore, but it was still there between us, what he told me, and he knew I remembered, and sometimes when we were out drinking, me and somebody and him and Polly, and then we'd call it a night and go home, he'd grin at me. What I don't know is how you can be like that with a guy, then shoot him and leave him to bleed to death while you sit outside waiting for your old man and everybody. This morning we put him next to Kingsley and I was hugging Mom from one side and the old man hugging her from the other, and it seemed to me I had two brothers down there for no reason. Kingsley wouldn't agree, and he wouldn't like it that I don't vote anymore, or read the newspapers, or even watch the news. All Ray did was fall in love and not get over it when she got weird the way women do sometimes.

So I sit out here in the skiff and it's like they're both out here with me. I can feel them, and I wish I'd see them come walking across the lake. And I'd say, Why didn't you guys do something else? Why didn't you wait to be drafted, or go to Canada? Why didn't you find another girl? I'd tell them I'm going to sell this—and oh shit it starts now, the crying, the big first one, and I let it come and I shout against it over the water: 'I'm going to *sell* this fucking *house*, you *guys*. And the one in *town*, and I'm moving in with *Mom* and the *old man*; I'm going to get them to sell *theirs* too and get the fuck *out* of here, take them down to *Flor*ida and live in a *con*do. We'll go fishing. We'll buy a boat, and fish.'

Bless Me, Father

A T EASTER VACATION Jackie discovered that her father was committing adultery, and four days later—after thinking of little else—she wrote him a letter. She was a dark, attractive girl whose brown eyes were large and very bright. She would soon be nineteen, she had almost completed her freshman year at the University of Iowa, and she knew, rather proudly, that her eyes had lost some of their innocence. This had happened in the best possible way: she hadn't actually done anything new, but she had been exposed to new people, like Fran, her roommate, who was a practicing nonvirgin. Fran's boy friend was a drama student and sometimes Jackie double-dated with them, and they went to parties where people went outside and smoked marijuana. Jackie had also drunk bourbon and ginger at football games and got herself pinned to Gary Nolan. Being pinned to Gary did not interfere with her staying in the state of grace; every Sunday she went to the Folk Mass at the chapel, and she usually received Communion, approaching the altar rail to the sound of guitars. It had been a good year for growing up: seven months ago she had been so naive that she never would have caught her father, much less written him a letter.

Before writing the letter, she talked to Fran, then Gary. The night she got back from vacation she told Fran; they talked until two in the morning, filling the room with smoke, pursing their lips, waving their hands. As sophisticated as Fran was, she agreed with Jackie that her father was wrong, that her parents' marriage was in danger, and that her mother must be delivered from this threat of terrible and gratuitous pain. Again and again they sighed, and said in gloomy, disillusioned, yet enduring voices that something had to be done. The next night she talked to Gary. There was a movie he wanted to see, but she asked him if they couldn't go drink beer. I have to talk to you, she said.

They sat facing each other in a booth at the rear, where it was dark, and using fake identification cards they drank beer, and she watched his eyes reflecting the sorrow and distraction in her own. Her story lasted for three beers; then, as she ended by saying she would write her father a letter, her tone changed. Now she was purposeful, competent, striking back. This shift caught Gary off guard, nearly spoiling his evening. He had liked it much better when she had so obviously needed his comfort. So he nodded his head, agreeing that a letter was probably the thing to do, but he looked at her with compassion, letting her know how well he understood her, that she was not as cool as she pretended to be, and that a letter to her father would never ease the pain in her heart. Then he took her out to his car, drove to the stadium and parked in its shadow, and soothed her so much that, on the following Saturday, she went to confession and told the priest she had indulged in heavy petting one time.

By then, she had written and mailed the letter. It was seven pages long, using both sides of the stationery, and she had read the first draft to Fran, then written another. Five days later she had heard nothing. When she mailed the letter, she had thought there were only two possible results: either her father would break off with the woman and renew his fidelity to her mother, or he would ignore the letter (although she didn't see how he could possibly do that; the letter was there at his office; her knowledge of him was there; and—this was it—his knowledge of himself was there too: he could not ignore these things). But after a week she was afraid: she saw other alternatives, even more evil than the affair itself. Feeling trapped, he might confront her mother with the truth, push a divorce on her. Or he might bolt: resign his position at the bank and flee with the other woman to California or Mexico, leaving her mother to live her life, shamed and hurt, in Chicago. She thought of the awful boomerangs of life, how the letter—written to save the family—could very well leave her a scandaled half-orphan; as the last unmarried child, she saw herself bravely seeking peace for her mother, taking her on trips away from their lovely house that was now hollow, echoing, ghost-ridden.

Then, at seven o'clock on a Wednesday morning, exactly one week after she had mailed the letter, her father phoned. He woke her up. By the time she was alert enough to say no, she had already said yes. Then she lit a cigarette and got back in bed. From the other bed, Fran asked who was that on the phone.

'My father. He's driving down to lunch.'

'Oh Lord.'

When he arrived at the dormitory she was waiting on the front steps, for it was a warm, bright day. He was wearing sunglasses, and he smiled easily as he came up the walk, as though—trouble or not—he was glad to see her. He was a short man who at first seemed fat until you noticed he was simply rounded, his chest and hips separated by a very short waist; he kept himself in good condition, swimming every day in their indoor pool at home, and he could still do more laps than she could. Jackie rose and went down the steps. When he leaned forward to kiss her, she turned her cheek, receiving his lips a couple of inches from hers.

He followed her to the Lincoln, opened the door for her, and she directed him to the bar and grill where she and Gary had talked, then led him to the same booth, where it was dark even in the afternoon and people couldn't distinguish your face unless they walked past you. He wanted a drink before lunch, and Jackie ordered iced tea.

'Nothing stronger?' he said.

'They won't serve me.'

She thought now he would wait until his Scotch came.

'You said you saw her at the train station,' he said.

She nodded and put her purse on the table and offered him a cigarette; he said no, they were filtered, and she lit one and looked past his shoulder.

'When I was getting off I saw you nod your head to somebody, and I looked that way and saw her getting into a taxi.'

Then she tried to look into his eyes, but the best she could do was his mouth.

'She's a blonde,' she said.

'A lot of blondes nowadays. When I was a kid—before TV, you know—the blondes in movies were always bad. If a woman was blonde and smoked, you knew right away she was bad.'

The drinks came and she told the waiter she'd have a hamburger with everything but onions; her father ordered a salad, then winked and patted his belly, and she thought of him naked with that blonde, whom she would see forever in a black coat stepping into a taxi.

'Then you heard me on the phone. On Holy Saturday, you said.'

She nodded and sipped her tea. She was smoking fast, deeply, knowing she would need another as soon as she finished this one, while he sat calmly, drinking without a cigarette, and it struck her that perhaps he was a corrupt, remorseless man. She tried to remember the last time he had received Communion. Of course at Easter he had stayed in the pew while she and her mother went to the altar rail; returning to the pew, she had kept her head bowed, hoping he was watching her. She didn't know about Christmas because, while she was on a date, her parents had gone to midnight Mass. She couldn't remember the Sunday of Thanksgiving vacation, but she knew he had received last summer, kneeling beside her. So apparently he still had the faith, but he sat calmly, enclosing a mortal heart, one year away from fifty: the decade of sudden death when a man had to be careful not only about his body but his soul as well. Now she was shaking another cigarette from her pack.

'How much do you smoke?' he said.

'A pack.' It was a lie, but one she also told herself.

'I should have paid you not to, the way some parents do.'

'Or set an example,' she said quickly, but then she flushed and lowered her eyes. She wasn't ready to fight him and, looking into her glass of tea, she thought if her own husband was ever unfaithful, she didn't want to know about it.

'I suppose that's best,' he said. 'What if you made a mistake?'

'Did I?'

'No, I just wanted to see if you'd be disappointed.'

'That's sick,' she said. 'It really is.'

'Suppose your mother had seen that letter.'

'I sent it to the bank.'

'Letters get seen. Suppose I was sick or something, and they'd sent it home?'

'People get heard talking on the phone too.'

'That's right, they do. And I sounded like a—wait a second.'

He took her letter and a pair of glasses from his inside coat pocket, put on his glasses, and scanned the pages.

'Here it is: "That voice on the phone was not yours. I might as well be honest and say it was the voice of a silly old man. I was so ashamed that I couldn't move"—'

'Daddy—'

'Wait: "I would think at least your respect for Mother would keep you from making a phone call to your mistress right in our home".'

'Well it's true.'

'True? What's true?'

He took off the glasses and put them and the letter in his coat pocket.

'What you just read.'

'You think I don't respect your mother?'

'I'd think if you did you wouldn't be doing what you're doing.'

His smile seemed bitter, perhaps scornful, but his eyes had that look she had seen for years: loving her because she was a child.

'So you want me to stop seeing this woman before your mother gets hurt.'

'Yes.'

'And go to confession.'

'I hope you will.'

'Just like that.'

'Don't you still believe in it?'

'Sure. Do you?'

'Of course I do.'

'Are you a virgin?'

'Me!' She leaned toward him, keeping her voice low. 'Oh, that's petty. That's so petty and mean and perverted. *Yes*, I am.'

'What, then? Semivirgin? Never mind: I didn't come for that. Anyway, I went to confession.'

'You did?'

Now the waiter was at their booth, and she was thankful for that, because she felt she ought to be happy now, but she wasn't, and she didn't know what to say next. She watched her hamburger descending, then looked over her father's shoulder, blinking as though looking up from a book: a group of boys and girls came in and sat at a long table in the front. When the waiter left, she said: 'That's wonderful.'

'Is it?'

'Well, of course it is.'

'*I* don't feel so good about it.'

'I won't listen to that. I'm not interested in how *hard* it is to break up with some—'

'Wait—I didn't feel good while it was going on, either. You think I *like* being involved with this woman?'

'But you're *not* involved, Daddy. Not if you've been to confession.'

'You sound like the priest. I told him the first mistake was sleeping with her. He bought that, all right. But he wouldn't buy it when I told him I felt just as sinful about leaving her. She's alone, you know. She didn't cry when I broke it off, she's too old for that, but I know she hurts now. It's not love, it's—'

'I should hope not.'

'It's a lie. Don't you know that?'

'What is?'

'Adultery. A sweet lie, sometimes a happy lie, but a lie. You know what happens? We'd see each other for an hour or two, and that's not real. What's real is with your mother. The other's just a game, like you and that boy in a car someplace.'

'Would you *please* get over this compulsion of yours? Accusing me of what *you're* doing?'

'Compulsion—that's a good word. Now I'm compulsive, old, and silly. Is that right?'

'Well, you have to be old, but you don't have to be silly.'

'That's absolutely right. And you don't have to be selfish.'

'Selfish?'

'Sure. Why did you write a letter like that and hurt your father?'

'I didn't want to hurt you.'

'Come on.'

'I was worried about Mother.'

'Come on.'

'I *was*.'

He finished his salad and pushed the bowl away; then, smoking, he watched her eating, and now the hamburger was dry and heavy, something to hurry and be done with.

'You did it for yourself,' he said.

'That's not true.'

'Sure it is. It's okay for Richard Burton but not your father.'

'It's not okay for him either. I think they're disgusting.'

'Not glamorous and wicked? Not silly, anyway. Or old. You think your mother doesn't know about it?'

'*Does* she?'

'Probably. The point is, we've been married twenty-five years and you can never know what we're like, mostly because it's none of your business. You know what she said two nights ago? After dinner? She said: You must have broken up with your girl friend; you're not being so sweet to me anymore. Joking, you see. Smiling. So I smiled back and said: Sure, you know how it is. That's all we said. Last night I took her out for beer and pizza and a cowboy show—'

In her confusion Jackie thought she might suddenly cry, for she knew the story was sentimental, even corny, but it touched her anyway. She looked at her watch: she had missed gym.

'I'll tell you this too, so you'll know it,' he said. 'I don't know one man who's faithful. Not in here anyway.' He tapped his forehead. 'Or whatever it is.' His dropping hand gestured toward his chest. 'Some don't get many chances. Or they're afraid to see a chance.'

'That letter didn't do a bit of good, did it? Come on, I've already missed one class.'

'I told you, I broke it off. And you know why? For you and me.'

'Sorry,' she said. 'I'm not one of those daughters.'

'Jesus—don't they teach anything but psychology around here? Listen, Jackie: we'll have a good summer, and I don't want suspicious looks every time I walk out of the house.'

'I don't believe you anymore. I don't think you even broke it off.'

'That's right: I drove two hundred and fifty miles to lie to an eighteen-year-old kid.'

'All right. You broke up with her.'

'But I'm not saying it right. I should be happy, I should be thanking you and blowing my nose. Right, Peter Pan?'

'What?'

'You used to read Peter Pan, over and over. That's what you were playing: Peter Pan, make everybody happy, save Wendy and Tiger Lily. Or maybe you were Tinker Bell. Remember? She flew ahead because she was jealous and she wanted the boys to shoot Wendy.'

'Oh *stop* it.'

'Okay. That was mean.'

He reached across the table and touched her face, then trailed his fingers down her cheek.

'It just happens that I don't like to tell people goodbye, especially if it's a woman I've slept with. It reminds me of dying.'

'I have to get back,' she said. 'I have a class.'

He signalled the waiter, paid, and left a two dollar tip on the table. She slipped out of the booth and walked out, feeling him behind her as though she were being stalked; on the sidewalk she stopped, blinking in the sun. Then his hand was on her arm and he led her to the car. As they rode to the dormitory she watched students on the sidewalks, hoping to see Gary, for she could not be alone now and she could not go to math, which was the same as being alone, only worse. They passed the classroom buildings and, looking ahead now, she saw Fran climbing the dormitory steps; when her father stopped, she opened the door.

'Wait,' he said. 'Sit a minute and cool off.'

He shifted on the seat, hitching his right leg up, and faced her. At first she thought she would look straight ahead through the windshield but she didn't really know what she wanted to do, so—sitting straight—she turned her face to him.

'When you come home you'll have to carry your load, the same as Mother.'

'Meaning what?'

'Meaning don't look at me that way anymore. Mother doesn't.'

'She must be terribly hurt.'

'The difference between you and your mother is she knows me and you don't. Here: take this.'

Now the letter was out of his pocket, crossing the space between them, into her lap.

'Read it over tonight and see who you wrote it for.'

'For *her*,' she said, looking down at her own handwriting of a week ago.

'Think it over. And take this.'

Raising himself, he got his wallet; she was shaking her head as, barely looking at them, he pulled out some bills and pressed them into her hand. She left her fingers open.

'Get a dress or take your boy friend to dinner. Go on, take it.'

The top one was a five, and it was a thick stack; she folded it and dropped it in her purse.

'I'm not buying you, either. It's just a present.'

'All right.'

She was looking down, her warm cheek profiled to him, knowing it was a humble posture, but she could not lift her eyes.

'I want you to be straightened out by June.'

'Maybe I shouldn't come home.'

'Yes you will. And you'll be all right too. Now give me a kiss.'

She leaned toward him and kissed his mouth, then she was hugging him and, closing her eyes, she rubbed them quickly on his coat. He got out and came around her side, held the door open, and walked with her up the sidewalk and dormitory steps.

'Be careful driving back,' she said.

'Always.' Then he was grinning, shrugging his shoulders. 'What the hell, I've been to confession.'

She smiled, and held it while he got into the car, put on his sunglasses, waved, and drove off. Then she went inside and took the elevator to her floor. Fran was lying on her bed, wearing a slip.

'What happened?'

Jackie shook her head, went to the window, and looked down at the girls walking to class.

'What did he say?'

'He broke up with her.'

'Great! So it's okay now.'

Jackie left the window and lay on her bed.

'I'm going to cut this afternoon,' she said. 'Do you think we can find Dick and Gary?'

'Sure.'

'Let's go someplace. Maybe to a movie, then out for dinner. It's on me.'

'How much did he give you?'

'I don't know, but it's enough.'

'Okay,' Fran said. 'We won't tell the boys how you got it, though.'

'No,' Jackie said, 'we won't.'

She closed her eyes. When Fran was dressed, she got up and they went down the elevator and out into the sunlight to find the boys.

Goodbye

ON A SUNDAY morning in June, Paul and Judith finished cleaning their apartment, left the key in the mailbox, and drove across town to the house Paul had left on a grey and windy day last March. It was the first house his father had ever bought: a small yellow one with a green door, a picture window, a car port. His father had bought it four years ago, when they moved from Lafayette to Lake Charles; it was a new house, built for selling in a residential section where at first there were half a dozen houses and wide, uncut fields where cottontails and meadowlarks lived. There were few trees. *My prairie*, Paul's mother called it. Now the fields were lawns and everywhere you looked there was a house, but still she said to friends: *Come out to the prairie and see us*. She said this in front of Paul's father too, her tone joking on the surface, yet no one could fail to hear the caverns of shame and bitterness beneath it. *Come to my little yellow house on the prairie*, she said.

Now, with hangered dresses lying on the back seat, and his new Marine uniform with the new gold bars hanging in a plastic bag from the hook above the window, he came in sight of the house, rectangular and yellow against the pale blue of the hot afternoon, and he felt a sense of dread, as though he were a child who had done something foolish and disobedient, and now must go home and pay the price. But he was also in luck (though he couldn't actually call it that, for he had planned it, and left enough cleaning and packing for after Mass so they wouldn't arrive in time to have lunch with his father): his mother's Chevrolet stood alone in the car port, his father's company car was gone, and glancing at his watch, Paul imagined him about now within sight of the oaks, the fairways, the limp red flags. He reached across the overnight bag and took Judith's hand, this nineteen-year-old blond girl who he knew had saved him from something as intangible as love and fear. He held her hand until he had to release it to turn left at what he still thought of as his street, then right into the driveway where, as though in echo of his incompetent boyhood, he depressed the clutch too late, and the Ford stopped with a shudder.

When he had unloaded what they needed for the night, he went to the kitchen. In the refrigerator were two six-packs of Busch-Bavarian beer. There were also cantaloupes, which he and Judith could not afford, and for a moment he allowed himself to believe his last day and night at home would be a series of simple, tangible exchanges of love: his father, who rarely drank beer, had bought some for him; he would drink it, as he would eat the roast tonight and the cantaloupes tomorrow. But when he took a beer into the living room, where his mother and Judith sat with demitasses poised steady and graceful above their pastel laps, his mother said: 'Oh, you found your beer.' Then to Judith: 'His Daddy brought two six-packs home yesterday and I said those children will never drink all that, but all he said was Paul likes his beer. And I got some cantaloupes, for your breakfast tomorrow.'

'Good,' he said, and sat in his father's easy chair.

After a while his mother went to her room for a nap. Judith got a magazine from the rack and sat on the couch, under a large watercolor of magnolias, painted long ago by a friend of his parents. Paul was looking at *Sports Illustrated* when his mother called him to the bedroom. She stood at the foot of her bed, wearing a slip and summer robe.

'Would you get my pen from under the bed?' she said loudly, motioning with her head toward the living room and Judith. 'Your young body can bend better than mine.'

'Your pen?' He even started to bend over, to look; he would have crawled under the bed if she hadn't stopped him with a hand on his arm, a finger to her lips.

'I went to see Monsignor,' she whispered. 'To see if you and Judith were bad. I —'

'You did *what*?'

Her hand quickly tightened on his arm, her fingers rose to her lips; he whispered: 'You did *what?*'

'I had to know, Paul, and it's good I went, he was very nice, he said you were both very good young people, that the bad ones don't get into trouble—'

'You mean pregnant?'

Nodding quickly, her finger to her lips again: '—that only the innocent ones did because they didn't plan things.'

'Mother—Mother, why did you have to ask him that? Why didn't you *know* that?'

'Well because—'

'What's *wrong* with you?'

But he did not want to know, not ever—turning from her, leaving the room, down the hall past the photographs of him and his sisters, Amy and Barbara; he had only this afternoon and tonight to be at home, and he did not want to know anything more. Judith was looking at him.

'I think I'll go run,' he said.

'In this heat? After drinking a beer?'

'Yes.'

'But your things are packed. And they're clean.'

'I'll unpack them and you can throw them in the washer when I finish.'

Under the early afternoon sun he ran two miles on hot blacktop; for a while he ran in anger, then it left him when he was too hot to think of anything but being hot. When he got back his mother was sleeping. He took a beer into the shower and stayed a long time.

At six-thirty his mother began watching the clock, her eyes quick and trapped. She was in the pale green kitchen, moving through the smell of roast; Paul and Judith sat at the table, drinking beer.

'Don't y'all want to go to the living room instead of this hot old kitchen? You don't have to stay in here with me.'

Paul told her no, he didn't like the smell of air-conditioned rooms, he wanted to smell cooking. He was watching the clock too. Certainly she must remember the meals after Amy and Barbara had gone: if she didn't talk, the three of them ate to the sounds of silverware on china. There was nothing else her memory could give her, unless she had dreamed this night of goodbyes out of some memory of her own childhood, with the five brothers and four sisters, the loud meals at that long table where he too had sat as a child and watched black hands lowering bowls and platters, and had daydreamed beneath the voices, the laughter of the Kelleys, who had once had money and perhaps dignity and now believed they had lost both because they had lost the first. The lawyer father had died in debt, with his insurance lapsed, and the sons had sold their house, whose grounds were so big that, when Paul played there, he had not needed to imagine size: it seemed as large as Sherwood Forest. Jews bought the house, tore the vines from its brick walls, and painted the first story pink. Maybe they had got around to painting the top story; he didn't know. He hadn't been to New Iberia in years, and when his mother went she refused to pass the house.

He watched her at the stove. If his father missed the cocktail hour, Paul would be spared while she suffered; and more: he knew by now, after those nights—one or two a month—that when his father came home late for dinner, drunk (she called it tight), gentle, and guilty, Paul sided with him; and in the face of his mother's pique they played a winking, grinning game of two men who by their natures were bound to keep the sober women waiting at their stoves. He even drew pleasure from it, though as a boy he had loved his mother more than anyone on earth, he loved her still, he had always been able to talk with her, although now he had things to say that she didn't want to hear: hardly reason enough to make her the sheep he offered for a few warm and easy (not really: faked, strained) moments with his father. But he would probably do it again. Since waking from her nap, she had not tried to speak to him alone; she had kept them with Judith; and her voice and eyes asked his forgiveness.

By seven-thirty, when the roast was done, they had moved with their drinks to the living room: Paul in his father's chair, his head resting on the doily, on the same spot (from Vaseline hair tonic, two drops a day, and Paul used it too) faintly soiled by his father's head. His mother, sitting wtih Judith on the couch, was not wearing a watch; but at exactly seven-thirty, she asked Paul the time.

'All right, he'd rather drink out there with his friends than with his own family. All right: I'm used to that. I've lived with it. But not the dinner. He can't do this to the dinner. Call him, Paul. I'm sorry, Judith: families should be quiet about these things. Paul, call your father.'

'Not me.' He shook his head. 'No: not me.'

When he was a boy in Lafayette she had sometimes told him to call the golf course and ask his father how long before he'd be home. He did it, feeling he was an ally against his father, whose irritation—*All right: tell her I'm coming*—was not, he knew, directed at him; was even in collusion with him; but that knowledge didn't help. Also, at thirteen and fourteen and then fifteen his voice hadn't changed yet, so he was doubly humiliated: when he asked for his father the clerk always said: *Yes ma'am, just a second*—

'Then I'll call,' his mother said. 'Should I call him, Judith, or should we just go ahead and eat without him?'

'Maybe we could wait another few minutes.'

'All right. Fifteen. I'll wait until quarter to eight. Paul, fix your mother a drink. I might as well get tight, then. That's what they say: join your husband in his vices.'

'Drinking isn't Daddy's vice.'

'No, who said it was? It's that *golf* that's his vice. I might as well have married a sea captain, Judith, at least then I wouldn't be out here on my prairie—'

'You could live by the sea,' Judith said, 'and have a widow's walk.'

Paul took his mother's glass and pushed through the swinging kitchen door, out of the sound and smell of air-conditioning, into the heat, and the fragrance of roast.

At twenty before ten, they sat down to dinner. His mother set Paul's plate at the head of the table, but Paul said no, Daddy might come home while we're eating. He sat opposite Judith. His mother said they should have eaten at eight-fifteen. It took fifteen minutes to drive home from the club, and at eight o'clock she had gone to her room, and slid the door shut in a futile attempt at privacy in a house too small to contain what it had to. They heard her voice: hurt, bitter, whining. And at once—though his mother was right, his father wrong by something as simple as an hour and a half—he was against her. Maybe if she didn't whine, if she had served dinner at seven-thirty and said the hell with him, the old bastard can eat it cold when he gets home, maybe then he would have joined her. But he knew that wasn't true either, that it wasn't her style he resented so much as her vision—or lack of it—which allowed her to have that style and feel it was her due. When perhaps all the time his father, by staying away, was telling her: *You shouldn't have planned this, you are not helping us all but failing us all, and I choose not to bear the pain of it.* But if that were true, then his father's method was cowardly, and his cowardice added to or even created the problem he couldn't face.

For nearly three hours after the call his mother went on with the recitation of betrayal which was her attack. It was not continuous. Often enough, with the voice of someone waiting for a phone call that will change her life, she was able to talk of other things: guesses about what their new life would be like, what sort of people they would meet at Quantico (all educated, I'm sure; a lot of Northerners too; I hope y'all get along); and it was a blessing there wasn't a war, Paul was lucky, too young for Korea and now it looked like there would be peace for a long time unless those Russians did something crazy; she said his father had been saved from war too, he had grown up between them, so Paul was the first Clement to be in the service; there had been three Kelleys, her nephews, in World War II, they had all fought and all come home; but no one in the family had ever been a Marine lieutenant. And she spoke to Judith of food prices and ways to save; she offered recipes; and once she mentioned the child: she said she hoped Judith would be able to go back to college after the baby came. Always, though, she returned to the incredible and unpredictable violation of her evening; again and again she told them, with anger posing as amazement, how his father had said they were playing gin and time had slipped up on him, had taken him by surprise, had passed him by. And he had said he was coming. Thirty minutes ago, and the way he drives it only takes ten minutes. An hour ago. With all that drinking from—from four, four-thirty on, that's when they finish—maybe he was in an accident.

'Paul, you'd better call and see if he's left, maybe he's—'

Around a mouthful of mayonnaised pineapple, Paul said no.

'Well, all right, youth is callous, you know he was in an accident before, he was lucky it was so clearly the other man's fault, because he had been drinking, he had played golf that day, and then we went out to eat with the Bertrands. He's a wonderful driver, Judith.

But how could—oh, that *mis*erable man, we'll have to go get him. He won't be able to drive.'

Paul thought they wouldn't have to, that surely his father would weave in, blinking, flirting with Judith in his deep, mellow drinking voice, averting his eyes from the woman whose face showed years of waiting not only for him but for all that she wanted—money, prominence, perhaps even love: or perhaps only that, and was it impossible, and if so, who had made it impossible?—and dealing her a series of bourbon-thickened apologies, renunciations, promises. But it didn't happen. At ten-forty the dishwasher was doing its work, the women had wiped and swept every crumb from the table and floor, sponged every spot of grease from the stove, and drunk second cups of coffee. Then his mother said: 'Oh that *man*. I'm going to bed, I've had a lovely evening with you two anyway; Paul, give me a kiss, and you and your wife go get him.'

'Why don't we just leave him alone?'

'He's been drinking for seven *hours*, he's got to come *home*.'

'He can handle it.'

'All right, I won't go to bed, I'll go alone, and we'll leave his car at the club all night for everyone to see in the morning, if he doesn't have any pride, why should I care, his friends would think it's funny, oh look there's old Paul's car; I wish that damn company had never got him into the club, I don't know if Paul told you this, Judith, but his company pays the dues, we don't have that kind of money; when they transferred him from Lafayette he said he wouldn't come unless they got him into the club and paid his dues, because there's no golf course here, and they did it, it's all they've ever done for him all these years, and I wish they'd never done that—'

Paul was about to say *But think how unhappy he'd be*, when he realized that was precisely what she meant, and perhaps not only for vengeance but also to cut off all his avenues of escape and force him to find happiness for her and with her, or find none at all.

'—well, I'm used to it, I don't care, I'm past caring now—'

'Mother.'

'—in Lafayette he left me and married the golf course, and now he's married to his old country club, he might as well bring a bed—'

'Mother, we'll go.'

'No, you don't have to, I can—'
'Go to bed, if you want. We'll go.'

The shells of the parking lot were white in the moonlight. Paul stopped beside his father's car in the shadow of palmettos and told Judith she might as well wait outside, because his father would be in the locker room. She said she'd wait at the wharf, and he touched her hand, then slid out of the car and went slowly to the front door, where he paused and looked out at the lake; on that wharf he had first kissed Judith. Then he went in, past loud men with their wives at tables in the bar, into the locker room. The four men sat at a card table between rows of tall green wall lockers; his father's back was turned. Mr. Clay looked up and said: 'Young man you know, Paul.'

His father turned, the reddening of his already sun-red face starting up at once, with his grin; then as he beckoned to a chair he began to cough, that deep, liquid body-wrenching cough that Paul had heard for years, a cough from about four hundred thousand cigarettes and two or three lies his father told himself: *a holder helps, filters make a difference, sometimes switching brands.* Now he came out of it, patted his chest and swallowed while his eyes watered; his voice was weak: 'Hi, Son. Have a seat and we'll get you a drink.'

'Judith's waiting outside.'

'Oh? Did your momma come out too? We could buy 'em a drink, couple of good-looking women, we could handle that—'

'She's home.'

'Oh.' He looked at the cards on the table, took a drink from his bourbon and water. 'Did you drink all that beer?'

'Just about.'

'You all packed and ready?'

'Yep.'

'This boy would like to be called Lieutenant by you old bastards. Second lieutenant, United States Marine Corps. He'll do my *fightin'* for me.'

'He can do something else for you too, you old hoss.'

'When do you leave, son?' Mr. Clay said.

'Tomorrow.'

'Tomorrow?' He looked at Paul's father. Then he stood up.

'Well, I'm going home and boil me an egg.'

'Me too,' another said. 'Before y'all win my house and bird dog too.'

His father rose, grinning, lighting a cigarette, and Paul tensed for the cough, but it didn't come; it was down there, waiting.

They walked through the bar, his father weaving some, his shoulders forward in a subtle effort to balance his velocity and weight.

'Judith's down at the wharf.'

'Oh?' Then the cough came. Paul stood watching him; he thought of his father collapsing: he would catch him before his face struck the shells, carry him to the car. His father brought up something from deep in his body and spit. 'Okay, good. We'll go see Judith at the wharf.'

They crunched over shells, then walked quietly on damp earth sloping to the wharf, then onto it, walking the length of it, their footsteps loud, over the lapping of waves on the pilings and the shore. Ahead of them, at the wharf's end, Judith's moonlit hair was silver.

'Hi, darling,' his father said, and put his arm around her; Paul moved to the other side, and the three of them stood arm in arm, looking out at the black water shimmering under the moon.

'I wanted to see it before we left,' Judith said.

'Is this where y'all did it?'

He felt Judith stiffen then relax, and then he felt her hugging his father.

'No,' he said. 'No, it's where we first kissed.'

They started back, still arm in arm; holding Judith, Paul was guiding his father. Judith said: 'Will you be all right?'

'That car responds to me, darling. You can come with me, though, for company; one of y'all.'

They left the wharf and started up the gentle slope. When they reached the shells Judith said: 'Okay.' Paul was looking straight ahead, at the palmettos before the shadowed colonial front of the club. He felt his father looking at Judith.

'How come my bride doesn't know I got to get drunk to tell my boy goodbye? We had our first kiss on a porch swing, his momma and me. That's where we courted in those days. Maybe that's why nothing happened.'

'What *did* happen?' Paul said.

They crossed the deep shells. He thought his father had not heard, or, hearing, hadn't understood. But when they reached the company car, his father said: 'God knows, Son.' Then he opened the door and got in.

Judith waited, looking up at Paul. His father started the engine. Then Paul turned quickly away, toward his own car, Judith got in with his father, and he followed them home, watching their heads moving as they talked. The house was quiet, and they crept in and went to bed.

In the morning they were together for about an hour. The talk was of the details of departure, and their four voices called from room to room, from house to car, and filled the kitchen as they ate cantaloupes and bacon and eggs. No one mentioned last night; it showed on no one's face. At the door he kissed and embraced his quietly weeping mother. 'There goes our last one,' she said. 'We should have had more.' He looked through tears into his father's damp eyes, and they hugged fiercely, without a word. He did not look at them again until he had backed out of the driveway: they stood in their summer robes, his father's hand resting on his mother's shoulder. They waved. His father coughed, his lifted arm faltering, dropping; then he recovered, and waved again. Paul waved back, and drove down the road.

Leslie in California

W HEN THE ALARM rings the room is black and grey; I smell Kevin's breath and my eye hurts and won't open. He gets out of bed, and still I smell beer in the cold air. He is naked and dressing fast. I get up shivering in my nightgown and put on my robe and go by flashlight to the kitchen, where there is some light from the sky. Birds are singing, or whatever it is they do. I light the gas lantern and set it near the stove, and remember New England mornings with the lights on and a warm kitchen and catching the school bus. I won't have to look at my eye till the sun comes up in the bathroom. Dad was happy about us going to California; he talked about sourdough bread and fresh fruit and vegetables all year. I put water on the stove and get bacon and eggs and milk from the ice chest. A can of beer is floating, tilting, in the ice and water; the rest are bent in the paper bag for garbage. I could count them, know how many it takes. I put on the bacon and smoke a cigarette, and when I hear him coming I stand at the stove so my back is to the door.

'Today's the day,' he says.

They are going out for sharks. They will be gone five days, maybe more, and if he comes back with money we can have electricity again. For the first three months out here he could not get on a boat, then yesterday he found one that was short a man, so last night he celebrated.

'Hey, hon.'

I turn the bacon. He comes to me and hugs me from behind,

rubbing my hips through the robe, his breath sour beer with mint.

'Let me see your eye.'

I turn around and look up at him, and he steps back. His blond beard is damp, his eyes are bloodshot, and his mouth opens as he looks.

'Oh, hon.'

He reaches to touch it, but I jerk my face away and turn back to the skillet.

'I'll never do that again,' he says.

The bacon is curling brown. Through the window above the stove I can see the hills now, dark humps against the sky. Dad liked the Pacific, but we are miles inland and animals are out there with the birds; one morning last week a rattlesnake was on the driveway. Yesterday some men went hunting a bobcat in the hills. They say it killed a horse, and they are afraid it will kill somebody's child, but they didn't find it. How can a bobcat kill a horse? My little sister took riding lessons in New England; I watched her compete, and I was afraid, she was so small on that big animal jumping. Dad told me I tried to pet some bobcats when I was three and we lived at Camp Pendleton. He was the deer camp duty officer one Sunday, and Mom and I brought him lunch. Two bobcats were at the edge of the camp; they wanted the deer hides by the scales, and I went to them saying here, kitty, here, kitty. They just watched me, and Dad called me back.

'It wasn't you,' Kevin says. 'You know it wasn't you.'

'Who was it?'

My first words of the day, and my voice sounds like dry crying. I clear my throat and grip the robe closer around it.

'I was drunk,' he says. 'You know. You know how rough it's been.'

He harpoons fish. We came across country in an old Ford he worked on till it ran like it was young again. We took turns driving and sleeping and only had to spend motel money twice. That was in October, after we got married on a fishing boat, on a clear blue Sunday on the Atlantic. We had twenty-five friends and the two families and open-faced sandwiches and deviled eggs, and beer and wine. On the way out to sea we got married, then we fished for cod and drank, and in late afternoon we went to Dad's for a fish fry with a fiddle band. Dad has a new wife, and Mom was up from

Florida with her boy friend. Out here Kevin couldn't get on a boat, and I couldn't even waitress. He did some under-the-table work: carpenter, mechanic, body work, a few days here, a few there. Now it's February, a short month.

'Hon,' he says behind me.

'It's three times.'

'Here. Let me do something for that eye.'

I hear him going to the ice chest, the ice moving in there to his big hands. I lay the bacon on the paper towel and open the door to pour out some of the grease; I look at the steps before I go out. The grease sizzles and pops on the wet grass, and there's light at the tops of the hills.

'Here,' he says, and I shut the door. I'm holding the skillet with a pot holder, and I see he's wearing his knife, and I think of all the weapons in a house: knives, cooking forks, ice picks, hammers, skillets, cleavers, wine bottles, and I wonder if I'll be one of those women. I think of this without fear, like I'm reading in the paper about somebody else dead in her kitchen. He touches my eye with ice wrapped in a dish towel.

'I have to do the eggs.'

I break them into the skillet and he stands behind me, holding the ice on my eye. His arm is over mine, and I bump it as I work the spatula.

'Not now,' I say.

I lower my face from the ice; for awhile he stands behind me, and I watch the eggs and listen to the grease and his breathing and the birds, then he goes to the chest and I hear the towel and ice drop in.

'After, okay?' he says. 'Maybe the swelling will go down. Jesus, Les. I wish I wasn't going.'

'The coffee's dripped.'

He pours two cups, takes his to the table, and sits with a cigarette. I know his mouth and throat are dry, and probably he has a headache. I turn the eggs and count to four, then put them on a plate with bacon. I haven't had a hangover since I was sixteen. He likes carbohydrates when he's hung over; I walk past him, putting the plate on the table, seeing his leg and arm and shoulder, but not his face, and get a can of pork and beans from the cupboard. From there I look at the back of his head. He has a bald spot the size of a quarter. Then I go to the stove and heat the beans on a high flame, watching them, drinking coffee and smoking.

'We'll get something,' he says between bites. 'They're out there.'

Once, before I met him, he was in the water with a swordfish. He had harpooned it and they were bringing it alongside, it was thrashing around in the water, and he tripped on some line and fell in with it.

'We'll get the lights back on,' he says. 'Go out on the town, buy you something nice. A sweater, a blouse, okay? But I wish I wasn't going today.'

'I wish you didn't hit me last night.' The juice in the beans is bubbling. 'And the two before that.'

'I'll tell you one thing, hon. I'll never get that drunk again. It's not even me anymore. I get drunk like that, and somebody crazy takes over.'

I go to his plate and scoop all the beans on his egg yellow. The coffee makes me pee, and I leave the flashlight and walk through the living room that smells of beer and ashtrays and is grey now, so I can see a beer can on the arm of a chair. I sit in the bathroom where it is darkest, and the seat is cold. I hear a car coming up the road, shifting down and turning into the driveway, then the horn. I wash my hands without looking in the mirror; in the gas light of the kitchen, and the first light from the sky, he's standing with his bag and harpoon.

'Oh, hon,' he says, and holds me tight. I put my arms around him, but just touching his back. 'Say it's okay.'

I nod, my forehead touching his chest, coming up, touching, coming up.

'That's my girl.'

He kisses me and puts his tongue in, then he's out the door, and I stand on the top step and watch him to the car. He waves and grins and gets in. I hold my hand up at the car as they back into the road, then are gone downhill past the house. The sun is showing red over the hills, and there's purple at their tops, and only a little green. They are always dry, but at night everything is wet.

I go through the living room and think about cleaning it, and open the front door and look out through the screen. The house has a shadow now, on the grass and dew. There are other houses up here, but I can't see any of them. The road goes winding up into the hills where the men hunted yesterday. I think of dressing and filling the canteen and walking, maybe all morning, I could make a sandwich and bring it in my jacket, and an orange. I open the screen and look up the road as far as I can see, before it curves around a hill in the sun. Blue is spreading across the sky. Soon the road will warm, and I think of rattlesnakes sleeping on it, and I shut the screen and look around the lawn where nothing moves.

The New Boy

ASATURDAY NIGHT IN summer: his mother and two sisters had dates, and he did not want to greet the boys and the man, so he sat by the swimming pool, with his back to the house, and gazed at the lake and the woods beyond it. The house was on the crest of a ridge and, past the pool, the lawn was a long slope down to the lake. The sun was low over the trees, and their shadows spread toward him on the water. When he heard the last car, most of the lake was dark and the sun was nearly gone beyond the trees. The cars would return in the same order: Stephanie by twelve, Julie by two now that she was eighteen, then his mother; he would wake as each one turned into the driveway, and sleep after the front door closed and light footsteps had gone from kitchen to bathroom to bedroom. Stephanie was sixteen and stayed longest at the front door and in the kitchen; his mother was quickest at the door and did not stop at the kitchen unless a man came in for a drink; then Walter slept and woke again when the car started in the driveway, and he listened to his mother climbing the stairs and going to her room. Now she called him, and he looked over his shoulder at her standing behind the screen door.

'I'm going now.'

'Have a good time.'

When the car was gone, he rose and walked around the pool, then downhill to the lake, darker now than the sky. The sun showed through the woods as burning leaves. Then it was gone, leaving him in the black and grey solitude that touched him, and gave him the peaceful joy of sorrow that was his alone, that singled him out from all others. A sound intruded: above the frogs' croaking and the flutter and soft plash of stirring geese, so familiar that they were, to him, audible silence, he heard now the rhythmic splashes and lapping of a swimmer. He looked to his right, near the shore, where purple loose-strife stood, deflowered by night, like charcoal strokes three feet tall. Beyond their tops he saw a head and arms and the small white roil of water at the feet. The swimmer angled toward him. Above and behind him, he felt the presence of his house: that place where, nearly always, he could go when he did not want something to happen. He stared at the head and arms coming to him. They rose: slender chest and waist of a boy walking through the dark water, then light bathing suit and legs, and the boy stepped onto the bank and shook his head, sprinkling Walter's face, then he pushed his hair back from his forehead. He was neither taller nor broader than Walter, who glanced at the boy's biceps and did not see in them, either, the source of his fear.

'It's against the law to swim in there,' he said. 'That's a reservoir.'

'I pissed in it too. Let's swim in your pool.'

'How do you know I have one?'

'You live here?'

'Yes.'

'Everybody on this road's got one. I can see all the backyards from the sun deck.'

'Don't you have one?'

'It's empty.' He started walking up the slope. 'Which house?'

'Straight ahead.'

Walter followed him up to the lighted house and stood at the shallow end while the boy went to the deep end and dived in and swam back, then stood.

'I have to go put on my suit.'

'Turn on the underwater lights.'

He turned them on with the switch near the door and went upstairs; his room looked over the pool, and in the dark he stood at the window and undressed, watching the boy splashing silver as he moved fast through the water that was greener now in the light from the bottom of the pool. Naked, he looked beyond at the slope and lake and, on its far side, the trees like a tufted black wall. He put on his damp trunks and went down the carpeted hall and stairs and out through the kitchen, then ran across flagstones to the side of the pool, glimpsing the boy to his left, in the deep end, and dived, opening his eyes to bubbles and the pale bottom coming up at him. He touched it with his fingers. Under the night sky the water felt heavy, deeper. He arched his back and started to rise; the boy was up there, breaststroking, then bending into a dive, coming down at Walter, under his lifted arms: a shoulder struck his chest, an arm went around it, then the boy was behind him, the arm moved and was around his neck, tightening and pulling, and he went backward toward the bottom, and with both hands jerked at the wrist and forearm, cool and slick under his prying fingers. His jaws were clamped tight on the pressure rising from his chest. He released some, and bubbles rose toward the dark air. He rolled toward the bottom, touched it for balance with a hand, swung his feet down to it, and thrust upward with straightening legs; he had exhaled again; he released the boy's arm and stroked upward and kicked and kept his mouth closed against the throbbing emptiness in his chest, then breathed water and rose to the air choking, inhaling, coughing. The boy's arm had left his throat. He did not look behind him. Slowly he swam away, head out of the water, coughing; he climbed out of the pool and, bent over, coughed and spat on the flagstones. He heard the feet behind him.

'You're crazy,' he said, then straightened and turned and looked at the boy's eyes. He had seen them before, on school playgrounds: amused, playful, and with a shimmer of affection, they had looked at him as knowingly as his family and his closest friends did. Boys with those eyes never fought in fury; they rarely fought at all. They threw your books in the mud, pushed you against walls, pulled your hair, punched your arm or stomach, shamed and goaded you, while watching boys and girls urged you to fight. Two years ago, when he was twelve, he had leaped into those voices, onto the bully, and they rolled grappling in the dust, then he was on his back, shoulders pinned by knees, fists striking his face before someone pulled the boy away. For the rest of the school year he was free; and for the rest of his boyhood, for he knew that the months of peace were worth the fear and pain of the first quick fight, so he was ready for that, and so was left alone. This boy's eyes were

brown; Walter swung his right fist at them and struck the nose.
The boy raised a hand to it, and looked at blood on the fingers. He
wiped them on his trunks; blood had reached his lip now.

'I didn't know you were scared,' the boy said.

'Scared my ass.'

'I mean underwater.'

'I couldn't breathe.'

The boy folded his arms.

'I could.'

'Let's go inside and fix your nose.'

'Let's go inside and eat.'

The boy turned and dived. Swimming underwater, he pinched
and rubbed his nose, and blood wafted from his fingers, became
the green-tinted pale blue of the pool. He swam to the other side;
Walter walked around the pool and they went into the kitchen.
The boy stood at the bar. Looking into the refrigerator, Walter
said: 'Peaches, grapes, liverwurst, cheese—four kinds of cheese—'
He turned and looked at the boy; his eyes had not changed.

In the still heat of Sunday morning he slept long and woke, clam-
my, to the voices of his sisters and mother rising from the terrace.
Every day in summer his sisters slept late, and his mother did on
weekends, and he loved those mornings, going downstairs, quiet
and alone, to eat cereal and read the baseball news, feeling in the
kitchen silence their sleeping behind the three closed doors above
him. They woke loudly, talking in the hall and from one bathroom
door to another, and through bedroom doors as they altered their
hair and faces; their voices came down the stairs and into the
kitchen, then they entered, red-lipped and tan and scented; talking,
they turned on the radio and made coffee and lit cigarettes. It
seemed that always at least one of them was smoking, at least one
was talking, and all three of them were now, on the terrace beneath
his window; he had not waked when they came home in the night,
so his own night of sleep seemed long; and, having no place to go,
he still felt that he was late. He looked down at them sitting at the
glass table; their hair, chestnut in three seasons, was lighter; they
wore two-piece bathing suits, and his mother and Julie drank
Bloody Marys; Stephanie had a glass of wine. His mother let her
drink wine at dinner and at Sunday brunch, and only Walter

knew that when she drank at brunch she got drunk, for they stayed at the table longer than at any dinner except Thanksgiving and Christmas, and neither Julie nor his mother was sober enough to notice her rose cheeks and shining eyes. He put on his trunks and made his bed and moved past their rooms, glancing at their beds that would not be made until old Nora from Ireland came to work Monday afternoon, down the stairs into the undulant sound of their voices. He stepped into the sunlight and Stephanie said: 'Well finally.'

They smiled at him; they wished him a good morning and he returned it; Julie said why couldn't she meet someone as good-looking as her brother; his mother puckered her lips for a kiss and he gave her one. Their hair and bathing suits were dry. He stood above them in the warmth of the sun and their love, and his for them; their eyes flushed his cheeks, and he left: went to the deep end and dived in and swam fast laps of the pool until he was winded, then returned to them. Someone had poured him a glass of orange juice. His mother blew smoke and said: 'Spinach crepes, kid. Can you handle it?'

'Sure.'

Stephanie looked down at herself and said: 'I shouldn't handle anything.'

'You're not fat,' he said.

'I need to lose seven pounds.'

'Bull.'

'She does,' his mother said. 'But not today.'

'Do it gradually,' Julie said. 'Give yourself three weeks.'

'That's August. I'd like to get into my bathing suit before August.'

He looked through the glass table at her black pants like a wide belt around her hips.

'You're in it,' he said.

'And look what shows,' and she pinched flesh above the pants.

'You have to be really skinny to wear those things,' he said, then grinned, looking through glass at his mother's and Julie's flat skin above the maroon and blue swaths, and Julie said: 'Okay, everybody stare at Walter's pelvis.'

He stood and, profiled to them, he drew in his stomach muscles, expanded his chest, flexed his left arm, and looked down at them over the rising and falling curve of his bicep as he rotated his wrist.

'Our macho man,' Julie said, and his father was there: not a memory of the broad, hairy chest, and hair curling over the gold watchband as he read the Sunday paper before swimming his laps, but his father in Philadelphia, in that apartment of leaves: plants growing downward from suspended pots and upward from pots on tables and floor, his father like a man reading in a jungle clearing; he sat and drank juice and his mother said: 'Were you up late last night?'

'No.'

'What did you do?'

'Nothing.'

He picked up a green cigarette pack, let it fall, pushed it toward Stephanie. He looked beyond Julie at Canadian geese on the lake; his mother and the girls were talking again, and he leaned back in the canvas deck chair and looked up at the blue sky, then closed his eyes and turned his face to the sun, and breathed deeply into the chill of his lie until it was gone, and his mother went to the kitchen, and he opened his eyes and watched the girls talking. They rarely said anything he wanted to know, but he liked hearing their voices and watching their faces and hands: they spoke of clothes, and he looked with tender amusement at their passionate eyes, their lips closing on cigarettes with sensuous pouts he knew they had practiced; hair fell onto their cheeks, and their hands rose to it and lightly swept it back, as if stroking a spider web. From the house behind him, his mother came with a broad tray: a bottle of white wine in an ice bucket, a bowl of fruit, four plates with crepes, a glass of milk, and ringed napkins. He believed Julie—but maybe Stephanie—had asked one Sunday: *What did you do with Dad's napkin ring?* But since he could not remember the answer, he was not sure anyone had ever asked; perhaps he had dreamed it, or had imagined someone asking, and had waited for that; he slipped linen from silver, and his mother asked him to pour the wine. For over a year of Sundays and dinners he had poured the wine, but always he waited for his mother to ask him: he disliked doing what his father had done, felt artificial and very young and disloyal too, as if he were helping to close the space his father had left behind; and he disliked her never saying that she wanted him to pour because his father was gone. While his sisters nibbled and moaned and sipped, he ate fast, head down, waiting for his mother to strike back, knowing she was watching yet would not tell him the truth: that she wanted him to eat with slow appreciation of her work. She would tell him that eating fast was bad for— Then he heard the squeak-skid of brakes and tires and turned to see him at the edge of the terrace, straddling his bicycle, bare-chested, wearing cut-off jeans and sneakers without socks. Walter nodded to him, ate the last of the crepe, and stood, looking at his mother as he swallowed and wiped his mouth.

'I'm going bike riding.'

'Who's that?'

'Mark Evans.' Walking away, he looked back over his shoulder and said: 'They moved in yesterday.'

In the woods near the road he and Mark lay face down in the shadow of trees and looked through branches and brown needles of a larger fallen branch of pine; Mark had dragged it from deeper in the woods, where their bicycles were chained to a tree. Moist dead leaves were cool against Walter's flesh. Out in the sunlight the white handkerchief hung: folded over a length of fishing line tied to trees on either side of the narrow road, it was suspended three feet above the blacktop, motionless in the still air.

'It's like waiting in ambush,' Walter said.

'It's better at night. It looks like a ghost at night.'

'It looks like one now.'

The first car that came around the curve down the road to their left was green and foreign; Walter pressed his palms and bare toes against the earth and saw a second shape behind the windshield, a woman, and then two more figures in the back, and now the driver's face: a man beyond the hood, wearing sunglasses, right hand at the top of the wheel, peering now, shifting down, slowing and slowing, the woman's hands in front of her, pushing toward the windshield, then her head out of the window saying 'What *is* it?' and the children leaning forward, arms and hands out of the windows, and the man stopped and got out, he was tall and wore a suit, and Walter pressed against the leaves and watched him holding the line and looking down both of its ends; then breaking it, and watching the handkerchief fall, and standing with fists on his hips, turning his head from one side of the road to the other as he spoke: 'I want you boys to think about something while you're in there laughing and having your fun. You could kill somebody. You could make somebody swerve into another car. I've got two kids in mine. You could have caused something you'd regret for the rest of your lives.' Then he went back to his car. Before he got in, his wife said: 'Don't just leave it in the road.'

'I don't want to touch it.'

She opened the door but he said 'Let's go' and got in and shifted and drove slowly by, his wife hunting the woods, her eyes sweeping the fallen pine branch. Then the car was hidden by trees, and he listened to it going faster up the road, and laughing, he stood and squeezed Mark's shoulders and hopped and skipped in a circle, pulling Mark with him, forcing the sound of his laughter faster when it slowed and louder when it lulled; he stopped dancing and laughing, but still quivering with jubilance, he squeezed Mark's shoulder and shouted: 'I don't want to *touch* it.'

When he rode his bicycle up the driveway, the sun was low above the trees across the lake, and his mother and sisters were still at the glass table; then, coming out of the garage, he saw that it was not still but again: his mother and Julie wore dresses and Stephanie wore shorts; beyond them, downwind, smoke rose from charcoal in the wheeled grill.

'I'll be right down,' he said.

'I'm coming up,' his mother said.

He went into the pale light of the house, up the stairs, hearing the screen door open and shut, and the clack of her steps on the kitchen floor then muted by carpets as she followed him up. His room was sunlit. He looked down at Julie and Stephanie, then turned to face the door a moment before she entered it. Her dress was white and, between its straps, a pearl necklace lay on her tan skin. She had a cigarette in one hand and a drink in the other: a tall, clear one with a piece of lime among the bubbles and ice.

'Did you have a good day?'

'Yes.'

'Where did you go?'

'Bike riding.'

She put her drink on the chest of drawers and flicked ashes into her hand.

'That's quite a workout.'

'We went to the woods too.'

'You were right across the lake?'

'The big woods. By the highway.'

'Oh. You said—Mark?—moved here yesterday? When did you meet him?'

'Last night.'

'Where?'

'Here. He was looking around.'

'Well, I don't want to'—she glanced at her drink, drew on her cigarette, flicked ashes in her hand—'I don't want to make a big thing out of it, but why didn't you tell me?'

'I don't know.'

'You really don't? That's so—I don't know, it's so—*strange*.' With forefinger and thumb of her ash-hand she picked up her drink. 'Well. Will you do something for me? Ask him to come over some-time when I'm home. We'll have dinner. Will you do that?'

'I'll ask him.'

He looked at the cigarette burning close to her fingers.

'Good. I like meeting your friends. You have time to shower be-fore dinner, pal.'

'I was about to.'

She smiled and left, and he followed her to the door and said to her back as she moved down the hall, gingerly holding the drink and cigarette: 'Will I have time to swim? After my shower?'

'Plenty of time,' she called over her shoulder. 'It's pork.'

The apartment in Philadelphia smelled of the city, not only exhaust but something else that came through the open windows: a stale-ness, as though Philadelphia itself were enclosed by ceiling and walls, and today's breeze carried to his lungs yesterday's cement and stirred dust; when the windows were closed, the apartment's motionless air had no smell, and that too, for Walter, was Phila-delphia. With his father in the apartment she had filled with plants was blond Jenny, who, that first morning when he visited them for a weekend, knocked on his door, and he woke remembering where he was and said *Yes*, and she came in with a tray holding hot choc-olate and bread she had baked last night, wrapped in hot foil—*that child*, his mother had said, *that child. With those clothes from Nashville by way of Hollywood. What is she? There aren't any more hippies. I'm sorry, children, he's your father but I cannot*

*can not live quietly through this mad time. She was born the year
we were married and I've spent twenty-two years giving my life to
my husband and my home and now it feels like I was just taking
care of him while she did nothing but get taller and busty so he
could leave with her—*Jenny sat on the bed and talked to him while
he drank the chocolate and ate the bread and liked her, and understood his father loving her, and so shared his father's guilt. He was
the first to visit; in two weeks Stephanie would come, and then
Julie, because there was only the one guest room, his father said,
and his mother said: *He's protecting that girl from handling all of
you at once.* Jenny said: *You probably don't like breakfast in bed,*
and he said: *No, not even when I'm sick,* and she blushed, smiling
at herself, and said: *I don't either. I'll stop trying so hard. Are you
all right?* At first he thought she meant the bed, the room, his
hunger, then looking at her he knew she didn't, and he said: *Yes.
And Stephanie and Julie? They'll be all right. They're not now?
They'll get better. Is your Mom? No. That's why they're not.
It's awful. I wish—* He wanted to hear the wish: perhaps behind her
worried blue eyes she wished his father had no wife, no children,
that he and his mother and Julie and Stephanie were dead or had
never lived; now sadly he saw them, the woman and girls he had
left at home: they were in the living room, talking, then they van-
ished; for moments their voices lingered in the room and then faded
with them into space. *There's too much to wish,* she said; *there's
nothing to wish. I just have to hope. For what? That nobody's
hurt too badly for too long.* Sunday night he boarded an airplane
for the second time in three days and in his life; he had spent most
of the flight Friday afternoon imagining the weekend, making himself shy and awkwardly intrusive in his father's new home and life
before he saw either. He had met Jenny, had eaten dinner in restaurants with her and his father and sisters; but that was all. Sunday
in the plane he liked being alone with the small light over his head
and the black sky at his cool window; a man sat beside him, but
he was alone: no one knew him, and when the stewardess spoke to
him as though he were either boy or man, he felt that his age as
well as his name had remained on the earth. Philadelphia was done;
Philadelphia was good; he could go back, and now he was going
home.

His mother and sisters ate dinner in Boston, then met him at the airport, and he sat in the back seat with Stephanie; the night was cool, and in the closed car he remembered what he had forgotten to remember until now: Jenny and his father smelled of soap and cloth and flesh, and no smoke drifted toward his face through the still air of their rooms. He started to say this, nearly said: *At least she doesn't smoke*; then he knew he must not.

'So how was it,' Stephanie said, and watching his mother in part-profile, hair and upper cheek, her hand on the wheel, smoke pluming from her mouth he could not see, he told of the weekend without once saying *Jenny*. For the next few nights, when at dinner they questioned him or he remembered something about the weekend that he wanted to make alive again with words so it would be more than just a memory, he glanced from his sisters to his mother's face, her eyes quick and lips severely set, and said *Dad* and *we* and all but twice was able to avoid saying even *they*, until finally he could no longer bear the shame of loving two women and betraying them both, and he kept his memories in silence. Then Stephanie went to Philadelphia and came back, and he watched his mother's face at the dinners and said nothing or little and began to rid himself of shame, and in the week after Julie's visit he knew he had never had reason for shame, that he had not been afraid to tell his mother he loved Jenny too, that it was not him but she who needed the lie; and, loving her, he felt detached and older, and at times he was lonely.

The extended family, she calls us. I hope we can be like sisters someday; she actually said that. What did you say? I wanted to say Right, airhead: incest. She gives him three eggs a week. She doesn't know what to call him. When she talks about him to us. She said that. She feels funny when she says Walter and funny when she says Your father. So what does she do? She takes turns. And if she's talking to him she says Hon. Or Darling. No: nobody says darling except in books. She watches his salt too. And every day before dinner they go to this health club and swim. How cute. She's the one who needs it, old thunder thighs. She had a pimple. She looks out of those big blue eyes and talks about how much he cares about us, and I wanted to tell her if he cares so much why is he here with you, and she's got a pimple on her chin—

He watched them: their faces over plates of food glowed with malice, the timbre of their voices was sensually wicked, their throaty laughter mischievous. They were eerie and fascinating; he had never seen them like this. He knew his silence was not disloyal to his father and Jenny; sometimes he gave his mother's eyes what they had to see: he smiled, even laughed.

At night the handkerchief was a pale shape in the air, then lit by headlights, and he knew that to the driver it had suddenly appeared without locomotion or support, and the cars stopped faster, and the voices from them were more frightened and then more angry. One night they rode past the woods to the bridge over the highway and leaned on the steel fence and watched the four lanes of cars coming to them and passing below. They pressed against the vertical railings and pissed arcs dropping into headlights.

'I've got to shit,' he said, and started for the woods.

'Wait. We can use that.'

He stopped and looked at Mark, then down at the cars.

'You think I'm going to squat on that little fence and shit over the highway?'

Near the bridge the woods ended at a small clearing before the slope going steeply down to the highway. Among beer bottles and cans Mark found a paper bag.

'It won't do anything,' Walter said. 'When it hits the car. *If* it hits it.'

'You have any matches?'

'No.'

'We'll get some. Go on.'

He started to go into the woods, but Mark turned and walked back to the bridge, so he squatted in the clearing and looked at bottles and tire tracks in the grass that was high enough to tickle his shins, and wondered when the teenagers parked here; he had seen them: once there were three or four cars and boys and girls sitting on fenders or standing, but the other times it was only one car nestled in the shadows of the woods, dully and for an instant reflecting his mother's headlights as she drove off the bridge. Always he had seen them from his mother's car, when they had been to a movie or dinner and were coming home late. Carrying the bag away from his body, he went onto the bridge, his face turned to the breeze.

'If we wait, we can get some parkers,' he said.

'Get our asses whipped too.'

'We could sneak through the woods. Let the air out of the back tires, then throw this in the front window.'

'What do you think he'll be doing while all that hissing is going on?'

'Getting out and beating our asses. We could get close enough to listen, though. Maybe even look in.'

'Now you're talking. Maybe we can think up a trap. Something he'd drive into and couldn't get out of. Let's go find a front porch to burn your dinner on.'

With headlights on, they rode fast over the winding road past the woods and then open country where the lighted houses were separated by low ridges and shallow draws and trees planted in lines and orchards, and up Walter's driveway, onto the terrace, where he placed the bag beside his kickstand. In the kitchen they looked on counters and in drawers and behind the bar.

'They use lighters.'

He went upstairs with Mark following, into his mother's room, and switched on the ceiling light, standing a moment looking at her wide bed covered with light blue, and felt behind him Mark breathing the air of the room while his eyes probed it. He moved to the dresser, and when Mark pulled open a drawer of the chest at another wall, he raised his face and looked at himself in the mirror. Then he looked down, and between a hairbrush and an ashtray saw a glossy black matchbook bearing a name in gold script.

'Let's go,' he said, and crossed the room and closed the drawer as Mark's hand, dropping a stack of silk pants, withdrew.

He did not know any of the neighbors well enough to choose a target, so with lights off they rode to the last house before the woods and walked their bicycles up the long driveway between tall trees, and lay them on the ground where the pavement curved and rose through open lawn to the garage beside the house. Upstairs one room was lighted, and light came through the two high windows on either side of the small front porch with a low narrow roof and two columns. At the base of a tree they lay on their bellies and watched the windows, and Mark whispered: 'Don't ever think your shit doesn't stink,' and they pressed hands against their mouths and laughed through their noses. Then, crouching, they ran to the front porch and listened and heard nothing. Walter set the bag near the screen door and unfolded its top and listened again, then struck the match and held the flame to one corner of the opening and then another, and stood, and when fire was moving down the sides, Mark pressed the doorbell and held it chiming inside the house, then they ran to the tree, and Walter dived beside it and rolled behind it next to Mark. The door swung inward, a short, wide man stepped into its frame, then said something fast and low, and pushed open the screen and with one foot stomped the flames smaller and smaller to embers and smoke, then he cursed, and Mark was running and Walter was too, hearing cursing and heavy running steps coming as he ran beside his bicycle down the driveway and jumped onto the seat, passing Mark before the road, where he turned and pumped for the woods.

Across the glass table Mark's wet hair was sleek in the sunlight. He sat beside Julie; the sun, nearing the trees across the lake, was behind and just above him, so that Walter squinted at him. Walter's mother had thawed chicken, then when she came home early from the boutique she had bought after going to court with his father, she said she had decided on hamburgers because some people were clumsy about eating barbecued chicken with a knife and fork and she didn't want to make it hard on him. Walter had said Mark could eat chicken with his hands, and she said she knew he could and Walter would like to, and that's what she meant about making it hard on Mark.

She could clean the bones of a chicken with knife and fork as daintily as if she were eating lima beans, so he liked watching her with a hamburger: it was thick and it dripped catsup and juice from the meat and tomatoes and pickles; she leaned over the plate and opened her mouth wide enough to close on both buns, yet with that width of jaws she took only a small bite from the edge and lowered the hamburger, then sat straight to chew with her lips closed. Julie's and Stephanie's bites were larger but still small, and neither had to use a napkin. He and Mark had stayed in the pool until now, so his mother was asking questions between eating: Where he was from and what his father did and did his mother work, how many brothers and sisters and where had he gone to school. Some of this was new to Walter; the rest of it he had learned in the woods, during the heat of afternoons as they lay on cool shadowed grass and spoke to avoid silence. His mother's questions ended before her hamburger did; she held her wineglass toward Walter and he filled it, then she said: 'And your sisters,' and he reached to their places and poured, then held the bottle over Mark's glass of milk, and Mark said: 'Go ahead.'

'Just two more years,' his mother said, and she leaned toward him and tousled his wet hair. 'This boy of mine,' she said to Mark, and dried her hand with her napkin.

'He'll be doing more than wine in two more years,' Julie said.

'A lot more,' Stephanie said, and smiled at Mark.

'Like what?' Walter said.

'You'll have a girl,' Julie said.

'Maybe not.'

'You will. Some girl will take care of that.'

'Wow,' he said to Mark. 'I'll have a *date*.'

'In the *car*,' Mark said.

'With a *girl*.'

'And you'll love it,' his mother said. 'You two guys will beg for the car and start looking in the mirror. We have blueberry pie and ice cream.'

'Tell me you didn't,' Stephanie said. 'Not *blue*berry. I'm going to be very fat tonight.'

'You might get an older man,' his mother said. 'Dessert is for these boys who swim and ride bikes all day.'

'I swam this morning,' Stephanie said, and stood, and then Julie and his mother did, and when he pushed back his chair she said: 'Stay with your guest. We'll do it,' and they were all in motion, clearing and wiping the table and setting it again with ashtrays and cigarette packs and plates and three demitasses and a silver coffee-pot, and pie and ice cream for everyone, though he and Mark had the biggest slices and scoops. When his mother reached for her cig-arettes, he stood and said: 'Let's go down to the lake.'

He rolled his napkin and pushed it into the ring, and when Mark started to, he told him to leave it, the guest napkin gets washed.

Near the bank of the lake he found a small flat rock and skimmed it hitting once on the sunlit surface and three times in the shadows before it sank. He paced up and down, looking for another rock, and Mark lay on the grass in the sun, and said: 'They're pretty.'

He sat beside Mark and looked at the flowers of purple loose-strife and then at a crow rising from the trees.

'Sometimes I wish I lived with my father.'

'Can you?'

'They never asked me to.'

He did not like the sound of his voice; in its softening he heard tears coming, and for a long time he had not cried about anything. He sat up and plucked a blade of grass and chewed it. Julie did not like the monthly visits to his father because she missed her boy friend, and Stephanie did not like them because she could not smoke there and she missed her boy friend, and neither one of them had forgiven his father. He would like to spend the school year with his father and Jenny and the summer here, and he knew now that for a long time he had made himself believe his father had never asked or even hinted because the apartment was too small.

'Do they fuck?' Mark said.

'Who?'

He pointed a thumb over his shoulder, and Walter turned and looked up the hill; sunlight splashed bronze on their hair.

'How would *I* know?' he said, and looked at his bare toes in the grass.

'Lots of ways, if you wanted to.'

'I never thought about it.'

'You're weird.'

'Sometimes I think about it. When they go out.'

He was awake when they came home, starting with Stephanie at eighteen minutes past midnight on his luminous digital clock and ending with his mother at three twenty-nine, and if he slept at all he did not know it, for even if he did, he still saw in his mind what he saw awake. *Too much*, Mark had said as Walter's hand rose from Stephanie's drawer with the third plastic case like a clam shell, and he snapped it open and it was empty too. *Everybody's fucking but you. I'll have to jerk off tonight.* But not him: he lay on the warm sheet in the cooling night air and listened for them, and then to them: the downstairs footsteps when the sound of the car was gone—a sound that chilled him with yearning hatred, as though he were bound to the bed by someone he could not hit—then steps climbing the stairs and into their bedrooms that he felt part of now (and was both ashamed and vengeful because Mark was part of them too) and, in there, slower and lighter steps so that for moments he did not hear them and then did again, at another part of the room. He tried to think but could not: tried to focus on each of them, force the other two from his mind, and reasonably say to himself: *Dad has Jenny and she ought to have someone too* or *Julie's eighteen and people when they're eighteen* but he could get no further and did not even try with Stephanie, for as soon as he focused on one, the other two were back in his room, among its shadows and furniture, and they all merged: naked, their legs embracing the cruelly plunging bodies of the two boys and one man he knew, and he saw their three open-mouthed wild-haired faces, and heard sounds he had not known he knew: fast, heavy breath and soft cries and grunts and, between their legs, sloshing thuds; heard these as he waited and as they climbed the stairs and turned on faucets and flushed toilets—Did it drip out of them and drop spreading and slowly sinking like thick sour milk, droplets left on that hair he had never seen, and did they—*wipe* it then with paper, the motion of arm and hand, the expressions on their faces as common as if nothing were there and in the water below their—again: naked—flesh but piss? Or did it stay in the diaphragm that Mark said was shaped like half an orange peel with the fruit gone? He tightened his legs and arms, shook his head on the pillow, shut his eyes to a darker dark; between his legs he felt nothing. When did they take it out? And how did their faces look when they took it out? He saw them frowning, nauseated, wickedly pleased. Once he had a large boil on his leg and the doctor froze it and lanced it, and for weeks he had to fight his memory when he ate. He could not imagine them now in clothes, nor in bathing suits, nor simply eating on the terrace or at the kitchen or dining room table; he tried to remember them in winter, fur-covered, leaving the house and walking with short, careful steps over the icy sidewalk, moving into the vapor of their breath as it wafted about their heads. But he could not, as though all he had known of them clothed was a mask that tonight he had pulled from their faces. When at last his mother's steps ended, he imagined them all settled between sheets, their legs closed now, at rest, and he thought: *They must stink.*

He woke to a bird's shriek and sunlight, and went barefooted down the hall, looking at each door closed on the darkened blind-drawn cool of the room and bed and soft breathing of sleep, and out of the house and onto his bicycle. He rode toward the woods. He was hungry and thirsty and had not brushed his teeth, so the taste of night was still in his mouth, and he opened it to the breeze. Then he was there: the fragrance of pines sharper among the other smells of green life and earth and the old dappled leaves moist and soft under his feet as he walked his bicycle without trail or pattern between and under tall trees and around brush, the sweat from his ride drying now, cooling him in the shade as he moved farther into the woods that had waked while he slept: above him squirrels rustled leaves as they moved higher and birds fluttered from perches, and twice he heard the sudden flight of a rabbit. In a glade lit by the sun he stood up his bicycle and lay on his back with hands clasped behind his head and closed his eyes. The sun warmed his face, and beneath his eyelids he felt the heat and saw specks of red and orange in the darkness, and he tried to see them as he had known them, but he could not dress them, could not cover their nakedness, and could not keep them naked alone: behind his eyes they slowly revolved, coupling with the two boys and the man, and he tried to see nothing at all but the speckled dark, and then tried to see the food his stomach wanted, the juice for his dry throat, and then tried to concentrate his rage only on the two boys and the man whose faces had the glazed look of a dog's above the bitch's back, but he could not do that either, and the sounds from the six writhing bodies were louder than the woods.

He stood and moved out of the sunlight, into the shade of a maple, and unzipped and pissed, then stroked, shutting his eyes against the softness his hand encircled, seeing an infected and oozing orange peel, the softness even receding as though trying to withdraw from his abrasive fingers. He opened his eyes. Then he lay on his belly in the sunlight and pressed his cheek against the earth and held its grass with both hands.

We had to leave before you came home. We went shopping in Boston and will be back before dinner. Mark was looking for you and said he'd be back after lunch. Love, Mom, and a smiling line for a mouth drawn inside a circle with two eyes and a nose. He left the note on the table in front of him while he ate cereal and a peanut butter sandwich, then he took the small garbage basket from under the sink and went upstairs. He went to Stephanie's room first. It was still darkened, and he opened the blinds and looked at the tossed-back top sheet and bedspread and stuffed brown bear and blue rabbit near a pillow; actors and singers watched him from the walls; he opened the drawer and took out the case and opened it with a click that tensed his arms. *It's more like a hollowed-out mushroom*; then he realized he was holding his breath, and he let it out, and breathing fast and shallow he turned the case over and watched the diaphragm drop softly among banana peels and milk carton and tuna fish can. As he put the case under silk in the drawer, he knew why he had gone to her room first: the youngest, only a few years removed from the time when pranks on each other were as much part of their days as laughter.

The basket was wicker and lined with a plastic bag. He brought it to Julie's room and opened her blinds and was crossing the floor when his name rose from outside, into the room; he stool still, gripping the basket, while Mark called again, then rang the back doorbell and called and then was quiet, but Walter could feel him down there, and he stood looking at the soft yellow wall, listening to the slow breeze and a car coming and passing by, then crept to the window and looked down at the empty terrace. Quickly he took the case from the drawer and emptied it in the basket.

In his mother's room he did not open the blinds; he walked softly as though she were sleeping there; he glanced at the sheets and pillows, and quietly slid open the drawer where last night Mark had found it, the first one they had found, while Walter was opening leather boxes of jewelry at her dresser and telling Mark to start in another room so they could work faster. He put the basket on the floor and held the open case in both hands. He lifted it closer to his eyes. He looked at it until his breathing slowed; and when he stopped hearing his breathing, he was suddenly tired, and as he lowered one hand and turned the other and watched the brief white descent, he wanted to sleep.

Their voices woke him, and when they started up the stairs, he turned quietly onto his side, his back to the door, and heard the girls with soft-crackling shopping bags going into their rooms and his mother coming to his; she stopped at the doorway and he breathed as though asleep until she turned and went to her room. He opened his eyes to the lake and trees and the low sun. He waited until he heard showers in all three bathrooms. Then he ran on tiptoes down the hall and stairs, and at the terrace he sprinted: past the pool and down toward the widening lake, and fell forward and struck with knees and palms, and rolled and stood and ran again, weight on his heels now, leaping when his balance shifted forward: running and leaping to the bottom of the hill where he could not stop: with short flat-footed steps he went across the narrow mud bank and into the water deep as his knees and then was sitting in it. He stood and looked up at the house, and higher and beyond it at the sky. Then he eased backward into the water and floated. Behind him the geese stirred and he listened to their wings as they rose and settled again. He backstroked toward the middle, then floated. Now the trees were on his left and he looked at their green crowns and the sky and waited for his mother's voice calling from the terrace.

The Captain

For Gunnery Sergeant Jim Beer

HIS SON WORE a moustache. Over and between tan faces and the backs of heads with hair cut high and short, and green-uniformed shoulders and chests and backs, Harry saw him standing with two other second lieutenants at the bar. His black moustache was thick. Only one woman was at happy hour, a blond captain: she had a watchful, attractive face that was pretty when she laughed. Harry stepped forward one pace, then another, and stood with his back to the door, breathing the fragrance of liquor and cigarette smoke, as pleasing to him as the smell of cooking is to some, and feeling through his body the loud talk and laughter and shouts, as though he watched a parade whose music coursed through him. In his own uniform wth captain's bars and ribbons, he wanted to stand here and have one Scotch. He did not feel that he stood to the side of the gathered men, but at their head, looking down the axis of their gaiety. A tall man, he did look down at most of them, and he wanted to watch his son from this distance. But there were no waitresses, so he went to the bar and spoke over Phil's shoulder: 'There's one nice thing about a moustache.'

The eyes in the turning face were dark and happy. Then Harry was hugging him, and Phil's arms were around his waist, tighter and tighter, and Phil leaned back and lifted him from the floor, the metal buttons of their blouses clicking together, then scraping as Phil lowered him, and introduced him to the two lieutenants as *my father, Captain LeDuc, retired*. Harry shook hands, not hearing their names, focusing intsead on their faces and tightly tailored

blouses and the silver shooting badges on their breasts: both wore
the crossed rifles and crossed pistols of experts, and above those,
like Phil, they wore only the one red and gold ribbon that showed
they were in the service during a war they had not seen. He saw
them scanning his four rows of ribbons, pretended he had not, and
turned to Phil, letting his friends look comfortably at the colored
rectangles of two wars and a wound and one act that had earned
him a Silver Star. Beside Phil's crossed rifles was the Maltese cross
of a sharpshooter. The bartender emptied the ashtray, and Phil ordered another round and a Scotch and water, and Harry said:
'What happened with the .45?'

'I choked up. What bothers me is knowing I'm better and having
to wear this till next year. *Then* I'll—' He smiled and his eyes lowered and rose. 'Jesus.'

'Good,' Harry said. 'If we couldn't forget, we'd never enjoy
anything after the age of ten. Or five.'

Phil turned to his friends standing at his left and said he had just
told his father he didn't like having to wear the sharpshooter badge
until he qualified again next year, and the three of them laughed
and joked about rice paddies and Monday and jungle and Charlie,
and Harry saw the bartender coming with their drinks and paid
him, thinking of how often memory lies, of how so often the lies
are good ones. When he was twenty-four years old, he had learned
on Guadalcanal that the body could endure nearly anything, and
after that he had acted as though he believed it could endure everything: could work without sleep or rest or enough food and
water, heedless of cold and heat and illness; could survive penetra-
tion and dismemberment, so that death in combat was a matter of
bad luck, a man with five bullets in him surviving another pierced
by only one. He was so awed by the body's strength and vulnera-
bility that he did nothing at all about prolonging its life. This re-
fusal was rooted neither in confidence nor an acceptance of fate.
His belief in mystery and chance was too strong to allow faith in
exercising and in controlling what he ate and drank and when he
smoked. Phil had forgotten who he was and where he was going;
was that how the mind survived? The body pushed beyond pain,
and the mind sidestepped. How else could he stand here, comfortable, proud of his son, when his own mind held images this room
of cheerful peace could not contain? He raised a knee and drew

his pack of cigarettes from his sock, and Phil gave him a light with a Zippo bearing a Marine emblem, and said: 'What's the one nice thing about a moustache?'

'If I have to tell you, you're fucking up on more than the .45.'

'They don't give out badges for that.'

'One girl?'

'No.'

'Good. It's too rough on them.'

'They'll *all* miss me, Pop.'

'I'd rather be in the middle of it. I didn't have a girl, when I was in the Pacific. But, Jesus, I was never warm in the Reservoir, not for one minute, there was always *some*thing cold—'

'Frozen Chosin,' one of the lieutenants said, and drank and eyed Harry's ribbons over the glass.

'—Right: *I* was frozen. *Every*body: we'd come on dead Chi*nese* frozen. And tell you the truth, I didn't think we'd get out, more fucking Chinese than snow, but I'd rather have been freezing my ass off and trying to keep it from getting between a Chinaman's bullet and thin air than back home like your mother. How do you keep waking up every day and doing what there is to do when you know your man is getting shot at? Ha.' He looked from Phil to the two lieutenants watching him, respectfully embarrassed, then back at Phil, whose dark saddened eyes had never looked at him this way before, almost as a father gazing at a son, and in a rush of age he saw himself as father of a man grown enough to give him pity. 'I guess I'm fucking well about to find out.'

'Fucking-A,' Phil said, and clapped his shoulder and turned to his drink.

At three in the morning, a half-hour before the alarm, his heart woke him, its anticipatory beat freeing him as normally caffeine did from that depth of sleep whose paradox he could not forgive: needing each night that respite so badly that finally nothing could prevent his having it, then each morning having to rise from it with coffee and tobacco so that he could resume with hope those volitive hours that would end with his grateful return to the oblivion of dreams. He coughed and swallowed, and coughed again and swallowed that too. Phil was in a sleeping bag on an air mattress in the middle of the small room. Last night after dinner at the officers' club, where they had talked of hunting and today's terrain, they had spread out on Phil's desk a map he got from the sportsmen's club when he drew their hunting area from a campaign hat three nights earlier, and Harry looked, nodded, and listened while Phil, using a pencil as a pointer, told him about the squares of contoured earth on the map that Harry could not only read more quickly, and more accurately, but also felt he knew anyway because, having spent most of his peacetime career at Camp Pendleton, he felt all its reaches were his ground. But he remained amused, and nearly agreed when Phil showed him two long ridges flanking a valley, and said this was the place to get a deer and spend the whole Saturday without seeing one of the other eight hunters who had drawn the same boundaries.

'It'll take us too long to walk in,' Harry said.

'I got the CO's jeep. I told him you were coming to hunt.'

At three-fifteen by the luminous dial of his Marine-issued wristwatch that he felt he had not stolen but retired with him, he quietly left the bed and stood looking down at Phil. He lay on his back, a pillow under his head, all but his throat and face hidden and shapeless in the bulk of the sleeping bag. His face was paled by sleep and the dark, eyeless save for brows and curves, and his delicate breathing whispered into the faint hum, the constant tone of night's quiet. Harry had not watched him sleeping since he was a boy, and now he was pierced as with a remembrance of fatherhood, but of something else too, as old as the earth's dust: in the darkened bedrooms of Phil and the two daughters he had felt this tender dread; and also looking at the face of a woman asleep, even some he did not love when he woke in the night: his children and the women devoid of anger and passion and humor and pain, so that he yearned during their fragile rest to protect them from and for whatever shaped their faces in daylight.

'Lieutenant,' he said, his deep voice, almost harsh, snapping both him and Phil into the day's hunt: 'The good thing about a moustache is you can smell her all night while you sleep, and when you wake up you can lick it again.'

The eyes opened and stared from a face still in repose; the mouth was slower to leave sleep, then it smiled and Phil said: 'You ex-enlisted men talk dirty.'

They dressed and went quickly down the corridor, rifles slung on their shoulders, Phil carrying in one hand a pack with their breakfast and lunch; they wore pistol belts with canteens and hunting knives, and jeans, and sweat shirts over their shirts, and windbreakers; Harry wore a wide-brimmed straw hat. Still, the act of arming himself to go into the hills made him feel he was in uniform, and as Phil drove the open jeep through fog, Harry shivered and pushed his hat tighter on his head and watched both flanks, an instinct so old and now useless that it amused him. He had learned to use his senses as an animal does, and probably as his ancestors in Canada and New Hampshire had, though not his father, whose avocation was beer and cards and friends in his kitchen or theirs, the men's talk with the first beers and hands of penny ante poker in French and English, then later only in the French that had crossed the ocean centuries before the invention of things, so in the flow of words that Harry never learned he now and then heard engine and car and airplane and electric fan. So in 1936, never having touched a rifle or pistol, he went into the Marine Corps with a taste for beer and a knowledge of poker acquired in his eighteenth year and last at home, when his father said he was old enough to join the table, and he trained with young men who had killed game since boyhood, and would learn cards in the barracks and drinking in bars. Four years later he returned home; in the summer evening he walked from the bus station over climbing and dropping streets of the village to the little house where his father sat on the front steps with a bottle of beer; he had not bathed yet for the dinner that Harry could smell cooking; he had taken off his shirt, and his undershirt was wet and soiled; sweat streaked the dirt on his throat and arms, and he hugged Harry and called to the family, took a long swallow of beer, handed the bottle to Harry, and said: 'I got you a job at the foundry.' Two days later, Harry took a bus to the recruiting office and reenlisted.

The jeep descended into colder air; fog hid the low earth, so that Harry could not judge the distance from the road to the dark bulk of hills on both sides. He stopped looking, and at once felt exposed and alert; he smiled and shook his head and leaned toward the dashboard to light a cigarette. He could see no stars; the wet moon was pallid, distant. He watched the road, grey fog paled and swathed yellow by the headlights, and said: 'There was a battalion cut off, when the Chinese came in.'

'*What?*'

He turned to Phil and spoke away from the rushing air, loudly over the vibrating moan of the jeep: the Chosin Reservoir, the whole Goddamned division was surrounded and a battalion cut off, and they had to go through Chinese to get there and break the battalion out and bring it to the main body. So they could retreat through all those Chinese to the sea. The battalion was pinned down about five miles away, so they started on foot, with a company on each flank playing leapfrog over the hills: two battalions, one of them Royal Marines, and their colonel was in command. A feisty little bastard. 'I've never *liked Li*meys, but the Royal Ma*rines* are *good*.' He guessed he liked Limey troops, it was just the country that pissed him off. The reason Marines had such good liberty in Australia in World War II was the Aussies were off in Africa fighting for England. Even the chaplain probably got laid. 'They loved M*arines* and still *do*, and if you ever get a chance to go to Austra*li*a, *take* it.' Their boys were fighting the Goddamn Germans, so it was the Marines keeping Australia safe, and they'd go there for R and R and get all the thanks too. The Limeys were good at that, getting other people to go off and fight in somebody else's yard. 'Do you read *hi*story?'

'Not since *coll*ege.'

'You've *got* to.' He shivered and caught his hat before it blew off, and the jeep climbed into lighter fog. 'If you're going to be a ca*reer* man, you've got to start *study*ing this stuff *now*. Not just *tac*tics and *strat*egy; but how these wars get *start*ed, and *why*, and who *starts* them.'

'I *will*. What about that bat*ta*lion?'

The flank companies kept making contact in the hills, and the troops in the road would assault and clear that hill, then start moving again; but they were moving too slowly, it was one firefight after another, so the colonel called back for trucks and brought the people down from the hills, and they all mounted up in the trucks and hauled ass down the road till they got hit; then they'd pile out and attack, and when they'd knocked out whatever it was or it had run off to some other hill, they'd hi-diddle-diddle up the road again—

'Holy *shit*.'

'I never felt so *much* like a moving *target*.' He rode shotgun in a six-by; the driver was a corporal and he pissed all over himself; he was good, though; he just kept cussing and shifting gears; probably he was praying too; maybe it was all praying: Jesus Christ God-*damn*—pissssss—shit *Jesus*— From the front of the six-by he watched the hills, but what good was it to watch where it's going to come from, when you're moving so fast that you know you can't see anything till you draw fire? He felt like he was searching the air for a bullet. He told the corporal he wished he were up there and the Chinese were down here. Probably that was a prayer too— Harry grabbed his hat as the brim slapped the crown; he put it in his lap, and the air was cool on his bald spot. '*De*-fense is *best*, you know. Or don't they *tell* you *that*.' 'Course they don't, Marines always attack; but with helicopters you can go behind them and cut off their line of supply and defend that. 'Read Lid*del Hart*. And learn *Span*ish. That's where it's *going* to *be*.'

'*Where?*'

'*Mex*ico to Ti*erra* del *Fue*go. We got the batta*li*on out.'

He twisted and reached behind his left hip for his canteen.

'So the *colo*nel was *right*.'

'*Sure* he was.' He gargled, then swallowed, and drank again and offered the canteen to Phil, who shook his head. 'We *lost* people we might *not* have, if we'd *done* it the *right* way. But we had to *do* it the *fast* way.'

The jeep climbed, and above him the fog was thinning; to his right he could see a ridge outlined clearly against the sky.

'Have you *seen* your *moth*er yet?'

'Last *night*. She and the *girls*. We had *din*ner. *Cath*erine's screwed up.'

'Not *dope?*'

'*No*. She doesn't *think* I should *go*. At the same *time* she—' He shrugged, glanced at Harry, then watched the road.

'Loves her *broth*er,' Harry said.

'Yes.'

'Just the *wom*en? No *boy* friends?'

'I *don't* think they *like* Marines.'

'*Fuck* 'em.'

'I'll leave *that* to *Cath*erine and *Joyce*.'

'*Ea*sy now. My *daugh*ters are *vi*rgins.'

'*Right.*'

'I wish your *ski*pper had left the *top* on the *jeep.*'

'*—soon.*'

'*What?*'

'To*day* will be *hot.*'

Harry nodded and put on his hat, pressing it down, and watched the suspended motion of fog above the road.

The deer camp duty officer's table was near the fire. He wore hunting clothes and was rankless, as all the hunters were, but was in charge of the camp, logging hunters in and out, and recording their kills, because he had drawn the duty from a hat. A hissing gas lantern was on the table near his log book, and above him shadows cast by the fire danced in trees. Harry and Phil gave him their names and hunting area; he was in his midthirties, looked to Harry like a gunnery sergeant or major; they spoke to him about fog and the cold drive, and he wished them luck as they moved away, to the fire where two men squatted with skillets of eggs and others stood drinking coffee from canteen cups. The fire was in a hole; a large coffeepot rested on two stones at the edge of the flames. Harry poured for both of them, shook the pot, and a lance corporal emerged from the darkness; he wore faded green utilities and was eating a doughnut. He took the pot from Harry and shook it, then placed it beside the hole and returned to the darkness. The two men cooking eggs rose and brought the crackling skillets to the edge of the fire's light, where three men sat drinking coffee. The lance corporal came back with a kettle and put it on the stones, then sat cross-legged and smoked. His boots shone in the fire's light. From above, Harry watched him: he liked his build, lean and supple, and the cocky press of his lips, and his wearing his cap visor so low over his eyes that he had to jut out his chin to see in front of him. Phil crouched and held a skillet of bacon over the fire, and Harry stepped closer to the lance corporal; he wanted to ask him why he was in special services, in charge of a hobby shop or gym or swimming pool, drawing duty as a fire-builder and coffee-maker. Looking down at his starched cap and polished boots and large, strong-looking hands, he wished he could train him, teach him and care for him, and his wish became a yearning: looking at Phil wrapping a handkerchief around the skillet handle, he wished he could train him too. He circled the lance corporal and sat heavily on the earth beside Phil.

'I *used* to be graceful.'

'Civilians are entitled to a beer gut. We forgot a spatula.'

'Civilian my ass. Here.'

He drew his hunting knife and handed it to Phil; behind him, and beyond the line of trees, a car left the road and stopped. Bacon curled over the knife blade; Phil lifted strips free of the skillet, lowered the pale sides into the grease, and said: 'The eggs will break.'

'I'll cook them.'

'Fried?'

'Lieutenant, I've spent more time in chow lines than you've spent in the Marine Corps.'

Three hunters came out of the trees and stood at the table to his left. The lance corporal flipped his cigarette into the flames and crossed his arms on his knees and watched the kettle.

'They use spatulas,' Phil said.

'True enough. But I will turn the eggs. How they come out is in the hands of the Lord.'

'Bless us o Lord in this thy omelet.'

'Over easy. Do you go to Mass?'

'Sometimes. Do you?'

'On Sundays.'

Across the fire the three men rubbed their hands in the heat. A car left the road, then another, and doors opened and slammed, and voices and rustling, cracking footsteps came through the trees. The lance corporal rose without using his hands and took the coffeepot into the darkness.

'Where does he go?' Harry said.

'He's like an Indian.'

'He's like an Oriental.'

Then he heard the water boiling and, as he looked, steam came from the spout. From the pack he took bread, eggs, and paper plates. Phil spread bacon on a plate, then Harry dug a small hole with the knife and poured in some of the bacon grease and covered it. Kneeling, he fried four slices of bread, then broke six eggs, one-handed, into the skillet and was watching the bubbling whites and browning edges when he heard cars on the road; he glanced up at the dimmed stars and lemon moon; the fog was thinner, and smoke rose darkly through its eddying grey. In the skillet the eggs joined, and he was poised to separate them with his knife, then said: 'Look what we have.'

'Your basic sunnyside pie.'

'It's beautiful.'

He slanted the skillet till grease moved to one side, and with the blade he slapped it over the eggs. He held the skillet higher and watched the yellows, and the milky white circling them; he slid his knife under the right edge, gently moved it toward the center, and stopped under the first yolk. Phil held a paper plate, and Harry tilted the skillet over it, working the knife upward as connected eggs slid over the blade and rim, onto the plate.

'I hate to break it,' Phil said. 'Should we freeze it?'

'In our minds.'

Phil took their cups to the coffeepot; Harry watched him pouring, and waited for him to sit at the plate resting on loose dirt. They did not separate the eggs. On the road, cars approached like a convoy that had lost its intervals, and Harry and Phil ate quietly, slowly, watching the disc become oval, then oblong, then a yellow smear for the last of their bread. Men circled them and the fire. Phil reached for the skillet, and Harry said: 'I'll do it.'

He tossed dirt into it and rubbed the hot metal, then wiped it with a paper towel; he stabbed the knife into the earth and worked it back and forth and deeper, and wiped it clean on his trousers. He held his cigarettes toward Phil, but he was shaking one from his own pack. They sat facing the fire, smoking with their coffee. The lance corporal put on a fresh log, and Harry watched flames licking around its bottom and up its sides; above and around him the voices were incoherent, peaceful as the creaking of windblown trees.

Under a near-fogless sky, a half-hour before dawn, he reached the northern and highest peak of the narrow ridge, and walked with light steps, back and forth and in small circles, until his breathing slowed and his legs stopped quivering. Then he sat facing the bare spine of dirt and rock that dipped and rose and finally descended southward, through diaphanous fog, to the jeep. He heard nothing in the sky or on the earth save his own breathing. He rested his rifle on his thighs and watched both sides of the ridge: flat ground to the east until a mass of iron-grey hills; the valley, broken by a dark stand of trees, was to the west; beyond that was the ridge where Phil hunted.

The air and earth were the grey of twilight; then, as he looked down the western slope, at shapes of rocks and low thickets, the valley and Phil's ridge became colors, muted under vanishing mist: pale green patches of grass and brown earth and a beige stream bed. The trees were pines, growing inside an eastward bend of the stream. Brown and green brush spread up the russet slope of Phil's ridge, and beyond it was the light blue of the sea. Harry stood, was on his feet before he remembered to be quiet and still, and watched the blue spreading farther as fog rose from it like steam. He turned to the scarlet slice of sun crowning a hill. From the strip of rose and golden sky, the horizon rolled toward him: peaks and ridges, gorges and low country, and scattered green of trees among the arid yellow and brown. He faced the ocean, saw whitecaps now, and took off his hat and waved it. On the peak of Phil's ridge he could see only rocks. The sea and sky were pale still; he stood watching as fog dissolved into their deepening blue, the sky brightened, and he could see the horizon. He sat facing it.

At eight o'clock he started walking down the ridge: one soft step, then waiting, looking down both slopes; another step; after three he saw Phil: a flash of light, a movement on the skyline. Then Phil became a tiny figure, and Harry stayed abreast of him. Soon the breeze shifted, came from the sea, and he could smell it. Near midmorning he flushed a doe: froze at the sudden crack of brush, as her bounding rump and darting body angled down the side of the ridge; in the valley she ran south, and was gone.

He sat and smoked and watched a ship gliding past Phil, its stacks at his shoulders. Then he stood and took off his jacket and sweat shirt and hung them from his belt. He caught up with Phil, and stalked again. When the sun was high and sparkling the sea, the ridge dropped more sharply, and he unloaded his rifle and slung it from his shoulder, and went down to the jeep. Phil sat on the hood. Behind him was open country and a distant range of tall hills. Harry sat on the hood and drank from his canteen.

'Saved ammo,' Phil said.

'I almost stepped on a doe.'

'How close?'

'Three steps and a good spit.'

'I've never been that close.'

'Neither have I.'

'Pretty quiet, Pop.'

'She startled me. If she'd been a buck, I would have missed.'

They ate sandwiches, then lay on their backs in the shade of the jeep. Harry rested his hat on his forehead so the brim covered his eyes.

'Are you staying for dinner?' Phil said.

'No. I don't like driving tired.'

'We can go back now, if you want.'

'Let's hunt. What will you do tomorrow?'

'Make sure my toothbrush is packed.'

'No girl?'

'There isn't one. I mean no *one*. So why choose now, right? I'll go out with the guys and get drunk.'

'Only way to go. What time Monday?'

'I don't even want to say.'

'They love getting guys up in the dark.'

His boots were warm. He looked out from under the hat: sunlight was on his ankles now; he looked over his feet at the low end of Phil's ridge.

'Orientals can hide on a parade field. Chinese would crawl all night from their lines to ours. A few feet and wait. All night lying out there, no sound, nothing moving, and just before dawn they'd be on top of us. And *Jap*anese: they were like leaves.'

'Except that tank.'

'What tank?'

'Your Silver Star.'

'That was a pillbox.'

'It was?'

'Sure. Did you think I'd go after a tank?'

'Not much difference. Why didn't I know that?'

'Too many war stories, too many Marines; probably a neighbor told *his* kid about a tank.'

'I told *them*. Was it on Tarawa?'

'Yes.'

'At least I got that right.'

'It's not important. It's just something that happened. We were pinned down on the beach. The boxes had interlocking fire. I remember my mouth in the sand, then an explosion to my right front. It was a satchel charge, and a kid named Winslow Brimmer was the one who got it there.'

'Winslow Brimmer?'

'He was a mean little fart from Baltimore. Nobody harassed him about his name. He took whatever was left of his squad to that box, and all but two of them bought it. Then I was running with a flamethrower on my back. If you can call that running.'

'Where did you get the flamethrower?'

'The guy with it was next to me, and he was dead. So I put it on and moved out.'

'Jesus.'

'It was easier than Brimmer's because he had knocked out the one on their left. I had more fresh air than he did.'

'Not much.'

'I can remember doing it, but it's like somebody told me I did it, and that's why I remember. The way it can be after a bad drunk. I don't remember what I felt just before, or what I thought. I remember getting the flamethrower off him and onto me, and that should have taken a while, but it doesn't seem like it. I remember running, but I don't remember hearing anything, not with all those weapons firing, and I don't remember getting there. I was there, and then I burned them. They must have made sounds, but I only remember the smell.'

'Was that when you were wounded?'

'No. That was the next day.'

'I wish I had been there.'

'No you don't. The Navy dropped us in deep water—'

'I know.'

'Dead troops bobbing in it and lying on the reef and the beach. Fuck Tarawa.'

He opened his eyes to the sun, and squinted away from it at the sky. A hawk glided toward the earth, veered away, and climbed west over the ridge.

'You reflected the sun this morning,' he said. 'That's how I saw you.'

'My watch.'

He looked at the chrome band on Phil's wrist.

'Goddamn it, leave that civilian shit at home and get one from supply.'

'It's in my room.'

'Sorry.'

'Okay, Captain.'

He closed his eyes, listening to Phil's breathing. The sun on his face woke him, and he stiffened and pressed his palms against the ground, then knew where he was. Phil was gone. He stood, wiping sweat from his eyes; Phil leaned against the back of the jeep, eating a plum.

'Have some fruit.'

Harry took a peach from the pack and stood beside him.

'Do you want to swap ridges?' Phil said.

'Not unless you do.'

'No, I'm fine.'

'Mine's like home now.'

'We'll probably get back here around six. Thirty minutes to the camp to sign out. Then about forty.'

'Plenty of time. I make it in under three hours. 'Course, there's always the Jesus factor.'

'Like getting a deer.'

'If we do, I'll help you clean it.'

'And take it home with you.'

'Right.'

'All set?'

'Need my hogleg.'

He took the rifle from the back seat and slung it from his shoulder.

'How do you like the .308?' Phil said.

'It's good.'

'Have you zeroed it in?'

'Not this year.'

They walked into the valley and up the hard, cracked earth of the stream bed to the pine trees, and stood in their shade.

'I like the smell of pine,' Harry said. 'Up there I can smell the ocean. Did you see it this morning, when the sun came up?'

'Beautiful.'

'Now we get the sunset. Ready?'

'I'm off.'

'Take care, then.'

'You too.'

They turned from each other and Harry walked out of the trees, into the sunlight, then he lengthened his stride toward the ridge.

Sorrowful Mysteries

WHEN GERRY FONTENOT is five, six, and seven years old, he likes to ride in the car with his parents. It is a grey 1938 Chevrolet and it has a ration stamp on the windshield. Since the war started when Gerry was five, his father has gone to work on a bicycle, and rarely drives the car except to Sunday Mass, and to go hunting and fishing. Gerry fishes with him, from the bank of the bayou. They fish with bamboo poles, corks, sinkers, and worms, and catch perch and catfish. His father wears a .22 revolver at his side, for cottonmouths. In the fall Gerry goes hunting with him, crouches beside him in ditches bordering fields, and when the doves fly, his father stands and fires the twelve-gauge pump, and Gerry marks where the birds fall, then runs out into the field where they lie, and gathers them. They are soft and warm as he runs with them, back to his father. This is in southern Louisiana, and twice he and his father see an open truck filled with German prisoners, going to work in the sugar cane fields.

He goes on errands with his mother. He goes to grocery stores, dime stores, drugstores, and shopping for school clothes in the fall, and Easter clothes in the spring, and to the beauty parlor, where he likes to sit and watch the women. Twice a week he goes with her to the colored section, where they leave and pick up the week's washing and ironing. His mother washes at home too: the bed-clothes, socks, underwear, towels, and whatever else does not have to be ironed. She washes these in a wringer washing machine; he likes watching her feed the clothes into the wringer, and the way they come out flattened and drop into the basket. She hangs them on the clothesline in the backyard, and Gerry stands at the basket and hands them to her so she will not have to stoop. On rainy days she dries them inside on racks, which in winter she places in front of space heaters. She listens to the weather forecasts on the radio, and most of the time is able to wash on clear days.

The Negro woman washes the clothes that must be ironed, or starched and ironed. In front of the woman's unpainted wooden house, Gerry's mother presses the horn, and the large woman comes out and takes the basket from the back seat. Next day, at the sound of the horn, she brings out the basket. It is filled with ironed, folded skirts and blouses, and across its top lie dresses and shirts on hangers. Gerry opens the window his mother has told him to close as they approached the colored section with its dusty roads. He smells the clean, ironed clothes, pastels and prints, and his father's white and pale blue, and he looks at the rutted dirt road, the unpainted wood and rusted screens of the houses, old cars in front of them and tire swings hanging from trees over the worn and packed dirt yards, dozens of barefoot, dusty children stopping their play to watch him and his mother in the car, and the old slippers and dress the Negro woman wears, and he breathes her smell of sweat, looks at her black and brown hand crossing him to take the dollar from his mother's fingers.

On Fridays in spring and summer, Leonard comes to mow the lawn. He is a Negro, and has eight children, and Gerry sees him only once between fall and spring, when he comes on Christmas Eve, and Gerry's father and mother give him toys and clothes that Gerry and his three older sisters have outgrown, a bottle of bourbon, one of the fruit cakes Gerry's mother makes at Christmas, and five dollars. Leonard receives these at the back door, where on Fridays, in spring and summer, he is paid and fed. The Fontenots eat dinner at noon, and Gerry's mother serves Leonard a plate and a glass of iced tea with leaves from the mint she grows under the faucet behind the house. She calls him from the back steps, and he comes, wiping his brow with a bandanna, and takes his dinner to the shade of a sycamore tree. From his place at the dining room table, Gerry watches him sit on the grass and take off his straw hat; he eats, then rolls a cigarette. When he has smoked, he brings his plate and glass to the back door, knocks, and hands them to whoever answers. His glass is a jelly glass, his plate blue china, and his knife and fork stainless steel. From Friday to Friday the knife and fork lie at one side of a drawer, beside the compartments that hold silver; the glass is nearly out of reach, at the back of the second shelf in the cupboard for glasses; the plate rests under serving bowls in the china cupboard. Gerry's mother has told him and his sisters not to use them, they are Leonard's, and from Friday to Friday, they sit, and from fall to spring, and finally forever when one year Gerry is strong enough to push the lawn mower for his allowance, and Leonard comes only when Gerry's father calls him every Christmas Eve.

Before that, when he is eight, Gerry has stopped going on errands with his mother. On Saturday afternoons he walks or, on rainy days, rides the bus to town with neighborhood boys, to the movie theater where they watch westerns and the weekly chapter of a serial. He stands in line on the sidewalk, holding his quarter that will buy a ticket, a bag of popcorn, and, on the way home, an ice-cream soda. Opposite his line, to the right of the theater as you face it, are the Negro boys. Gerry does not look at them. Or not directly: he glances, he listens, as a few years later he will do with girls when he goes to movies that draw them. The Negroes enter through the door marked *Colored*, where he supposes a Negro woman sells tickets, then climb the stairs to the balcony, and Gerry wonders whether someone sells them popcorn and candy and drinks up there, or imagines them smelling all the bags of popcorn in the dark beneath them. Then he watches the cartoon and previews of next Saturday's movie, and he likes them but is waiting for the chapter of the serial whose characters he and his friends have played in their yards all week; they have worked out several escapes for the trapped hero and, as always, they are wrong. He has eaten his popcorn when the credits for the movie appear, then a tall man rides a beautiful black or white or palomino horse across the screen. The movie is black and white, but a palomino looks as golden and lovely as the ones he has seen in parades. Sitting in the dark, he is aware of his friends on both sides of him only as feelings coincident with his own: the excitement of becoming the Cisco Kid, Durango Kid, Red Ryder, the strongest and best-looking, the most courageous and good, the fastest with horse and fists and gun. Then it is over, the lights are on, he turns to his friends, flesh again, stands to leave, then remembers the Negroes. He blinks up at them standing at the balcony wall, looking down at the white boys pressed together in the aisle, moving slowly out of the theater. Sometimes his eyes meet those of a Negro boy, and Gerry smiles; only one ever smiles back.

In summer he and his friends go to town on weekday afternoons to see war movies, or to buy toy guns or baseballs, and when he meets Negroes on the sidewalk, he averts his eyes; but he watches them in department stores, bending over water fountains marked *Colored*, and when they enter the city buses and walk past him to the rear, he watches them, and during the ride he glances, and listens to their talk and laughter. One hot afternoon when he is twelve, he goes with a friend to deliver the local newspaper in the colored section. He has not been there since riding with his mother, who has not gone for years either; now the city buses stop near his neighborhood, and a Negro woman comes on it and irons the family's clothes in their kitchen. He goes that afternoon because his friend has challenged him. They have argued: they both have paper routes, and when his friend complained about his, Gerry said it was easy work. Sure, his friend said, you don't have to hold your breath. You mean when you collect? No, man, when I just ride through. So Gerry finishes his route, then goes with his friend: a bicycle ride of several miles ending, or beginning, at a neighborhood of poor whites, their houses painted but peeling, their screened front porches facing lawns so narrow that only small children can play catch in them; the older boys and girls play tapeball on the blacktop street. Gerry and his friends play that, making a ball of tape around a sock, and hitting with a baseball bat, but they have lawns big enough to contain them. Gerry's father teaches history at the public high school, and in summer is a recreation director for children in the city park, and some nights in his bed Gerry hears his father and mother worry about money; their voices are weary, and frighten him. But riding down this street, he feels shamefully rich, wants the boys and girls pausing in their game to know he only has a new Schwinn because he saved his money to buy it.

He and his friend jolt over the railroad tracks, and the blacktop ends. Dust is deep in the road. They ride past fields of tall grass and decaying things: broken furniture, space heaters, stoves, cars. Negro children are in the fields. Then they come to the streets of houses, turn onto the first one, a rutted and dusty road, and breathe the smell. It is as tangible as the dust a car raises to Gerry's face as it bounces past him, its unmuffled exhaust pipe sounding like gunfire, and Gerry feels that he enters the smell, as you enter a cloud of dust; and a hard summer rain, with lightning and thunder, would settle it, and the air would smell of grass and trees. Its base is sour, as though in the heat of summer someone has half-filled a garbage can with milk, then dropped in citrus fruit and cooked rice and vegetables and meat and fish, mattress ticking and a pillow, covered it, and left it for a week in the July sun. In this smell children play in the street and on the lawns that are dirt too, dust, save for strips of crisp-looking yellowish grass in the narrow spaces between houses, and scattered patches near the porches. He remembers the roads and houses and yards from riding with his mother, but not the smell, for even in summer they had rolled up the windows. Or maybe her perfume and cigarettes had fortified the car against the moment the laundry woman would open the back door, or reach through the window for her dollar; but he wonders now if his mother wanted the windows closed only to keep out dust. Women and men sit on the front porches, as Gerry and his friend slowly ride up the road, and his friend throws triangular-folded papers onto the yards, where they skip in rising dust.

It is late afternoon, and he can smell cooking too: hot grease and meat, turnip or mustard greens, and he hears talk and laughter from the shaded porches. Everything seems to be dying: cars and houses and tar paper roofs in the weather, grass in the sun; sparse oaks and pines and weeping willows draw children and women with babies to their shade; beneath the hanging tent of a willow, an old man sits with two crawling children wearing diapers, and Gerry remembers Leonard eating in the shade of the sycamore. Gerry's father still phones Leonard on Christmas Eve, and last year he went home with the electric train Gerry has outgrown, along with toy soldiers and cap pistols and Saturday serials and westerns, a growth that sometimes troubles him: when he was nine and ten and saw that other neighborhood boys stopped going to the Saturday movies when they were twelve or thirteen, he could not understand why something so exciting was suddenly not, and he promised himself that he would always go on Saturdays, although he knew he would not, for the only teenaged boy who did was odd and frightening:

he was about eighteen, and in his voice and eyes was the despera-
tion of a boy lying to a teacher, and he tried to sit between Gerry
and his friends, and once he did before they could close the gap,
and all through the movie he tried to rub Gerry's thigh, and Gerry
whispered *Stop it*, and pushed at the wrist, the fingers. So he knew
a time would come when he would no longer love his heroes and
their horses, and it saddened him to know that such love could not
survive mere time. It did not, and that is what troubles him, when
he wonders if his love of baseball and football and hunting and fishing and bicycles will die too, and wonders what he will love then.

He looks for Leonard as he rides down the road, where some
yards are bordered with colored and clear bottles, half-buried with
bottoms up to the sun. In others a small rectangle of flowers grows
near the porch, and the smell seems to come from the flowers too,
and the trees. He wants to enter one of those houses kept darkened
with shades drawn against the heat, wants to trace and define that
smell, press his nose to beds and sofas and floor and walls, the bos-
om of a woman, the chest of a man, the hair of a child. Breathing
through his mouth, swallowing his nausea, he looks at his friend
and sees what he knows is on his face as well: an expression of sus-
tained and pallid horror.

On summer mornings the neighborhood boys play baseball. One of
the fathers owns a field behind his house; he has mowed it with a
tractor, and built a backstop of two-by-fours and screen, laid out
an infield with a pitcher's mound, and put up foul poles at the edge
of the tall weeds that surround the outfield. The boys play every
rainless morning except Sunday, when all but the two Protestants
go to Mass. They pitch slowly so they can hit the ball, and so the
catcher, with only a mask, will not get hurt. But they pitch from a
windup, and try to throw curves and knuckleballs, and sometimes
they play other neighborhood teams who loan their catcher shin
guards and chest protector, then the pitchers throw hard.

One morning a Negro boy rides his bicycle past the field, on the
dirt road behind the backstop; he holds a fishing pole across the
handlebars, and is going toward the woods beyond left field, and
the bayou that runs wide and muddy through the trees. A few long
innings later, he comes back without fish, and stops to watch the
game. Standing, holding his bicycle, he watches two innings. Then,

as Gerry's team is trotting in to bat, someone calls to the boy: Do you want to play? In the infield and outfield, and near home plate, voices stop. The boy looks at the pause, the silence, then nods, lowers his kickstand, and slowly walks onto the field.

'You're with us,' someone says. 'What do you play?'

'I like first.'

That summer, with eight dollars of his paper route money, Gerry has bought a first-baseman's glove: a Rawlings Trapper, because he liked the way it looked, and felt on his hand, but he is not a good first baseman: he turns his head away from throws that hit the dirt in front of his reaching glove and bounce toward his body, his face. He hands the glove to the boy.

'Use this. I ought to play second anyway.'

The boy puts his hand in the Trapper, thumps its pocket, turns his wrist back and forth, looking at the leather that is still a new reddish brown. Boys speak their names to him. His is Clay. They give him a place in the batting order, point to the boy he follows.

He is tall, and at the plate he takes a high stride and a long, hard swing. After his first hit, the outfield plays him deeply, at the edge of the weeds that are the boys' fence, and the infielders back up. At first base he is often clumsy, kneeling for ground balls, stretching before an infielder has thrown so that some balls nearly go past or above him; he is fearless, though, and none of the bouncing throws from third and deep short go past his body. He does not talk to any one boy, but from first he calls to the pitcher: *Come babe, come boy;* calls to infielders bent for ground balls: *Plenty time, plenty time, we got him;* and, to hitters when Gerry's team is at bat: *Good eye, good eye.* The game ends when the twelve o'clock whistle blows.

'That it?' Clay says as the fielders run in while he is swinging two bats on deck.

'We have to go eat,' the catcher says, taking off his mask, and with a dirt-smeared forearm wiping sweat from his brow.

'Me too,' he says, and drops the bats, picks up the Trapper, and hands it to Gerry. Gerry looks at it, lying across Clay's palm, looks at Clay's thumb on the leather.

'I'm a crappy first baseman,' he says. 'Keep it.'

'You kidding?'

'No. Go on.'

'What you going to play with?'

'My fielder's glove.'

Some of the boys are watching now; others are mounting bicycles on the road, riding away with gloves hanging from the handlebars, bats held across them.

'You don't want to play first no more?'

'No. Really.'

'Man, that's some *glove*. What's your name again?'

'Gerry,' he says, and extends his right hand. Clay takes it, and Gerry squeezes the big, limp hand; releases it.

'Gerry,' Clay says, looking down at his face as though to memorize it, or discern its features from among the twenty white faces of his morning.

'Good man,' he says, and turning, and calling goodbyes, he goes to his bicycle, places his fishing pole across the handlebars, hangs the Trapper from one, and rides quickly up the dirt road. Where the road turns to blacktop, boys are bicycling in a cluster, and Gerry watches Clay pass them with a wave. Then he is in the distance, among white houses with lawns and trees; is gone, leaving Gerry with the respectful voices of his friends, and peace and pride in his heart. He has attended a Catholic school since the first grade, so knows he must despise those feelings. He jokes about his play at first base, and goes with his Marty Marion glove and Ted Williams Louisville Slugger to his bicycle. But riding home, he nestles with his proud peace. At dinner he says nothing of Clay. The Christian Brothers have taught him that an act of charity can be canceled by the telling of it. Also, he suspects his family would think he is a fool.

A year later, a Negro man in a neighboring town is convicted of raping a young white woman, and is sentenced to die in the electric chair. His story is the front-page headline of the paper Gerry delivers, but at home, because the crime was rape, his mother tells the family she does not want any talk about it. Gerry's father mutters enough, from time to time, for Gerry to know he is angry and sad because if the woman had been a Negro, and the man white, there would have been neither execution nor conviction. But on his friends' lawns, while he plays catch or pepper or sits on the grass, whittling branches down to sticks, he listens to voluptuous voices from the porches, where men and women drink bourbon and talk of niggers and rape and the electric chair. The Negro's name is Sonny Broussard, and every night Gerry prays for his soul.

On the March night Sonny Broussard will die, Gerry lies in bed and says a rosary. It is a Thursday, a day for the Joyful Mysteries, but looking out past the mimosa, at the corner streetlight, he prays with the Sorrowful Mysteries, remembers the newspaper photographs of Sonny Broussard, tries to imagine his terror as midnight draws near—why midnight? and how could he live that day in his cell?—and sees Sonny Broussard on his knees in the Garden of Olives; he wears khakis, his arms rest on a large stone, and his face is lifted to the sky. Tied to a pillar and shirtless, he is silent under the whip; thorns pierce his head, and the fathers of Gerry's friends strike his face, their wives watch as he climbs the long hill, cross on his shoulder, then he is lying on it, the men with hammers are carpenters in khakis, squatting above him, sweat running down their faces to drip on cigarettes between their lips, heads cocked away from smoke; they swing the hammers in unison, and drive nails through wrists and crossed feet. Then Calvary fades and Gerry sees instead a narrow corridor between cells with a door at the end; two guards are leading Sonny Broussard to it, and Gerry watches them from the rear. They open the door to a room filled with people, save for a space in the center of their circle, where the electric chair waits. They have been talking when the guard opens the door, and they do not stop. They are smoking and drinking and knitting; they watch Sonny Broussard between the guards, look from him to each other, and back to him, talking, clapping a hand on a neighbor's shoulder, a thigh. The guards buckle Sonny Broussard into the chair. Gerry shuts his eyes, and tries to feel the chair, the straps, Sonny Broussard's fear; to feel so hated that the people who surround him wait for the very throes and stench of his death. Then he feels it, he is in the electric chair, and he opens his eyes and holds his breath against the scream in his throat.

Gerry attends the state college in town, and lives at home. He majors in history, and is in the Naval ROTC, and is grateful that he will spend three years in the Navy after college. He does not want to do anything with history but learn it, and he believes the Navy will give him time to know what he will do for the rest of his life.

He also wants to go to sea. He thinks more about the sea than history; by Christmas he is in love, and thinks more about the girl than either of them. Near the end of the year, the college president calls an assembly and tells the students that, in the fall, colored boys and girls will be coming to the school. The president is a politician, and will later be lieutenant-governor. There will be no trouble at this college, he says. I do not want troops or federal marshals on my campus. If any one of you starts trouble, or even joins in on it if one of them starts it, I will have you in my office, and you'd best bring your luggage with you.

The day after his last examinations, Gerry starts working with a construction crew. In the long heat he carries hundred-pound bags of cement, shovels gravel and sand, pushes wheelbarrows of wet concrete, digs trenches for foundations, holes for septic tanks, has more money than he has ever owned, spends most of it on his girl in restaurants and movies and night clubs and bars, and by late August has gained fifteen pounds, most of it above his waist, though beneath that is enough for his girl to pinch, and call his Budweiser belt. Then he hears of Emmett Till. He is a Negro boy, and in the night two white men have taken him from his great-uncle's house in Mississippi. Gerry and his girl wait. Three days later, while Gerry sits in the living room with his family before supper, the news comes over the radio: a search party has found Emmett Till at the bottom of the Tallahatchie River; a seventy-pound cotton gin fan was tied to his neck with barbed wire; he was beaten and shot in the head, and was decomposing. Gerry's father lowers his magazine, removes his glasses, rubs his eyes, and says: 'Oh my Lord, it's happening again.'

He goes to the kitchen and Gerry hears him mixing another bourbon and water, then the back screen door opens and shuts. His mother and the one sister still at home are talking about Mississippi and rednecks, and the poor boy, and what were they thinking of, what kind of men *are* they? He wants to follow his father, to ask what memory or hearsay he had meant, but he does not believe he is old enough, man enough, to move into his father's silence in the backyard.

He phones his girl, and after supper asks his father for the car, and drives to her house. She is waiting on the front porch, and walks quickly to the car. She is a petite, dark-skinned Cajun girl, with fast and accented speech, deep laughter, and a temper that is fierce when it reaches the end of its long tolerance. Through generations the Fontenots' speech has slowed and softened, so that Gerry sounds more southern than French; she teases him about it, and often, when he is with her, he finds that he is talking with her rhythms and inflections. She likes dancing, rhythm and blues, jazz, gin, beer, Pall Malls, peppery food, and passionate kissing, with no fondling. She receives Communion every morning, wears a gold Sacred Heart medal on a gold chain around her neck, and wants to teach history in college. Her name is Camille Theriot.

They go to a bar, where people are dancing to the jukebox. The couples in booths and boys at the bar are local students, some still in high school, for in this town parents and bartenders ignore the law about drinking, and bartenders only use it at clubs that do not want young people. Gerry has been drinking at this bar since he got his driver's license when he was sixteen. He leads Camille to a booth, and they drink gin and tonics, and repeat what they heard at college, in the classroom where they met: that it was economic, and all the hatred started with slavery, the Civil War leaving the poor white no one about whom he could say: *At least I ain't a slave like him*, leaving him only: *At least I ain't a nigger*. And after the war the Negro had to be contained to provide cheap labor in the fields. Camille says it might explain segregation, so long as you don't wonder about rich whites who don't have to create somebody to look down on, since they can do it from birth anyway.

'So it doesn't apply,' she says.

'They never seem to, do they?'

'What?'

'Theories. Do you think those sonsabitches—do you think they tied that fan on before or after they shot him? Why barbed wire if he was already dead? Why not baling wire, or—'

The waitress is there, and he watches her lower the drinks, put their empty glasses on her tray; he pays her, and looks at Camille. Her face is lowered, her eyes closed.

Around midnight, when the crowd thins, they move to the bar. Three couples dance slowly to Sinatra; another kisses in a booth. Gerry knows they are in high school when the boy lights a cigarette and they share it: the girl draws on it, they kiss, and she exhales into his mouth; then the boy does it. Camille says: 'Maybe we should go north to college, and just stay there.'

'I hear the people are cold as the snow.'

'Me too. And they eat boiled food with some kind of white sauce.'

'You want some oysters?'

'Can we get there before they close?'

'Let's try it,' he says. 'Did you French-smoke in high school?'

'Sure.'

A boy stands beside Gerry and loudly orders a beer. He is drunk, and when he sees Gerry looking at him, he says: 'Woo. They *did* it to him, didn't they? 'Course now, a little nigger boy like that, you can't tell'—as Gerry stands so he can reach into his pocket—'could be he'd go swimming with seventy pounds hanging on his neck, and a bullet in his head'—and Gerry opens the knife he keeps sharp for fish and game, looks at the blade, then turns toward the voice: 'Emmett *Till* rhymes with *kill*. Hoo. Hot*damn*. Kill *Till*—'

Gerry's hand bunches the boy's collar, turns him, and pushes his back against the bar. He touches the boy's throat with the point of the knife, and his voice comes yelling out of him; he seems to rise from the floor with it, can feel nothing of his flesh beneath it: 'You like *death*? *Feel* it!'

He presses the knife until skin dimples around its point. The boy is still, his mouth open, his eyes rolled to his left, where the knife is. Camille is screaming, and Gerry hears *Cut his tongue out! Cut his heart out!* Then she is standing in front of the boy, her arms waving, and Gerry hears *Bastard bastard bastard*, as he watches the boy's eyes and open mouth, then hears the bartender speaking softly: 'Take it easy now. You're Gerry, right?' He glances at the voice; the bartender is leaning over the bar. 'Easy, Gerry. You stick him there, he's gone. Why don't you go on home now, okay?'

Camille is quiet. Watching the point, Gerry pushes the knife, hardly a motion at all, for he is holding back too; the dimple, for an instant, deepens and he feels the boy's chest breathless and rigid beneath his left fist.

'Okay,' he says, and releases the boy's shirt, folds the knife, and takes Camille's arm. Boys at the bar and couples on the dance floor stand watching. There is music he cannot hear clearly enough to name. He and Camille walk between the couples to the door.

Two men, Roy Bryant and John William Milan, are arrested, and through hot September classes Gerry and Camille wait for the trial.

Negroes sit together in classes, walk together in the corridors and across the campus, and surround juxtaposed tables in the student union, where they talk quietly, and do not play the jukebox. Gerry and Camille drink coffee and furtively watch them; in the classrooms and corridors, and on the grounds, they smile at Negroes, tell them hello, and get smiles and greetings. The Negro boys wear slacks and sport shirts, some of them with coats, some even with ties; the girls wear skirts or dresses; all of them wear polished shoes. There is no trouble. Gerry and Camille read the newspapers and listen to the radio, and at night after studying together they go to the bar and drink beer; the bartender is polite, even friendly, and does not mention the night of the knife. As they drink, then drive to Camille's house, they talk about Emmett Till, his story they have read and heard.

He was from Chicago, where he lived with his mother; his father died in France, in the Second World War. Emmett was visiting his great-uncle in Money, Mississippi. His mother said she told him to be respectful down there, because he didn't know about the South. One day he went to town and bought two cents' worth of bubble gum in Roy Bryant's store. Bryant's wife Carolyn, who is young and pretty, was working at the cash register. She said that when Emmett left the store and was on the sidewalk, he turned back to her and whistled. It was the wolf whistle, and that night Roy Bryant and his half-brother, John William Milan, went to the great-uncle's house with flashlights and a pistol, said *Where's that Chicago boy*, and took him.

The trial is in early fall. The defense lawyer's case is that the decomposed body was not Emmett Till; that the NAACP had put his father's ring on the finger of that body; and that the fathers of the jurors would turn in their graves if these twelve Anglo-Saxon men returned with a guilty verdict, which, after an hour and seven minutes of deliberation, they do not. That night, with Camille sitting so close that their bodies touch, Gerry drives on highways through farming country and cleared land with oil derricks and gas fires, and on bridges spanning dark bayous, on narrow blacktop roads twisting through lush woods, and gravel and dirt roads through rice fields whose canals shimmer in the moonlight. The windows are open to humid air whose rush cools his face.

When they want beer, he stops at a small country store; woods are behind it, and it is flanked by lighted houses separated by woods and fields. Oyster shells cover the parking area in front of the store. Camille will not leave the car. He crosses the wooden porch where bugs swarm at a yellow light, and enters: the store is lit by one ceiling light that casts shadows between shelves. A man and a woman stand at the counter, talking to a stout woman behind it. Gerry gets three six-packs and goes to the counter. They are only talking about people they know, and a barbecue where there was a whole steer on a spit, and he will tell this to Camille.

But in the dark outside the store, crunching on oyster shells, he forgets: he sees her face in the light from the porch, and wants to kiss her. In the car he does, kisses they hold long while their hands move on each others' backs. Then he is driving again. Twice he is lost, once on a blacktop road in woods that are mostly the conical silhouettes and lovely smell of pine, then on a gravel road through a swamp whose feral odor makes him pull the map too quickly from her hands. He stops once for gas, at an all-night station on a highway. Sweat soaks through his shirt, and it sticks to the seat, and he is warm and damp where his leg and Camille's sweat together. By twilight they are silent. She lights their cigarettes and opens their cans of beer; as the sun rises he is driving on asphalt between woods, the dark of their leaves fading to green, and through the insect-splattered windshield he gazes with burning eyes at the entrance to his town.

Anna

HER NAME WAS Anna Griffin. She was twenty. Her blond hair had been turning darker over the past few years, and she believed it would be brown when she was twenty-five. Sometimes she thought of dying it blond, but living with Wayne was still new enough to her so that she was hesitant about spending money on anything that could not be shared. She also wanted to see what her hair would finally look like. She was pretty, though parts of her face seemed not to know it: the light of her eyes, the lines of her lips, seemed bent on denial, so that even the rise of her high cheekbones seemed ungraceful, simply covered bone. Her two front teeth had a gap between them, and they protruded, the right more than the left.

She worked at the cash register of a Sunnycorner store, located in what people called a square: two blocks of small stores, with a Chevrolet dealer and two branch banks, one of them next to the Sunnycorner. The tellers from that one—women not much older than Anna—came in for takeout coffees, cigarettes, and diet drinks. She liked watching them come in: soft sweaters, wool dresses, polyester blouses that in stores she liked rubbing between thumb and forefinger. She liked looking at their hair too: beauty parlor hair that seemed groomed to match the colors and cut and texture of their clothing, so it was more like hair on a model or a movie actress, no longer an independent growth to be washed and brushed and combed and cut, but part of the ensemble, as the boots were. They all wore pretty watches, and bracelets and necklaces, and more than one ring. She liked the way the girls moved: they looked purposeful but not harried: one enters the store and stops at the magazine rack against the wall opposite Anna and the counter, and picks up a magazine and thumbs the pages, appearing even then to be in motion still, a woman leaving the job for a few minutes, but not in a hurry; then she replaces the magazine and crosses the floor and waits in line while Anna rings up and bags the cans and bottles and boxes cradled in arms, dangling from hands. They talk to each other, Anna and the teller she knows only by face, as she fills and caps Styrofoam cups of coffee. The weather. Hi. How are you. Bye now. The teller leaves. Often behind the counter, with other customers, Anna liked what she was doing; liked knowing where the pimientos were; liked her deftness with the register and bagging; was proud of her cheerfulness, felt in charge of customers and what they bought. But when the tellers were at the counter, she was shy, and if one of them made her laugh, she covered her mouth.

She took new magazines from the rack: one at a time, keeping it under the counter near her tall three-legged stool, until she finished it; then she put it back and took another. So by the time the girls from the bank glanced through the magazine, she knew what they were seeing. For they always chose the ones she did: *People, Vogue, Glamour*. She looked at *Playgirl*, and in *Penthouse* she looked at the women and read the letters, this when she worked at night, not because there were fewer customers then but because it was night, not day. At first she had looked at them during the day, and felt strange raising her eyes from the pictures to blink at the parking lot, whose presence of cars and people and space she always felt because the storefront was glass, her counter stopping just short of it. The tellers never picked up those magazines, but Anna was certain they had them at home. She imagined that too: where they lived after work; before work. She gave them large, pretty apartments with thick walls so they only heard themselves; stereos and color television, and soft carpets and soft furniture and large brass beds; sometimes she imagined them living with men who made a lot of money, and she saw a swimming pool, a Jacuzzi.

Near the end of her workday, in its seventh and eighth hours, her fatigue was the sort that comes from confining the body while giving neither it nor the mind anything to do. She was restless, impatient, and distracted, and while talking politely to customers and warmly to the regular ones, she wanted to be home. The apartment was in an old building she could nearly see from behind the counter; she could see the grey house with red shutters next to it. As soon as she left the store, she felt as if she had not been tired at all; only her feet still were. Sometimes she felt something else too, as she stepped outside and crossed that line between fatigue and energy: a touch of dread and defeat. She walked past the bank, the last place in the long building of bank Sunnycorner drugstore department store and pizza house, cleared the corner of the building, passed the dumpster on whose lee side teenagers on summer nights smoked dope and drank beer, down the sloping parking lot and across the street to the old near-yardless green wooden apartment house; up three flights of voices and television voices and the smell that reminded her of the weariness she had just left. It was not a bad smell. It bothered her because it was a daily smell, even when old Mrs. Battistini on the first floor cooked with garlic: a smell of all the days of this wood: up to the third floor, the top of the building, and into the apartment whose smells she noticed only because they were not the scent of contained age she had breathed as she climbed. Then she went to the kitchen table or the bed or shower or couch, either talking to Wayne or waiting for him to come home from Wendy's, where he cooked hamburgers.

At those times she liked her home. She rarely liked it when she woke in it: a northwest apartment, so she opened her eyes to a twilit room and, as she moved about, she saw the place clearly, with its few pieces of furniture, cluttered only with leavings: tossed clothes, beer bottles, potato chip bags, as if her night's sleep had tricked her so she would see only what last night she had not. And sometimes later, during the day or night, while she was simply crossing a room, she would suddenly see herself juxtaposed with the old maroon couch which had been left, along with everything else, by whoever lived there before she and Wayne: the yellow wooden table and two chairs in the kitchen, the blue easy chair in the living room, and in the bedroom the chest of drawers, the straight wooden chair, and the mattress on the floor, and she felt older than she knew she ought to.

The wrong car: a 1964 Mercury Comet that Wayne had bought for one hundred and sixty dollars two years ago, before she knew him, when the car was already eleven years old, and now it vibrated at sixty miles an hour, and had holes in the floorboard; and the wrong weapon: a Buck hunting knife under Wayne's leather jacket, unsheathed and held against his body by his left arm. She had not thought of the car and knife until he put the knife under his jacket and left her in the car, smoking so fast that between drags she kept the cigarette near her face and chewed the thumb of the hand holding it; looking through the wiper-swept windshield and the snow blowing between her and the closed bakery next to the lighted drugstore, at tall Wayne walking slowly with his face turned and lowered away from the snow. She softly kept her foot on the accelerator so the engine would not stall. The headlights were off. She could not see into the drugstore. When she drove slowly past it, there were two customers, one at the cash register and counter at the rear, one looking at display shelves at a side wall. She had parked and turned off the lights. One customer left, a man bareheaded in the snow. He did not look at their car. Then the other one left, a man in a watch cap. He did not look either, and when he had driven out of the parking lot to the highway it joined, Wayne said Okay, and went in.

She looked in the rearview mirror, but snow had covered the window; she looked to both sides. To her right, at the far end of the shopping center, the doughnut shop was open, and in front of it three cars were topped with snow. All the other stores were closed. She would be able to see headlights through the snow on the rear window, and if a cruiser came she was to go into the store, and if Wayne had not already started, she would buy cigarettes, then go out again, and if the cruiser was gone she would wait in the car; if the cruiser had stopped, she would go back into the store for matches and they would both leave. Now in the dark and heater-warmth she believed all of their plan was no longer risky, but doomed, as if by leaving the car and walking across the short space through soft angling snow, Wayne had become puny, his knife a toy. So it was the wrong girl too, and the wrong man. She could not imagine him coming out with money, and she could not imagine tomorrow or later tonight or even the next minute. Stripped of history and dreams, she knew only her breathing and smoking and heartbeat and the falling snow. She stared at the long window of the drugstore, and she was startled when he came out: he was running, he was alone, he was inside, closing the door. He said *Jesus Christ* three times as she crossed the parking lot. She turned on the headlights and slowed as she neared the highway. She did not have to stop. She moved into the right lane, and cars in the middle and left passed her.

'A *lot*,' he said.

She reached to him, and he pressed bills against her palm, folded her fingers around them.

'Can you see out back?' she said.

'No. Nobody's coming. Just go slow: no skidding, no wrecks. Jesus.'

She heard the knife blade sliding into the sheath, watched yellowed snow in the headlights and glanced at passing cars on her left; she held the wheel with two hands. He said when he went in he was about to walk around like he was looking for something because he was so scared, but then he decided to do it right away or else he might have just walked around the store till the druggist asked what he wanted and he'd end up buying toothpaste or something, so he went down along the side wall to the back of the store —he lit a cigarette and she said *Me too*; she watched the road and taillights of a distant car in her lane as he placed it between her fingers. —and he went around the counter and took out the knife and held it at the druggist's stomach: a little man with grey hair watching the knife and punching open the register.

She left the highway and drove on a two-lane road through woods and small towns.

'Tequila,' he said.

In their town all but one package store closed at ten-thirty; she drove to the one that stayed open until eleven, a corner store on a street of tenement houses where Puerto Ricans lived; on warm nights they were on the stoops and sidewalks and corners. She did not like going there, even on winter nights when no one was out. She stopped in front of it, looked at the windows, and said: 'I think it's closed.'

'It's quarter to.'

He went out and tried the door, then peered in, then knocked and called and tried the door again. He came back and struck the dashboard.

'I can't fucking be*lieve* it. I got so much money in my pockets I got no room for my hands, and we got one *beer* at home. Can you believe it?'

'He must've closed early—'

'No shit.'

'—because of the *snow*.'

She turned a corner around a used car lot and got onto the main street going downhill through town to the river.

'I could use some tequila,' she said.

'Stop at Timmy's.'

The traffic lights were blinking yellow so people would not have to stop on the hill in the snow; she shifted down and coasted with her foot touching the brake pedal, drove over the bridge, and parked two blocks from it at Timmy's. When she got out of the car, her legs were weak and eager for motion, and she realized they had been taut all the way home; and, standing at the corner of the bar, watching Johnny McCarthy pour two shots beside the drafts, she knew she was going to get drunk. She licked salt from her hand and drank the shot, then a long swallow of beer that met the tequila's burn as it rose, and held the shot glass toward grinning McCarthy and asked how law school was going; he poured tequila and said *Long but good*, and she drank that and finished her beer, and he poured two more shots and brought them drafts. She looped her arm around Wayne's and nuzzled the soft leather and hard bicep, then tongue-kissed him, and looked down the bar at the regulars, most of them men talking in pairs, standing at the bar that had no stools; two girls stood shoulder to shoulder and talked to men on their flanks. The room was long and narrow, separated from the dining room by a wall with a half-door behind the bar. Anna waved at people who looked at her, and they raised a glass or waved and some called her name, and old Lou, who was drinking beer alone at the other end of the bar, motioned to McCarthy and sent her and Wayne a round. Wayne's hand came out of his jacket and she looked at the bill in it: a twenty.

'Set up Lou,' he said to McCarthy. '*Lou*. Can I buy you a shot?'

Lou nodded and smiled, and she watched McCarthy pour the

Fleischmann's and bring it and a draft to Lou, and she wondered if she could tend bar, could remember all the drinks. It was a wonderful place to be, this bar, with her back to the door so she got some of the chill, not all stuffy air and smoke, and able to look down the length of the bar, and at the young men crowded into four tables at the end of the room, watching a television set on a shelf on the wall: a hockey game. It was the only place outside of her home where she always felt the comfort of affection. Shivering with a gulp of tequila, she watched Wayne arm-wrestling with Curt: knuckles white and hand and face red, veins showing at his temple and throat. She had never seen either win, but Wayne had told her that till a year ago he had always won.

'*Pull*,' she said.

His strength and effort seemed to move into the air around her, making her restless; she slapped his back, lit a cigarette, wanted to dance. She called McCarthy and pointed to the draft glasses, then Curt's highball glass, and when he came with the drinks, told him Wayne would pay after he beat Curt. She was humming to herself, and she liked the sound of her voice. She wondered if she could tend bar. People didn't fight here. People were good to her. They wouldn't— A color television. They shouldn't buy it too soon; but when? Who would care? Nobody watched what they bought. She wanted to count the money, but did not want to leave until closing. Wayne and Curt were panting and grunting; their arms were nearly straight up again; they had been going slowly back and forth. She slipped a hand into Wayne's jacket pocket, squeezed the folded wad. She had just finished a cigarette but now she was holding another and wondering if she wanted it, then she lit it and did. There was only a men's room in the bar. 'Draw?' Curt said; 'Draw,' Wayne said, and she hugged his waist and rubbed his right bicep and said: 'I ordered us and Curt a round. I didn't pay. I'm going piss.'

He smiled down at her. The light in his eyes made her want to stay holding him. She walked toward the end of the bar, past the backs of leaning drinkers; some noticed her and spoke; she patted backs, said *Hi How you doing Hey what's happening*; big curly-haired Mitch stopped her: Yes, she was still at Sunnycorner; where had he been? Working in New Hampshire. He told her what he did, and she heard, but seconds later she could not remember; she

was smiling at him. He called to Wayne and waved. She said I'll
see you in a minute, and moved on. At the bar's end was Lou. He
reached for her, raised the other arm at McCarthy. He held her
shoulder and pulled her to him.

'Let me buy you a drink.'

'I have to go to the ladies'.'

'Well, go to the ladies' and come back.'

'Okay.'

She did not go. Her shot and their drafts were there and she was
talking to Lou. She did not know what he did either. She used to
know. He looked sixty. He came every night. His grey hair was
short and he laughed often and she liked his wrinkles.

'I wish I could tend bar here.'

'You'd be good at it.'

'I don't think I could remember all the drinks.'

'It's a shot and beer place.'

His arm was around her, her fingers pressing his ribs. She drank.
The tequila was smooth now. She finished the beer, said she'd be
back, next round was hers; she kissed his cheek: his skin was cool
and tough, and his whiskers scraped her chin. She moved past the
tables crowded with the hockey watchers; Henry coming out of
the men's room moved around her, walking carefully. She went
through the door under the television set, into a short hall, glanced
down it into the doorless, silent kitchen, and stepped left into the
rear of the dining room: empty and darkened. Some nights she and
Wayne brought their drinks in here after the kitchen closed and
sat in a booth in the dark. The ladies' room was empty. 'Ah.'
Wayne was right: when you really had to piss, it was better than
sex. She listened to the voices from the bar, wanted to hurry back
to them. She jerked the paper, tore it.

Lou was gone. She stood where he had been, but his beer glass
was gone, the ashtray emptied. He was like that. He came and
went quietly. You'd look around and see him for the first time and
he already had a beer; sometime later you'd look around and he
was gone. Behind Wayne the front door opened and a blue cap and
jacket and badge came in: it was Ryan from the beat. She made
herself think in sentences and tried to focus on them, as if she were
reading: *He's coming in to get warm. He's just cold.* She waved at

him. He did not see her. She could not remember the sentences. She could not be afraid either. She knew that she ought to be afraid so she would not make any mistakes but she was not, and when she tried to feel afraid or even serious she felt drunker. Ryan was standing next to Curt, one down from Wayne, and had his gloves off and was blowing on his hands. He and McCarthy talked, then he left; at the door he waved at the bar, and Anna waved. She went toward Wayne, then stopped at the two girls: one was Laurie or Linda, she couldn't remember which; one was Jessie. They were still flanked by Bobby and Mark. They all turned their backs to the bar, pressed her hands, touched her shoulders, bought her a drink. She said tequila, and drank it and talked about Sunny-corner. She went to Wayne, told McCarthy to set up Bobby and Mark and Jessie—leaning forward: 'Johnny, what is it? Laurie or Linda?' 'Laurie.' She slipped a hand into Wayne's pocket. Then her hand was captive there, fingers on money, his forearm pressing hers against his side.

'I'll get it. Did you see Ryan?'

'Yes.'

She tried to think in sentences again. She looked up at Wayne; he was grinning down at her. She could see the grin, or his eyes, but not both at once. She gazed at his lips.

'You're cocked,' he said. He was not angry. He said it softly, and took her wrist and withdrew it from his pocket.

'I'll do it in the john.'

She wanted to be as serious and careful as he was, but looking at him and trying to see all of his face at once weakened her legs; she tried again to think in sentences but they jumped away from her like a cat her mind chased; when she turned away from him, looked at faces farther away and held the bar, her mind stopped struggling and she smiled and put her hand in his back pocket and said: 'Okay.'

He started to walk to the men's room, stopping to talk to some-one, being stopped by another; watching him, she was smiling. When she became aware of it, she kept the smile; she liked stand-ing at the corner of the bar smiling with love at her man's back and profile as he gestured and talked; then he was in the men's room. Midway down the bar McCarthy finished washing glasses and dried his hands, stepped back and folded his arms, and looked up and down the bar, and when he saw nothing in front of her he said: 'Anna? Another round?'

'Just a draft, okay?'

She looked in her wallet; she knew it was empty but she looked to be sure it was still empty; she opened the coin pouch and looked at lint and three pennies. She counted the pennies. Johnny put the beer in front of her.

'Wayne's got—'

'On me,' he said. 'Want a shot too?'

'Why not.'

She decided to sip this one or at least drink it slowly, but while she was thinking, the glass was at her lips and her head tilted back and she swallowed it all and licked her lips, then turned to the door behind her and, without coat, stepped outside: the sudden cold emptied her lungs, then she deeply drew in the air tasting of night and snow. 'Wow.' She lifted her face to the light snow and breathed again. Had she smoked a Camel? Yes. From Lou. Jesus. Snow melted on her cheeks. She began to shiver. She crossed the sidewalk, touched the frosted parking meter. One of her brothers did that to her when she was little. Which one? Frank. Told her to lick the bottom of the ice tray. In the cold she stood happy and clear-headed until she wanted to drink, and she went smiling into the warmth and voices and smoke.

'Where'd you go?' Wayne said.

'Outside to get straight,' rubbing her hands together, drinking beer, its head gone, shaking a cigarette from her pack, her flesh recalling its alertness outside as, breathing smoke and swallowing beer and leaning on Wayne, it was lulled again. She wondered if athletes felt all the time the way she had felt outside.

'We should get some bicycles,' she said.

He lowered his mouth to her ear, pushing her hair aside with his rubbing face.

'We can,' his breath in her ear; she turned her groin against his leg. 'It's about two thousand.'

'No, *Wayne*.'

'Ssshhh. I looked at it, man.'

He moved away, and put a bill in her hand: a twenty.

'Jesus,' she said.

'Keep cool.'

'I've never—' She stopped, called McCarthy, and paid for the round for Laurie and Jessie and Bobby and Mark, and tipped him a dollar. Two thousand dollars: she had never seen that much money in her life, had never had as much as a hundred in her hands at one time: not of her own.

'*Last* call.' McCarthy started at the other end of the bar, taking empty glasses, bringing back drinks. '*Last* call.' She watched McCarthy pouring her last shot and draft of the night; she faced Wayne and raised the glass of tequila: 'Hi, babe.'

'Hi.' He licked salt from his hand.

'I been forgetting the salt,' she said, and drank, looking at his eyes. She sipped this last one, finished it, and was drinking the beer when McCarthy called: 'That's *it*. I'm taking the glasses in *five minutes*. You don't have to go home—'

'—but you can't stay here,' someone said.

'Right. Drink up.'

She finished the beer and beckoned with her finger to McCarthy. When he came she held his hands and said: 'Just a quick one?'

'I can't.'

'Just half a draft or a quick shot? I'll drink it while I put my coat on.'

'The cops have been checking. I got to have the glasses off the bar.'

'What about a roader?' Wayne said.

'Then they'll all want one.'

'Okay. He's right, Anna. Let go of the man.'

She released his hands and he took their glasses. She put on her coat. Wayne was waving at people, calling to them. She waved: '*See* you people. Good *night*, Jessie. Laurie. Good *night*. See you, Henry. Mark. Bobby. Bye-bye, Mitch—'

Then she was in the falling white cold, her arm around Wayne; he drove them home, a block and a turn around the Chevrolet lot, then two blocks, while in her mind still were the light and faces and voices of the bar. She held his waist going up the dark stairs. He was breathing hard, not talking. Then he unlocked the door, she was inside, lights coming on, coat off, following Wayne to the kitchen where he opened their one beer and took a swallow and handed it to her and pulled money from both pockets. They sat down and divided the bills into stacks of twenties and tens and fives and ones. When the beer was half gone he left and came back from the bedroom with four Quaaludes and she said: 'Mmmm' and took two from his palm and swallowed them with beer. She picked up the stack of twenties. Her legs felt weak again. She was hungry. She would make a sandwich. She put down the stack and sat looking at the money. He was counting: '—thirty-five forty forty-five fifty—' She took the ones. She wanted to start at the lowest and work up; she did not want to know how many twenties there were until the end. She counted aloud and he told her not to.

'You don't either,' she said. 'All I hear is ninety-five hundred ninety-five hundred—'

'Okay. In our heads.'

She started over. She wanted to eat and wished for a beer and lost count again. Wayne had a pencil in his hand, was writing on paper in front of him. She counted faster. She finished and picked up the twenties. She counted slowly, making a new stack on the table with the bills that she drew, one at a time, from her hand. She did not keep track of the sum of money; she knew she was too drunk. She simply counted each bill as she smacked it onto the pile. Wayne was writing again, so she counted the last twelve aloud, ending with: '—and forty-*six*,' slamming it onto the fanning twenties. He wrote and drew a line and wrote again and drew another line, and his pencil moved up the columns, touching each number and writing a new number at the bottom until there were four of them, and he read to her: 'Two thousand and eighteen.'

The Quaalude bees were in her head now, and she stood and went to the living room for a cigarette in her purse, her legs wanting to go to the sink at her right but she forced them straight through the door whose left jamb they bumped; as she reached into her purse she heard herself humming. She had thought she was talking to Wayne, but that was in her head, she had told him *Two thousand and eighteen we can have some music and movies now* and she smiled aloud because it had come out as humming a tune she had never heard. In the kitchen Wayne was doing something strange. He had lined up their three glasses on the counter by the sink and he was pouring milk into them; it filled two and a half, and he drank that half. Then he tore open the top of the half-gallon carton and rinsed it and swabbed it out with a paper towel.

Then he put the money in it, and folded the top back, and put it in the freezer compartment, and the two glasses of milk in the refrigerator. Then she was in the bedroom talking about frozen money; she saw the cigarette between her fingers as she started to undress, in the dark now; she was not aware of his turning out lights: she was in the lighted kitchen, then in the dark bedroom, looking for an ashtray instead of pulling her sleeve over the cigarette, and she told him about that and about a stereo and Emmylou Harris and fucking, as she found the ashtray on the floor by the bed, which was a mattress on the floor by the ashtray; that she thought about him at Sunnycorner, got horny for him; her tongue was thick, slower than her buzzing head, and the silent words backed up in the spaces between the spoken ones, so she told him something in her mind, then heard it again as her tongue caught up; her tongue in his mouth now, under the covers on the cold sheet, a swelling of joy in her breast as she opened her legs for him and the night's images came back to her: the money on the table and the faces of McCarthy and Curt and Mitch and Lou, and Wayne's hand disappearing with the money inside the carton, and Bobby and Mark and Laurie and Jessie, the empty sidewalk where she stood alone in the cold air, Lou saying: *You'd be good at it.*

The ringing seemed to come from inside her skull, insistent and clear through the voices of her drunken sleep: a ribbon of sound she had to climb, though she tried to sink away from it. Then her eyes were open and she turned off the alarm she did not remember setting; it was six o'clock and she was asleep again, then wakened by her alarmed heartbeat: all in what seemed a few seconds, but it was ten minutes to seven, when she had to be at work. She rose with a fast heart and a headache that made her stoop gingerly for her clothes on the floor and shut her eyes as she put them on. She went into the kitchen: the one empty beer bottle, the ashtray, the milk-soiled glass, and her memory of him putting away the money was immediate, as if he had just done it and she had not slept at all. She took the milk carton from the freezer. The folded money, like the bottle and ashtray and glass, seemed part of the night's drinking, something you cleaned or threw away in the morning. But she had no money and she needed aspirins and coffee and doughnuts and cigarettes; she took a cold five-dollar bill and put the carton in the freezer, looked in the bedroom for her purse and then in the kitchen again and found it in the living room, opened her wallet and saw money there. She pushed the freezer money in with it and slung the purse from her shoulder and stepped into the dim hall, shutting the door on Wayne's snoring. Outside she blinked at sun and cold and remembered Wayne giving her twenty at the bar; she crossed the street and parking lot and, with the taste of beer in her throat and toothpaste in her mouth, was in the Sunnycorner before seven.

She spent the next eight hours living the divided life of a hangover. Drinking last night had stopped time, kept her in the present until last call forced on her the end of a night, the truth of tomorrow; but once in their kitchen counting money, she was in the present again and she stayed there through twice waking, and dressing, and entering the store and relieving Eddie, the all-night clerk, at the register. So for the first three or four hours while she worked and waited and talked, her body heavily and slowly occupied space in those brightly lit moments in the store; but in her mind were images of Wayne leaving the car and going into the drugstore and running out, and driving home through falling snow, the closed package store and the drinks and people at Timmy's and taking the Quaaludes from Wayne's palm, and counting money and making love for so drunk long; and she felt all of that and none of what she was numbly doing. It was a hangover that demanded food and coffee and cigarettes. She started the day with three aspirins and a Coke. Then she smoked and ate doughnuts and drank coffee. Sometimes from the corner of her eye she saw something move on the counter, small and grey and fast, like the shadow of a darting mouse. Her heart was fast too, and the customers were fast and loud, while her hands were slow, and her tongue was, for it had to wait while words freed themselves from behind her eyes, where the pain was, where the aspirins had not found it. After four cups of coffee, her heart was faster and hands more shaky, and she drank another Coke. She was careful, and made no mistakes on the register; with eyes trying to close she looked into the eyes of customers and Kermit, the manager, slim and balding, in his forties; a kind man but one who, today, made her feel both scornful and ashamed, for she was certain he had not had a hangover in twenty years. Around noon her blood slowed and her hands stopped trembling, and she was tired and lightheaded and afraid; it seemed there was always someone watching her, not only the customers and Kermit, but someone above her, outside the window, in the narrow space behind her. Now there were gaps in her memory of last night: she looked at the clock so often that its hands seemed halted, and in her mind she was home after work, in bed with Wayne, shuddering away the terrors that brushed her like a curtain windblown against her back.

When she got home he had just finished showering and shaving, and she took him to bed with lust that was as much part of her hangover as hunger and the need to smoke were; silent and hasty, she moved toward that orgasm that would bring her back to some calm mooring in the long day. Crying out, she burst into languor; slept breathing the scent of his washed flesh. But she woke alone in the twilit room and rose quickly from the bed, calling him. He came smiling from the living room, and asked if she were ready to go to the mall.

The indoor walk of the mall was bright and warm; coats unbuttoned, his arm over her shoulder, hers around his waist, they moved slowly among people and smells of frying meat, stopping at windows to look at shirts and coats and boots; they took egg rolls to a small pool with a fountain in its middle and sat on its low brick wall; they ate pizza alone on a bench that faced a displayed car; they had their photographs taken behind a curtain in a shop and paid the girl and left their address.

'You think she'll mail them to us?' Anna said.

'Sure.'

They ate hamburgers standing at the counter, watching the old man work at the grill, then sat on a bench among potted plants to smoke. On the way to the department store they bought fudge, and the taste of it lingered, sweet and rich in her mouth, and she wanted to go back for another piece, but they were in the store: large, with glaring white light, and as the young clerk wearing glasses and a thin moustache came to them, moving past television sets and record players, she held Wayne's arm. While the clerk and Wayne talked, she was aware of her gapped and jutting teeth, her pea jacket, and old boots and jeans. She followed Wayne following the clerk; they stopped at a shelf of record players. She shifted her eyes from one to the other as they spoke; they often looked at her, and she said: Yes. Sure. The soles of her feet ached and her calves were tired. She wanted to smoke but was afraid the clerk would forbid her. She swallowed the taste of fudge. Then she was sad. She watched Wayne and remembered him running out of the drug-store and, in the car, saying *Jesus Christ*, and she was ashamed that she was sad, and felt sorry for him because he was not.

Now they were moving. He was hugging her and grinning and his thigh swaggered against her hip, and they were among shelved television sets. Some of them were turned on, but to different chan-nels, and surrounded by those faces and bodies and colliding words, she descended again into her hangover. She needed a drink, a ciga-rette, a small place, not all this low-ceilinged breadth and depth, where shoppers in the awful light jumped in and out of her vision. Timmy's: the corner of the bar near the door, and a slow-sipped tequila salty dog and then one more to close the spaces in her brain and the corners of her vision, stop the tingling of her gums, and the crawling tingle inside her body as though ants climbed on her veins. In her coat pocket, her hand massaged the box of cigarettes; she opened it with a thumb, stroked filters with a finger.

'That's a good advertisement for the Sony,' Wayne said. 'Turn-ing on the RCA next to it.'

She wanted to cry. She watched the pictures on the Sony: a man and woman in a car, talking; she knew California from television and movies, and they were driving in California: the winding road, the low brown hills, the sea. The man was talking about dope and people's names. The clerk was talking about a guarantee. Wayne told him what he liked to watch, and as she heard hockey and baseball and football and movies she focused so hard on imagining this set in their apartment and them watching it from the couch that she felt like she had closed her eyes, though she had not. She followed them to the cash register and looked around the room for the cap and shoulders of a policeman to appear in the light that paled skin and cast no shadow. She watched Wayne counting the money; she listened to the clerk's pleased voice. Then Wayne had her arm, was leading her away.

'Aren't we taking them?'

He stopped, looked down at her, puzzled; then he laughed and kissed the top of her head.

'We pick them up out back.'

He was leading her again.

'Where are we going now?'

'Records. Remember? Unless you want to spend a fucking fortune on a stereo and just look at it.'

Standing beside him, she gazed and blinked at album covers as he flipped them forward, pulled out some, talked about them. She tried to despise his transistor radio at home, tried to feel her old longing for a stereo and records, but as she looked at each album he held in front of her, she was glutted with spending, and felt more like a thief than she had last night waiting outside the drugstore, and driving home from it. Again she imagined the apartment, saw where she would put the television, the record player; she would move the chest of drawers to the living room and put them on its top, facing the couch where— She saw herself cooking. She was cooking macaroni and cheese for them to eat while they watched a movie; but she saw only the apartment now, then herself sweeping it. Wayne swept it too, but often he either forgot or didn't see what she saw or didn't care about it. Sweeping was not hard but it was still something to do, and sometimes for days it seemed too much to do, and fluffs of dust gathered in corners and under furniture. So now she asked Wayne and he looked surprised and she was afraid he would be angry, but then he smiled and said Okay. He brought the records to the clerk and she watched the numbers come up on the register and the money going into the clerk's hand. Then Wayne led her past the corners and curves of washers and dryers, deeper into the light of the store, where she chose a round blue Hoover vacuum cleaner.

She carried it, boxed, into the apartment; behind her on the stairs Wayne carried the stereo in two boxes that hid his face. They went quickly downstairs again. Anna was waiting. She did not know what she was waiting for, but standing on the sidewalk as Wayne's head and shoulders went into the car, she was anxious and mute. She listened to his breathing and the sound of cardboard sliding over the car seat. She wanted to speak into the air between them, the air that had risen from the floorboard coming home from the mall as their talk had slowed, repeated itself, then stopped. Whenever that happened, they were either about to fight or enter a time of shy loneliness. Now grunting, he straightened with the boxed television in his arms; she grasped the free end and walked backward up the icy walk, telling him Not so *fast*, and he slowed and told her when she reached the steps and, feeling each one with her calves, she backed up them and through the door, and he asked if she wanted him to go up first and she said No, he had most of its weight, she was better off. She was breathing too fast to smell the stairway; sometimes she smelled cardboard and the television inside it, like oiled plastic; she belched and tasted hamburger, and when they reached the third floor she was sweating. In the apartment she took off her coat and went downstairs with him, and they each carried up a boxed speaker. They brought the chest into the living room and set it down against the wall opposite the couch; she dusted its top, and they put the stereo and television on it. For a while she sat on the couch, watching him connect wires. Then she went to the kitchen and took the vacuum cleaner from its box. She put it against the wall and leaned its pipes in the corner next to it and sat down to read the instructions. She looked at the illustrations, and thought she was reading, but she was not. She was listening to Wayne in the living room: not to him, but to speakers sliding on the floor, the tapping touch of a screwdriver, and when she finished the pamphlet she did not know what she had read. She put it in a drawer. Then, so that raising her voice would keep shyness from it, she called from the kitchen: 'Can we go to Timmy's?'

'Don't you want to play with these?'

'No,' she said. When he did not answer, she wished she had lied, and she felt again as she had in the department store when sorrow had enveloped her like a sudden cool breath from the television screens. She went into the living room and kneeled beside him, sitting on the floor, a speaker and wires between his legs; she nuzzled his cheek and said: 'I'm sorry.'

'I don't want to play with them either. Let's go.'

She got their coats and, as they were leaving, she stopped in the doorway and looked back at the stereo and television.

'Should we have bought it all in one place?' she said.

'It doesn't matter.'

She hurried ahead of him down the stairs and out onto the sidewalk, then her feet slipped forward and up and he caught her against his chest. She hooked her arm in his and they crossed the

street and the parking lot; she looked to her left into the Sunnycorner, two men and a woman lined at the counter and Sally
punching the register. She looked fondly at the warm light in there,
the colors of magazine covers on the rack, the red soft-drink refrigerator, the long shelves of bread.

'What a hangover I had. And I didn't make any mistakes.'

She walked fast, each step like flight from the apartment. They
went through the lot of Chevrolet pickups, walking single file between the trucks, and now if she looked back she would not be
able to see their lawn; then past the broad-windowed showroom of
new cars and she thought of their—his—old Comet. Standing on the
curb, waiting for a space in traffic, she tightly gripped his arm.
They trotted across the street to Timmy's door and entered the
smell of beer and smoke. Faces turned from the bar, some hands
lifted in a wave. It was not ten o'clock yet, the dining room was
just closing, and the people at the bar stood singly, not two or
three deep like last night, and the tables in the rear were empty.
McCarthy was working. Anna took her place at the corner, and he
said: 'You make it to work at seven?'

'How did you know?'

'Oh my *God*, I've got to be at work at seven; another tequila,
Johnny.'

She raised a hand to her laughter, and covered it.

'I made it. I made it and tomorrow I don't work till three, and
I'm going to have *two* tequila salty dogs and that's *all*; then I'm
going to bed.'

Wayne ordered a shot of Fleischmann's and a draft, and when
McCarthy went to the middle of the bar for the beer, she asked
Wayne how much was left, though she already knew, or nearly
did, and when he said *About two-twenty* she was ahead of his
answer, nodding but paying no attention to the words, the numbers, seeing those strange visitors in their home, staring from the
top of the chest, sitting on the kitchen floor; then McCarthy
brought their drinks and went away, and she found on the bar the
heart enclosing their initials that she and Wayne had carved, drinking one crowded night when McCarthy either did not see them or
pretended not to.

'I don't want to feel bad,' she said.

'Neither me.'

'Let's don't. Can we get bicycles?'

'All of one and most of the other.'

'Do you want one?'

'Sure. I need to get back in shape.'

'Where can we go?'

'The Schwinn place.'

'I mean riding.'

'All over. When it thaws. There's nice roads everywhere. I know some trails in the woods, and one of them goes to a pond. A big pond.'

'We can go swimming.'

'Sure.'

'We should have bought a canoe.'

'Instead of what?'

She was watching McCarthy make a Tom Collins and a gimlet.

'I don't know,' she said.

'I guess we bought winter sports.'

'Maybe we should have got a freezer and a lot of food. You know what's in the refrigerator?'

'You said you didn't want to feel bad.'

'I don't.'

'So don't.'

'What about you?'

'I don't want to either. Let's have another round and hang it up.'

In the morning she woke at six, not to an alarm but out of habit: her flesh alert, poised to dress and go to work, and she got up and went naked and shivering to the bathroom, then to the kitchen, where, gazing at the vacuum cleaner, she drank one of the glasses of milk. In the living room she stood on the cold floor in front of the television and stereo, hugging herself. She was suddenly tired, her first and false energy of the day gone, and she crept into bed, telling herself she could sleep now, she did not have to work till three, she could sleep: coaxing, as though her flesh were a small child wakened in the night. She stopped shivering, felt sleep coming upward from her legs; she breathed slowly with it, and escaped into it, away from memory of last night's striving flesh: she and Wayne, winter-pallid yet sweating in their long, quiet, coupled work at coming until they gave up and their fast dry breaths slowed

and the Emmylou Harris album ended, the stereo clicked twice
into the silence, a record dropped and Willie Nelson sang 'Stardust.'
'I should have got some ludes and percs too,' he said.
Her hand found his on the sheet and covered it.
'I was too scared. It was bad enough waiting for the *mo*ney. I
kept waiting for somebody to come in and blow me away. Even
him. If he'd had a gun, he could have. But I should have got some
drugs.'
'It wouldn't have mattered.'
'We could have sold it.'
'It wouldn't matter.'
'Why?'
'There's too much to get. There's no way we could ever get it
all.'
'A *lot* of it, though. *Some* of it.'
She rubbed the back of his hand, his knuckles, his nails. She did
not know when he fell asleep. She slept two albums later, while
Waylon Jennings sang. And slept now, deeply, in the morning, and
woke when she heard him turning, rising, walking barefooted and
heavily out of the room.
She got up and made coffee and did not see him until he came
into the kitchen wearing his one white shirt and one pair of blue
slacks and the black shoes; he had bought them all in one store in
twenty minutes of quiet anger, with money she gave him the day
Wendy's hired him; he returned the money on his first payday.
The toes of the shoes were scuffed now. She kept the shirt clean,
some nights washing it in the sink when he came home and hanging
it on a chair back near the radiator so he could wear it next day; he
would not buy another one because, he said, he hated spending
money on something he didn't want.
When he left, carrying the boxes out to the dumpster, she turned
last night's records over. She read the vacuum cleaner pamphlet,
joined the dull silver pipes and white hose to the squat and round
blue tank, and stepped on its switch. The cord was long and she
did not have to change it to an outlet in another room; she wanted
to remember to tell Wayne it was funny that the cord was longer
than their place. She finished quickly and turned it off and could
hear the records again.
She lay on the couch until the last record ended, then got the

laundry bag from the bedroom and soap from the kitchen, and left. On the sidewalk she turned around and looked up at the front of the building, old and green in the snow and against the blue glare of the sky. She scraped the car's glass and drove to the laundry: two facing rows of machines, moist warm air, gurgling rumble and whining spin of washers, resonant clicks and loud hiss of dryers, and put in clothes and soap and coins. At a long table women smoked and read magazines, and two of them talked as they shook crackling electricity from clothes they folded. Anna took a small wooden chair from the table and sat watching the round window of the machine, watched her clothes and Wayne's tossing past it, like children waving from a ferris wheel.

A Father's Story

M Y NAME IS Luke Ripley, and here is what
I call my life: I own a stable of thirty
horses, and I have young people who
teach riding, and we board some horses too. This is in northeastern
Massachusetts. I have a barn with an indoor ring, and outside I've
got two fenced-in rings and a pasture that ends at a woods with
trails. I call it my life because it looks like it is, and people I know
call it that, but it's a life I can get away from when I hunt and
fish, and some nights after dinner when I sit in the dark in the
front room and listen to opera. The room faces the lawn and the
road, a two-lane country road. When cars come around the curve
northwest of the house, they light up the lawn for an instant, the
leaves of the maple out by the road and the hemlock closer to the
window. Then I'm alone again, or I'd appear to be if someone
crept up to the house and looked through a window: a big-gutted
grey-haired guy, drinking tea and smoking cigarettes, staring out
at the dark woods across the road, listening to a grieving soprano.

My real life is the one nobody talks about anymore, except
Father Paul LeBoeuf, another old buck. He has a decade on me:
he's sixty-four, a big man, bald on top with grey at the sides; when
he had hair, it was black. His face is ruddy, and he jokes about
being a whiskey priest, though he's not. He gets outdoors as much
as he can, goes for a long walk every morning, and hunts and fishes
with me. But I can't get him on a horse anymore. Ten years ago I
could badger him into a trail ride; I had to give him a western
saddle, and he'd hold the pommel and bounce through the woods

with me, and be sore for days. He's looking at seventy with eyes that are younger than many I've seen in people in their twenties. I do not remember ever feeling the way they seem to; but I was lucky, because even as a child I knew that life would try me, and I must be strong to endure, though in those early days I expected to be tortured and killed for my faith, like the saints I learned about in school.

Father Paul's family came down from Canada, and he grew up speaking more French than English, so he is different from the Irish priests who abound up here. I do not like to make general statements, or even to hold general beliefs, about people's blood, but the Irish do seem happiest when they're dealing with misfortune or guilt, either their own or somebody else's, and if you think you're not a victim of either one, you can count on certain Irish priests to try to change your mind. On Wednesday nights Father Paul comes to dinner. Often he comes on other nights too, and once, in the old days when we couldn't eat meat on Fridays, we bagged our first ducks of the season on a Friday, and as we drove home from the marsh, he said: For the purposes of Holy Mother Church, I believe a duck is more a creature of water than land, and is not rightly meat. Sometimes he teases me about never putting anything in his Sunday collection, which he would not know about if I hadn't told him years ago. I would like to believe I told him so we could have philosophical talk at dinner, but probably the truth is I suspected he knew, and I did not want him to think I so loved money that I would not even give his church a coin on Sunday. Certainly the ushers who pass the baskets know me as a miser.

I don't feel right about giving money for buildings, places. This starts with the Pope, and I cannot respect one of them till he sells his house and everything in it, and that church too, and uses the money to feed the poor. I have rarely, and maybe never, come across saintliness, but I feel certain it cannot exist in such a place. But I admit, also, that I know very little, and maybe the popes live on a different plane and are tried in ways I don't know about. Father Paul says his own church, St. John's, is hardly the Vatican. I like his church: it is made of wood, and has a simple altar and crucifix, and no padding on the kneelers. He does not have to lock its doors at night. Still it is a place. He could say Mass in my barn. I know this is stubborn, but I can find no mention by Christ of maintaining buildings, much less erecting them of stone or brick, and decorating them with pieces of metal and mineral and elements that people still fight over like barbarians. We had a Maltese woman taking riding lessons, she came over on the boat when she was ten, and once she told me how the nuns in Malta used to tell the little girls that if they wore jewelry, rings and bracelets and necklaces, in purgatory snakes would coil around their fingers and wrists and throats. I do not believe in frightening children or telling them lies, but if those nuns saved a few girls from devotion to things, maybe they were right. That Maltese woman laughed about it, but I noticed she wore only a watch, and that with a leather strap.

The money I give to the church goes in people's stomachs, and on their backs, down in New York City. I have no delusions about the worth of what I do, but I feel it's better to feed somebody than not. There's a priest in Times Square giving shelter to runaway kids, and some Franciscans who run a bread line; actually it's a morning line for coffee and a roll, and Father Paul calls it the continental breakfast for winos and bag ladies. He is curious about how much I am sending, and I know why: he guesses I send a lot, he has said probably more than tithing, and he is right; he wants to know how much because he believes I'm generous and good, and he is wrong about that; he has never had much money and does not know how easy it is to write a check when you have every thing you will ever need, and the figures are mere numbers, and represent no sacrifice at all. Being a real Catholic is too hard; if I were one, I would do with my house and barn what I want the Pope to do with his. So I do not want to impress Father Paul, and when he asks me how much, I say I can't let my left hand know what my right is doing.

He came on Wednesday nights when Gloria and I were married, and the kids were young; Gloria was a very good cook (I assume she still is, but it is difficult to think of her in the present), and I liked sitting at the table with a friend who was also a priest. I was proud of my handsome and healthy children. This was long ago, and they were all very young and cheerful and often funny, and the three boys took care of their baby sister, and did not bully or tease her. Of course they did sometimes, with that excited cruelty children are prone to, but not enough so that it was part of her days. On the Wednesday after Gloria left with the kids and a

U-Haul trailer, I was sitting on the front steps, it was summer, and I was watching cars go by on the road, when Father Paul drove around the curve and into the driveway. I was ashamed to see him because he is a priest and my family was gone, but I was relieved too. I went to the car to greet him. He got out smiling, with a bottle of wine, and shook my hand, then pulled me to him, gave me a quick hug, and said: 'It's Wednesday, isn't it? Let's open some cans.'

With arms about each other we walked to the house, and it was good to know he was doing his work but coming as a friend too, and I thought what good work he had. I have no calling. It is for me to keep horses.

In that other life, anyway. In my real one I go to bed early and sleep well and wake at four forty-five, for an hour of silence. I never want to get out of bed then, and every morning I know I can sleep for another four hours, and still not fail at any of my duties. But I get up, so have come to believe my life can be seen in miniature in that struggle in the dark of morning. While making the bed and boiling water for coffee, I talk to God: I offer Him my day, every act of my body and spirit, my thoughts and moods, as a prayer of thanksgiving, and for Gloria and my children and my friends and two women I made love with after Gloria left. This morning offertory is a habit from my boyhood in a Catholic school; or then it was a habit, but as I kept it and grew older it became a ritual. Then I say the Lord's Prayer, trying not to recite it, and one morning it occurred to me that a prayer, whether recited or said with concentration, is always an act of faith.

I sit in the kitchen at the rear of the house and drink coffee and smoke and watch the sky growing light before sunrise, the trees of the woods near the barn taking shape, becoming single pines and elms and oaks and maples. Sometimes a rabbit comes out of the treeline, or is already sitting there, invisible till the light finds him. The birds are awake in the trees and feeding on the ground, and the little ones, the purple finches and titmice and chickadees, are at the feeder I rigged outside the kitchen window; it is too small for pigeons to get a purchase. I sit and give myself to coffee and tobacco, that get me brisk again, and I watch and listen. In the first year or so after I lost my family, I played the radio in the mornings. But I overcame that, and now I rarely play it at all. Once in the mail I received a questionnaire asking me to write down everything I watched on television during the week they had chosen. At the end of those seven days I wrote in *The Wizard of Oz* and returned it. That was in winter and was actually a busy week for my television, which normally sits out the cold months without once warming up. Had they sent the questionnaire during baseball season, they would have found me at my set. People at the stables talk about shows and performers I have never heard of, but I cannot get interested; when I am in the mood to watch television, I go to a movie or read a detective novel. There are always good detective novels to be found, and I like remembering them next morning with my coffee.

I also think of baseball and hunting and fishing, and of my children. It is not painful to think about them anymore, because even if we had lived together, they would be gone now, grown into their own lives, except Jennifer. I think of death too, not sadly, or with fear, though something like excitement does run through me, something more quickening than the coffee and tobacco. I suppose it is an intense interest, and an outright distrust: I never feel certain that I'll be here watching birds eating at tomorrow's daylight. Sometimes I try to think of other things, like the rabbit that is warm and breathing but not there till twilight. I feel on the brink of something about the life of the senses, but either am not equipped to go further or am not interested enough to concentrate. I have called all of this thinking, but it is not, because it is unintentional; what I'm really doing is feeling the day, in silence, and that is what Father Paul is doing too on his five-to-ten-mile walks.

When the hour ends I take an apple or carrot and I go to the stable and tack up a horse. We take good care of these horses, and no one rides them but students, instructors, and me, and nobody rides the horses we board unless an owner asks me to. The barn is dark and I turn on lights and take some deep breaths, smelling the hay and horses and their manure, both fresh and dried, a combined odor that you either like or you don't. I walk down the wide space of dirt between stalls, greeting the horses, joking with them about their quirks, and choose one for no reason at all other than the way it looks at me that morning. I get my old English saddle that has smoothed and darkened through the years, and go into the stall, talking to this beautiful creature who'll swerve out of a canter if a piece of paper blows in front of him, and if the barn catches fire and you manage to get him out he will, if he can get away from you, run back into the fire, to his stall. Like the smells that surround them, you either like them or you don't. I love them, so am spared having to try to explain why. I feed one the carrot or apple and tack up and lead him outside, where I mount, and we go down the driveway to the road and cross it and turn northwest and walk then trot then canter to St. John's.

A few cars are on the road, their drivers looking serious about going to work. It is always strange for me to see a woman dressed for work so early in the morning. You know how long it takes them, with the makeup and hair and clothes, and I think of them waking in the dark of winter or early light of other seasons, and dressing as they might for an evening's entertainment. Probably this strikes me because I grew up seeing my father put on those suits he never wore on weekends or his two weeks off, and so am accustomed to the men, but when I see these women I think something went wrong, to send all those dressed-up people out on the road when the dew hasn't dried yet. Maybe it's because I so dislike getting up early, but am also doing what I choose to do, while they have no choice. At heart I am lazy, yet I find such peace and delight in it that I believe it is a natural state, and in what looks like my laziest periods I am closest to my center. The ride to St. John's is fifteen minutes. The horses and I do it in all weather; the road is well plowed in winter, and there are only a few days a year when ice makes me drive the pickup. People always look at someone on horseback, and for a moment their faces change and many drivers and I wave to each other. Then at St. John's, Father Paul and five or six regulars and I celebrate the Mass.

Do not think of me as a spiritual man whose every thought during those twenty-five minutes is at one with the words of the Mass. Each morning I try, each morning I fail, and know that always I will be a creature who, looking at Father Paul and the altar, and uttering prayers, will be distracted by scrambled eggs, horses, the weather, and memories and daydreams that have nothing to do with the sacrament I am about to receive. I can receive, though: the Eucharist, and also, at Mass and at other times, moments and even minutes of contemplation. But I cannot achieve contemplation, as

some can; and so, having to face and forgive my own failures, I
have learned from them both the necessity and wonder of ritual.
For ritual allows those who cannot will themselves out of the secular to perform the spiritual, as dancing allows the tongue-tied man
a ceremony of love. And, while my mind dwells on breakfast, or
Major or Duchess tethered under the church eave, there is, as I
take the Host from Father Paul and place it on my tongue and
return to the pew, a feeling that I am thankful I have not lost in the
forty-eight years since my first Communion. At its center is excitement; spreading out from it is the peace of certainty. Or the
certainty of peace. One night Father Paul and I talked about faith.
It was long ago, and all I remember is him saying: Belief is believing in God; faith is believing that God believes in you. That is the
excitement, and the peace; then the Mass is over, and I go into the
sacristy and we have a cigarette and chat, the mystery ends, we are
two men talking like any two men on a morning in America, about
baseball, plane crashes, presidents, governors, murders, the sun, the
clouds. Then I go to the horse and ride back to the life people see,
the one in which I move and talk, and most days I enjoy it.

It is late summer now, the time between fishing and hunting, but a
good time for baseball. It has been two weeks since Jennifer left, to
drive home to Gloria's after her summer visit. She is the only one
who still visits; the boys are married and have children, and sometimes fly up for a holiday, or I fly down or west to visit one of
them. Jennifer is twenty, and I worry about her the way fathers
worry about daughters but not sons. I want to know what she's up
to, and at the same time I don't. She looks athletic, and she is: she
swims and runs and of course rides. All my children do. When she
comes for six weeks in summer, the house is loud with girls, friends
of hers since childhood, and new ones. I am glad she kept the girl
friends. They have been young company for me and, being with
them, I have been able to gauge her growth between summers. On
their riding days, I'd take them back to the house when their lessons
were over and they had walked the horses and put them back in
the stalls, and we'd have lemonade or Coke, and cookies if I had
some, and talk until their parents came to drive them home. One
year their breasts grew, so I wasn't startled when I saw Jennifer in

July. Then they were driving cars to the stable, and beginning to look like young women, and I was passing out beer and ashtrays and they were talking about college.

When Jennifer was here in summer, they were at the house most days. I would say generally that as they got older they became quieter, and though I enjoyed both, I sometimes missed the giggles and shouts. The quiet voices, just low enough for me not to hear from wherever I was, rising and falling in proportion to my distance from them, frightened me. Not that I believed they were planning or recounting anything really wicked, but there was a female seriousness about them, and it was secretive, and of course I thought: love, sex. But it was more than that: it was womanhood they were entering, the deep forest of it, and no matter how many women and men too are saying these days that there is little difference between us, the truth is that men find their way into that forest only on clearly marked trails, while women move about in it like birds. So hearing Jennifer and her friends talking so quietly, yet intensely, I wanted very much to have a wife.

But not as much as in the old days, when Gloria had left but her presence was still in the house as strongly as if she had only gone to visit her folks for a week. There were no clothes or cosmetics, but potted plants endured my neglectful care as long as they could, and slowly died; I did not kill them on purpose, to exorcise the house of her, but I could not remember to water them. For weeks, because I did not use it much, the house was as neat as she had kept it, though dust layered the order she had made. The kitchen went first: I got the dishes in and out of the dishwasher and wiped the top of the stove, but did not return cooking spoons and pot holders to their hooks on the wall, and soon the burners and oven were caked with spillings, the refrigerator had more space and was spotted with juices. The living room and my bedroom went next; I did not go into the children's rooms except on bad nights when I went from room to room and looked and touched and smelled, so they did not lose their order until a year later when the kids came for six weeks. It was three months before I ate the last of the food Gloria had cooked and frozen: I remember it was a beef stew, and very good. By then I had four cookbooks, and was boasting a bit, and talking about recipes with the women at the stables, and looking forward to cooking for Father Paul. But I never looked forward to cooking at night only for myself, though I made myself do it; on some nights I gave in to my daily temptation, and took a newspaper or detective novel to a restaurant. By the end of the second year, though, I had stopped turning on the radio as soon as I woke in the morning, and was able to be silent and alone in the evening too, and then I enjoyed my dinners.

It is not hard to live through a day, if you can live through a moment. What creates despair is the imagination, which pretends there is a future, and insists on predicting millions of moments, thousands of days, and so drains you that you cannot live the moment at hand. That is what Father Paul told me in those first two years, on some of the bad nights when I believed I could not bear what I had to: the most painful loss was my children, then the loss of Gloria, whom I still loved despite or maybe because of our long periods of sadness that rendered us helpless, so neither of us could break out of it to give a hand to the other. Twelve years later I believe ritual would have healed us more quickly than the repetitious talks we had, perhaps even kept us healed. Marriages have lost that, and I wish I had known then what I know now, and we had performed certain acts together every day, no matter how we felt, and perhaps then we could have subordinated feeling to action, for surely that is the essence of love. I know this from my distractions during Mass, and during everything else I do, so that my actions and feelings are seldom one. It does happen every day, but in proportion to everything else in a day, it is rare, like joy. The third most painful loss, which became second and sometimes first as months passed, was the knowledge that I could never marry again, and so dared not even keep company with a woman.

On some of the bad nights I was bitter about this with Father Paul, and I so pitied myself that I cried, or nearly did, speaking with damp eyes and breaking voice. I believe that celibacy is for him the same trial it is for me, not of the flesh, but the spirit: the heart longing to love. But the difference is he chose it, and did not wake one day to a life with thirty horses. In my anger I said I had done my service to love and chastity, and I told him of the actual physical and spiritual pain of practicing rhythm: nights of striking the mattress with a fist, two young animals lying side by side in heat, leaving the bed to pace, to smoke, to curse, and too passionate to question, for we were so angered and oppressed by our passion that we could see no further than our loins. So now I understand how people can be enslaved for generations before they throw down their tools or use them as weapons, the form of their slavery —the cotton fields, the shacks and puny cupboards and untended illnesses—absorbing their emotions and thoughts until finally they have little or none at all to direct with clarity and energy at the owners and legislators. And I told him of the trick of passion and its slaking: how during what we had to believe were safe periods, though all four children were conceived at those times, we were able with some coherence to question the tradition and reason and justice of the law against birth control, but not with enough conviction to soberly act against it, as though regular satisfaction in bed tempered our revolutionary as well as our erotic desires. Only when abstinence drove us hotly away from each other did we receive an urge so strong it lasted all the way to the drugstore and back; but always, after release, we threw away the remaining condoms; and after going through this a few times, we knew what would happen, and from then on we submitted to the calendar she so precisely marked on the bedroom wall. I told him that living two lives each month, one as celibates, one as lovers, made us tense and short-tempered, so we snapped at each other like dogs.

To have endured that, to have reached a time when we burned slowly and could gain from bed the comfort of lying down at night with one who loves you and whom you love, could for weeks on end go to bed tired and peacefully sleep after a kiss, a touch of the hands, and then to be thrown out of the marriage like a bundle from a moving freight car, was unjust, was intolerable, and I could not or would not muster the strength to endure it. But I did, a moment at a time, a day, a night, except twice, each time with a different woman and more than a year apart, and this was so long ago that I clearly see their faces in my memory, can hear the pitch of their voices, and the way they pronounced words, one with a Massachusetts accent, one midwestern, but I feel as though I only heard about them from someone else. Each rode at the stables and was with me for part of an evening; one was badly married, one divorced, so none of us was free. They did not understand this

Catholic view, but they were understanding about my having it, and I remained friends with both of them until the married one left her husband and went to Boston, and the divorced one moved to Maine. After both those evenings, those good women, I went to Mass early while Father Paul was still in the confessional, and received his absolution. I did not tell him who I was, but of course he knew, though I never saw it in his eyes. Now my longing for a wife comes only once in a while, like a cold: on some late afternoons when I am alone in the barn, then I lock up and walk to the house, daydreaming, then suddenly look at it and see it empty, as though for the first time, and all at once I'm weary and feel I do not have the energy to broil meat, and I think of driving to a restaurant, then shake my head and go on to the house, the refrigerator, the oven; and some mornings when I wake in the dark and listen to the silence and run my hand over the cold sheet beside me; and some days in summer when Jennifer is here.

Gloria left first me, then the Church, and that was the end of religion for the children, though on visits they went to Sunday Mass with me, and still do, out of a respect for my life that they manage to keep free of patronage. Jennifer is an agnostic, though I doubt she would call herself that, any more than she would call herself any other name that implied she had made a decision, a choice, about existence, death, and God. In truth she tends to pantheism, a good sign, I think; but not wanting to be a father who tells his children what they ought to believe, I do not say to her that Catholicism includes pantheism, like onions in a stew. Besides, I have no missionary instincts and do not believe everyone should or even could live with the Catholic faith. It is Jennifer's womanhood that renders me awkward. And womanhood now is frank, not like when Gloria was twenty and there were symbols: high heels and cosmetics and dresses, a cigarette, a cocktail. I am glad that women are free now of false modesty and all its attention paid the flesh; but, still, it is difficult to see so much of your daughter, to hear her talk as only men and bawdy women used to, and most of all to see in her face the deep and unabashed sensuality of women, with no tricks of the eyes and mouth to hide the pleasure she feels at having a strong young body. I am certain, with the way things are now, that she has very happily not been a virgin for years. That does not bother me. What bothers me is my certainty about it, just from watching her walk across a room or light a cigarette or pour milk on cereal.

She told me all of it, waking me that night when I had gone to sleep listening to the wind in the trees and against the house, a wind so strong that I had to shut all but the lee windows, and still the house cooled; told it to me in such detail and so clearly that now, when she has driven the car to Florida, I remember it all as though I had been a passenger in the front seat, or even at the wheel. It started with a movie, then beer and driving to the sea to look at the waves in the night and the wind, Jennifer and Betsy and Liz. They drank a beer on the beach and wanted to go in naked but were afraid they would drown in the high surf. They bought another six-pack at a grocery store in New Hampshire, and drove home. I can see it now, feel it: the three girls and the beer and the ride on country roads where pines curved in the wind and the big deciduous trees swayed and shook as if they might leap from the earth. They would have some windows partly open so they could feel the wind; Jennifer would be playing a cassette, the music stirring them, as it does the young, to memories of another time, other people and places in what is for them the past.

She took Betsy home, then Liz, and sang with her cassette as she left the town west of us and started home, a twenty-minute drive on the road that passes my house. They had each had four beers, but now there were twelve empty bottles in the bag on the floor at the passenger seat, and I keep focusing on their sound against each other when the car shifted speeds or changed directions. For I want to understand that one moment out of all her heart's time on earth, and whether her history had any bearing on it, or whether her heart was then isolated from all it had known, and the sound of those bottles urged it. She was just leaving the town, accelerating past a night club on the right, gaining speed to climb a long, gradual hill, then she went up it, singing, patting the beat on the steering wheel, the wind loud through her few inches of open window, blowing her hair as it did the high branches alongside the road, and she looked up at them and watched the top of the hill for someone drunk or heedless coming over it in part of her lane. She crested to an open black road, and there he was: a bulk, a blur, a thing running across her headlights, and she swerved left and her foot went for the brake and was stomping air above its pedal when she hit him, saw his legs and body in the air, flying out of her light, into the dark. Her brakes were screaming into the wind, bottles clinking in the fallen bag, and with the music and wind inside the car was his sound, already a memory but as real as an echo, that car-shuddering thump as though she had struck a tree. Her foot was back on the accelerator. Then she shifted gears and pushed it. She ejected the cassette and closed the window. She did not start to cry until she knocked on my bedroom door, then called: 'Dad?'

Her voice, her tears, broke through my dream and the wind I heard in my sleep, and I stepped into jeans and hurried to the door, thinking harm, rape, death. All were in her face, and I hugged her and pressed her cheek to my chest and smoothed her blown hair, then led her, weeping, to the kitchen and sat her at the table where still she could not speak, nor look at me; when she raised her face it fell forward again, as of its own weight, into her palms. I offered tea and she shook her head, so I offered beer twice, then she shook her head, so I offered whiskey and she nodded. I had some rye that Father Paul and I had not finished last hunting season, and I poured some over ice and set it in front of her and was putting away the ice but stopped and got another glass and poured one for myself too, and brought the ice and bottle to the table where she was trying to get one of her long menthols out of the pack, but her fingers jerked like severed snakes, and I took the pack and lit one for her and took one for myself. I watched her shudder with her first swallow of rye, and push hair back from her face, it is auburn and gleamed in the overhead light, and I remembered how beautiful she looked riding a sorrel; she was smoking fast, then the sobs in her throat stopped, and she looked at me and said it, the words coming out with smoke: 'I hit somebody. With the *car*.'

Then she was crying and I was on my feet, moving back and forth, looking down at her, asking *Who? Where? Where?* She was pointing at the wall over the stove, jabbing her fingers and cigarette at it, her other hand at her eyes, and twice in horror I actually looked at the wall. She finished the whiskey in a swallow and I stopped pacing and asking and poured another, and either the drink or the exhaustion of tears quieted her, even the dry sobs, and she told me; not as I tell it now, for that was later as again and again we relived it in the kitchen or living room, and, if in daylight, fled it on horseback out on the trails through the woods and, if at night, walked quietly around in the moonlit pasture, walked around and around it, sweating through our clothes. She told it in bursts, like she was a child again, running to me, injured from play. I put on boots and a shirt and left her with the bottle and her streaked face and a cigarette twitching between her fingers, pushed the door open against the wind, and eased it shut. The wind squinted and watered my eyes as I leaned into it and went to the pickup.

When I passed St. John's I looked at it, and Father Paul's little white rectory in the rear, and wanted to stop, wished I could as I could if he were simply a friend who sold hardware or something. I had forgotten my watch but I always know the time within minutes, even when a sound or dream or my bladder wakes me in the night. It was nearly two; we had been in the kitchen about twenty minutes; she had hit him around one-fifteen. Or her. The road was empty and I drove between blowing trees; caught for an instant in my lights, they seemed to be in panic. I smoked and let hope play its tricks on me: it was neither man nor woman but an animal, a goat or calf or deer on the road; it was a man who had jumped away in time, the collision of metal and body glancing not direct, and he had limped home to nurse bruises and cuts. Then I threw the cigarette and hope both out the window and prayed that he was alive, while beneath that prayer, a reserve deeper in my heart, another one stirred: that if he were dead, they would not get Jennifer.

From our direction, east and a bit south, the road to that hill and the night club beyond it and finally the town is, for its last four or five miles, straight through farming country. When I reached that stretch I slowed the truck and opened my window for the fierce air; on both sides were scattered farmhouses and barns and sometimes a silo, looking not like shelters but like unsheltered things the wind would flatten. Corn bent toward the road from a field on my right, and always something blew in front of me: paper, leaves, dried weeds, branches. I slowed approaching the hill, and went up it in second, staring through my open window at the ditch on the left side of the road, its weeds alive, whipping, a mad dance with the trees above them. I went over the hill and down and, opposite the club, turned right onto a side street of houses, and parked there, in the leaping shadows of trees. I walked back across the road to the club's parking lot, the wind behind me, lifting me as I strode, and I could not hear my boots on pavement. I walked up the hill, on the shoulder, watching the branches above me, hearing their leaves and the creaking trunks and the wind. Then I was at the top, looking down the road and at the farms and fields; the night was clear, and I could see a long way; clouds scudded past the half-moon and stars, blown out to sea.

I started down, watching the tall grass under the trees to my right, glancing into the dark of the ditch, listening for cars behind me; but as soon as I cleared one tree, its sound was gone, its flapping leaves and rattling branches far behind me, as though the greatest distance I had at my back was a matter of feet, while ahead of me I could see a barn two miles off. Then I saw her skid marks: short, and going left and downhill, into the other lane. I stood at the ditch, its weeds blowing; across it were trees and their moving shadows, like the clouds. I stepped onto its slope, and it took me sliding on my feet, then rump, to the bottom, where I sat still, my body gathered to itself, lest a part of me should touch him. But there was only tall grass, and I stood, my shoulders reaching the sides of the ditch, and I walked uphill, wishing for the flashlight in the pickup, walking slowly, and down in the ditch I could hear my feet in the grass and on the earth, and kicking cans and bottles. At the top of the hill I turned and went down, watching the ground above the ditch on my right, praying my prayer from the truck again, the first one, the one I would admit, that he was not dead, was in fact home, and began to hope again, memory telling me of lost pheasants and grouse I had shot, but they were small and the colors of their home, while a man was either there or not; and from that memory I left where I was and while walking in the ditch under the wind was in the deceit of imagination with Jennifer in the kitchen, telling her she had hit no one, or at least had not badly hurt anyone, when I realized he could be in the hospital now and I would have to think of a way to check there, something to say on the phone. I see now that, once hope returned, I should have been certain what it prepared me for: ahead of me, in high grass and the shadows of trees, I saw his shirt. Or that is all my mind would allow itself: a shirt, and I stood looking at it for the moments it took my mind to admit the arm and head and the dark length covered by pants. He lay face down, the arm I could see near his side, his head turned from me, on its cheek.

'Fella?' I said. I had meant to call, but it came out quiet and high, lost inches from my face in the wind. Then I said, 'Oh God,' and felt Him in the wind and the sky moving past the stars and moon and the fields around me, but only watching me as He might have watched Cain or Job, I did not know which, and I said it again, and wanted to sink to the earth and weep till I slept there in the weeds. I climbed, scrambling up the side of the ditch, pulling at clutched grass, gained the top on hands and knees, and went to him like that, panting, moving through the grass as high and higher than my face, crawling under that sky, making sounds too, like some animal, there being no words to let him know I was here with him now. He was long; that is the word that came to me, not tall. I kneeled beside him, my hands on my legs. His right arm was by his side, his left arm straight out from the shoulder, but turned, so his palm was open to the tree above us. His left cheek was cleanshaven, his eye closed, and there was no blood. I leaned forward to look at his open mouth and saw the blood on it, going down into the grass. I straightened and looked ahead at the wind blowing past me through grass and trees to a distant light, and I stared at the light, imagining someone awake out there, wanting someone to be, a gathering of old friends, or someone alone listening to music or painting a picture, then I figured it was a night light at a farmyard whose house I couldn't see. *Going*, I thought. *Still going.* I leaned over again and looked at dripping blood.

So I had to touch his wrist, a thick one with a watch and expansion band that I pushed up his arm, thinking *he's left-handed*, my three fingers pressing his wrist, and all I felt was my tough fingertips on that smooth underside flesh and small bones, then relief, then certainty. But against my will, or only because of it, I still don't know, I touched his neck, ran my fingers down it as if petting, then pressed, and my hand sprang back as from fire. I lowered it again, held it there until it felt that faint beating that I could not believe. There was too much wind. Nothing could make a sound in it. A pulse could not be felt in it, nor could mere fingers in that wind feel the absolute silence of a dead man's artery. I was making sounds again; I grabbed his left arm and his waist, and pulled him toward me, and that side of him rose, turned, and I lowered him to his back, his face tilted up toward the tree that was groaning, the tree and I the only sounds in the wind. Turning my face from his, looking down the length of him at his sneakers, I placed my ear on his heart, and heard not that but something else, and I clamped a hand over my exposed ear, heard something liquid and alive, like when you pump a well and after a few strokes you hear air and water moving in the pipe, and I knew I must raise his legs and cover him and run to a phone, while still I listened to his chest, thinking *raise with what? cover with what?* and amid the liquid sound I heard the heart, then lost it, and pressed my ear against bone, but his chest was quiet, and I did not know when the liquid had stopped, and do not know now when I heard air, a faint rush of it, and whether under my ear or at his mouth or whether I heard it at all. I straightened and looked at the light, dim and yellow. Then I touched his throat, looking him full in the face. He was blond and young. He could have been sleeping in the shade of a tree, but for the smear of blood from his mouth to his hair, and the night sky, and the weeds blowing against his head, and the leaves shaking in the dark above us.

I stood. Then I kneeled again and prayed for his soul to join in peace and joy all the dead and living; and, doing so, confronted my first sin against him, not stopping for Father Paul, who could have given him the last rites, and immediately then my second one, or, I saw then, my first, not calling an ambulance to meet me there, and I stood and turned into the wind, slid down the ditch and crawled out of it, and went up the hill and down it, across the road to the street of houses whose people I had left behind forever, so that I moved with stealth in the shadows to my truck.

When I came around the bend near my house, I saw the kitchen light at the rear. She sat as I had left her, the ashtray filled, and I looked at the bottle, felt her eyes on me, felt what she was seeing too: the dirt from my crawling. She had not drunk much of the rye. I poured some in my glass, with the water from melted ice, and sat down and swallowed some and looked at her and swallowed some more, and said: 'He's dead.'

She rubbed her eyes with the heels of her hands, rubbed the cheeks under them, but she was dry now.

'He was probably dead when he hit the ground. I mean, that's probably what killed—'

'Where was he?'

'Across the ditch, under a tree.'

'Was he—did you see his face?'

'No. Not really. I just felt. For life, pulse. I'm going out to the car.'

'What for? Oh.'

I finished the rye, and pushed back the chair, then she was standing too.

'I'll go with you.'

'There's no need.'

'I'll go.'

I took a flashlight from a drawer and pushed open the door and held it while she went out. We turned our faces from the wind. It was like on the hill, when I was walking, and the wind closed the distance behind me: after three or four steps I felt there was no house back there. She took my hand, as I was reaching for hers. In the garage we let go, and squeezed between the pickup and her little car, to the front of it, where we had more room, and we stepped back from the grill and I shone the light on the fender, the smashed headlight turned into it, the concave chrome staring to the right, at the garage wall.

'We ought to get the bottles,' I said.

She moved between the garage and the car, on the passenger side, and had room to open the door and lift the bag. I reached out, and she gave me the bag and backed up and shut the door and came around the car. We sidled to the doorway, and she put her arm around my waist and I hugged her shoulders.

'I thought you'd call the police,' she said.

We crossed the yard, faces bowed from the wind, her hair blowing away from her neck, and in the kitchen I put the bag of bottles in the garbage basket. She was working at the table: capping the rye and putting it away, filling the ice tray, washing the glasses, emptying the ashtray, sponging the table.

'Try to sleep now,' I said.

She nodded at the sponge circling under her hand, gathering ashes. Then she dropped it in the sink and, looking me full in the face, as I had never seen her look, as perhaps she never had, being for so long a daughter on visits (or so it seemed to me and still does: that until then our eyes had never seriously met), she crossed to me from the sink and kissed my lips, then held me so tightly I lost balance, and would have stumbled forward had she not held me so hard.

I sat in the living room, the house darkened, and watched the maple and the hemlock. When I believed she was asleep I put on *La Boheme*, and kept it at the same volume as the wind so it would not wake her. Then I listened to *Madame Butterfly*, and in the third act had to rise quickly to lower the sound: the wind was gone. I looked at the still maple near the window, and thought of the wind leaving farms and towns and the coast, going out over the sea to die on the waves. I smoked and gazed out the window. The sky was darker, and at daybreak the rain came. I listened to *Tosca*, and at six-fifteen went to the kitchen where Jennifer's purse lay on the table, a leather shoulder purse crammed with the things of an adult woman, things she had begun accumulating only a few years back, and I nearly wept, thinking of what sandy foundations they were: driver's license, credit card, disposable lighter, cigarettes, checkbook, ballpoint pen, cash, cosmetics, comb, brush, Kleenex, these the rite of passage from childhood, and I took one of them—her keys—and went out, remembering a jacket and hat when the rain struck me, but I kept going to the car, and squeezed and lowered myself into it, pulled the seat belt over my shoulder and fastened it and backed out, turning in the drive, going forward into the road, toward St. John's and Father Paul.

Cars were on the road, the workers, and I did not worry about any of them noticing the fender and light. Only a horse distracted them from what they drove to. In front of St. John's is a parking lot; at its far side, past the church and at the edge of the lawn, is an old pine, taller than the steeple now. I shifted to third, left the road, and, aiming the right headlight at the tree, accelerated past the white blur of church, into the black trunk growing bigger till it was all I could see, then I rocked in that resonant thump she had heard, had felt, and when I turned off the ignition it was still in my ears, my blood, and I saw the boy flying in the wind. I lowered my forehead to the wheel. Father Paul opened the door, his face white in the rain.

'I'm all right.'

'What happened?'

'I don't know. I fainted.'

I got out and went around to the front of the car, looked at the smashed light, the crumpled and torn fender.

'Come to the house and lie down.'

'I'm all right.'

'When was your last physical?'

'I'm due for one. Let's get out of this rain.'

'You'd better lie down.'

'No. I want to receive.'

That was the time to say I want to confess, but I have not and will not. Though I could now, for Jennifer is in Florida, and weeks have passed, and perhaps now Father Paul would not feel that he must tell me to go to the police. And, for that very reason, to confess now would be unfair. It is a world of secrets, and now I have one from my best, in truth my only, friend. I have one from Jennifer too, but that is the nature of fatherhood.

Most of that day it rained, so it was only in early evening, when the sky cleared, with a setting sun, that two little boys, leaving their confinement for some play before dinner, found him. Jennifer and I got that on the local news, which we listened to every hour, meeting at the radio, standing with cigarettes, until the one at eight o'clock; when she stopped crying, we went out and walked on the wet grass, around the pasture, the last of sunlight still in the air and trees. His name was Patrick Mitchell, he was nineteen years old, was employed by CETA, lived at home with his parents and brother and sister. The paper next day said he had been at a friend's house and was walking home, and I thought of that light I had seen, then knew it was not for him; he lived on one of the streets behind the club. The paper did not say then, or in the next few days, anything to make Jennifer think he was alive while she was with me in the kitchen. Nor do I know if we—I—could have saved him.

In keeping her secret from her friends, Jennifer had to perform so often, as I did with Father Paul and at the stables, that I believe the acting, which took more of her than our daylight trail rides and our night walks in the pasture, was her healing. Her friends teased me about wrecking her car. When I carried her luggage out to the car on that last morning, we spoke only of the weather for her trip —the day was clear, with a dry cool breeze—and hugged and kissed, and I stood watching as she started the car and turned it around. But then she shifted to neutral and put on the parking brake and unclasped the belt, looking at me all the while, then she was coming to me, as she had that night in the kitchen, and I opened my arms.

I have said I talk with God in the mornings, as I start my day, and sometimes as I sit with coffee, looking at the birds, and the woods. Of course He has never spoken to me, but that is not something I require. Nor does He need to. I know Him, as I know the part of myself that knows Him, that felt Him watching from the wind and the night as I knelt over the dying boy. Lately I have taken to arguing with Him, as I can't with Father Paul, who, when he hears my monthly confession, has not heard and will not hear anything of failure to do all that one can to save an anonymous life, of injustice to a family in their grief, of deepening their pain at the chance and mystery of death by giving them nothing—no one—to hate. With Father Paul I feel lonely about this, but not with God. When I received the Eucharist while Jennifer's car sat twice-damaged, so redeemed, in the rain, I felt neither loneliness nor shame, but as though He were watching me, even from my tongue, intestines, blood, as I have watched my sons at times in their young lives when I was able to judge but without anger, and so keep silent while they, in the agony of their youth, decided how they must act; or found reasons, after their actions, for what they had done. Their reasons were never as good or as bad as their actions, but they needed to find them, to believe they were living by them, instead of the awful solitude of the heart.

I do not feel the peace I once did: not with God, nor the earth, or anyone on it. I have begun to prefer this state, to remember with fondness the other one as a period of peace I neither earned nor deserved. Now in the mornings while I watch purple finches driving larger titmice from the feeder, I say to Him: I would do it again. For when she knocked on my door, then called me, she woke what had flowed dormant in my blood since her birth, so that what rose from the bed was not a stable owner or a Catholic or any other Luke Ripley I had lived with for a long time, but the father of a girl.

And He says: I am a Father too.

Yes, I say, as You are a Son Whom this morning I will receive; unless You kill me on the way to church, then I trust You will receive me. And as a Son You made Your plea.

Yes, He says, but I would not lift the cup.

True, and I don't want You to lift it from me either. And if one of my sons had come to me that night, I would have phoned the police and told them to meet us with an ambulance at the top of the hill.

Why? Do you love them less?

I tell Him no, it is not that I love them less, but that I could bear the pain of watching and knowing my sons' pain, could bear it with pride as they took the whip and nails. But You never had a daughter and, if You had, You could not have borne her passion.

So, He says, you love her more than you love Me.

I love her more than I love truth.

Then you love in weakness, He says.

As You love me, I say, and I go with an apple or carrot out to the barn.

The Times Are Never So Bad
was set in Linotype Janson by Service Typesetting, Austin, Texas. Janson is an old-style face, first issued by Anton Janson in Leipzig between 1660 and 1687, and is typical of the Low Country designs broadly disseminated throughout Europe and the British Isles during the seventeenth century. The Linotype version of this eminently readable and widely employed typeface is based upon type cast from the original matrices, now in the possession of the Stempel Type Foundry in Frankfurt, Germany.